The Carreta

The Jungle Novels

Government
The Carreta
March to the Montería
The Troza (unpublished)
The Rebellion of the Hanged
General from the Jungle

Other Books by B. Traven Published in English

The Death Ship
The Cotton-Pickers
The Treasure of the Sierra Madre
The Bridge in the Jungle
The White Rose
Stories by the Man Nobody Knows
The Night Visitor and Other Stories
The Creation of the Sun and the Moon

B. Traven

The Carreta

American Century Series

 HILL AND WANG ⟶ NEW YORK
A division of Farrar, Straus and Giroux

The Carreta

1

Andrés Ugalde was of pure Indian stock, a member of the great Tseltal tribe. He was a native of Lumbojvil, a finca in the Simojovel district. The full name of the finca was Santa María Dolorosa Lumbojvil.

Lumbojvil was the old Indian name of an Indian village, or commune, and it meant "cultivated land." After the Spanish conquest it was taken away from the Indians and the land was given or sold by the governor in command there to one of his followers, who made a finca, or landed estate, of it. The Indians, its original possessors, remained in the village because there was nowhere else for them to go. They remained partly from a sentimental attachment to the soil and the place where they had been born and partly because they quickly realized that very much the same fate awaited them wherever else they might go. They were no longer independent peasants on land of their own; the finquero, the new lord of the place, assigned them plots of land according to his own will and discretion, and thus they could cultivate crops for their own and their families' support. This took the place of wages for the labor which they owed as serfs to their new lord.

1

When the Spaniards took over the land of these village communities they adopted the old Indian names; otherwise the Indian population, which had been used to these names for centuries, would not have been able to indicate where they belonged. But lest they might forfeit the protection of their own gods, the Spaniards prefixed to the Indian name a good pious name of their own—in this case, Santa María Dolorosa.

In the course of time the Lumbojvil finca passed by sale and inheritance through many hands. But what never changed, however often the land was bought and sold, was the land itself and its original inhabitants. The same families continued to live on the finca as had lived there before the Spaniards came. True to the land and the soil, they waited quietly and patiently for the day when they would come into their own again.

Finally the finca came into the possession of don Arnulfo Partida, a Mexican of Spanish descent—a distinction of which he was very proud, although he had a great deal more Mexican and Indian blood in his veins than Spanish.

2

It was a very rare thing for a peon to get away from a finca to which he belonged. The father was a peon and the son a peon and the daughter a peon's wife. This was as good as a divine law; and if a peon ran away to start on a life of his own, the finquero gave five pesos to the head of the district council, who then had the peon apprehended by the police and brought back again. After a special punishment for his attempted escape there were the five pesos still to work off. But an Indian is so closely linked with his family and his relations and friends that a peon very seldom thinks of running away from the finca of which he is a part.

Andrés Ugalde got away from the finca without needing to

run away. It does not at all follow that it is always to the advantage of a peon to get away from the finca where he was born, even though he was born into virtual serfdom. It is more often than not to his disadvantage. The peon lacks the intelligence, that is, the experience, either to judge of things beforehand or to adapt himself readily to new circumstances, and the finquero has no desire whatever to see the peon's intelligence developed. If anything of the sort is undertaken by the State for reasons of its own, the finquero turns Monarchist, Bolshevik, or starts a revolution—anything to obstruct such a dangerous policy on behalf of his peons.

3

One of don Arnulfo's daughters was married and lived at Tenejapa. Tenejapa is a clean and pleasing little town inhabited partly by Mexicans—Ladinos—and partly by full-blooded Indians. The Indians and the Mexicans each live in a section of their own; but in the market and in all affairs of business they mix freely with each other, just as the inhabitants do in any other town in the world. The Mexicans have their own alcalde or mayor and the Indians their jefe or chief, or cacique or whatever they choose to call him.

Doña Emilia could not find servants to suit her in her new home. Perhaps she could not get used to the Tenejapa Indians; or perhaps she wanted to have familiar faces about her. In any case she wrote her father a letter, which she sent by an Indian, begging him to send her two girls from home. She mentioned Ofelia and Paulina as the two she would like best. They were already employed in the kitchen and about the house, and doña Emilia was used to them. While she was about it she asked as well for a handy boy, for her young husband was in urgent need of one to help in the store.

Don Arnulfo could not deny his daughter anything; besides,

she hinted in her letter that he would in due course be a grandfather—as she had discovered the week before. So he made haste to send the two girls she asked for, and also picked out the boy to go with them.

This boy was Andrés. Ofelia was his aunt, and as he was to go with her he did not so much mind the separation from the paternal jacalito, the mud hut in which he had been born.

It was the first time he would be away from home. His mother wept as she kneaded his posol for him, but his father was stoical and gave no sign of his feelings. All the same, the boy knew as between one man and another how deeply his father loved him and how sorely he felt the pain of parting from his only son. There was not the slightest movement of his features to betray this. There was only a flicker in the dark brown eyes, a light Andrés had never seen in them before; and this told him that his father loved him with a strength of which until that moment he had never thought him capable. For Criserio was a simple man who knew no more of life and of the world than his milpa—his corn patch—his bean field, his few sheep, and the fields and herds of his master could teach him. He was unable to express his feelings either in words or gestures; and it never entered his mind to express them.

This glitter in his father's eyes when Andrés took leave of his home was to have several years later a decisive influence over the course of his future life.

Andrés was then twelve years old.

4

The two girls were put on horseback, and their clothes and sheepskin rugs packed in bast mats and loaded on a mule. Andrés and the man who was sent with them, and who would take the animals back, went on foot. It was a three-day journey.

The girls, and the boy too, felt some alleviation of their homesickness when they saw doña Emilia's well-known face once more. She had, after all, been born on the same soil as they themselves. She was only a year older than Ofelia and only three years older than Paulina. They had grown up together, for the two Indian girls went into service at the master's house at a very early age. They had all worked together in the kitchen and in the household, laughed, cried, danced together, and knelt together before the images of the saints in the chapel of the finca, and had shared their secrets. Doña Emilia spoke their own language as easily as they themselves, and the girls knew enough Spanish to make themselves understood among Mexicans.

Doña Emilia had always been beloved in the families of her father's peons, though of course it might have been only as the crown prince is more beloved than the king. But she had always been ready to help the sick, and whenever she could had tried to redress the wrongs which in her own opinion or in the opinion of the peons were done by her father or his overseer. And so the two girls and the boy were quickly reconciled to their new surroundings by the presence of their young mistress, in whom they already had confidence.

5

Don Leonardo was a comerciante, a merchant. He had a tienda de abarrotes, a store with all sorts of merchandise—sugar, coffee, maize, beans, soap, flour, brandy, preserves, shoes, lamps, hatchets, ready-made clothing, cotton goods, ribbons, gramophones, patent medicines, tobacco, holy images, ink, bottled beer, perfumes, saddlery, cartridges—a Wanamaker Department Store in miniature, which for Tenejapa, a half-Mexican, half-Indian town of about a thousand inhabitants, suggested the splendors of a metropolis.

Don Leonardo was easily able to run this giant concern singlehanded. In a crisis, if a woman came in for a three-centavo candle and at the same moment someone wanted two centavos' worth of turpentine, doña Emilia could always leap to his assistance. But it did not often happen that there were two customers in the store at the same time; it could only happen on a market day. On an ordinary day, there might be an Indian squatting at the door at half-past five in the morning ready to come in the moment the door was opened; he might buy a quinto's worth (five centavos) of tobacco leaf. Two hours later a child would appear to buy ground coffee for a medio (six centavos). At ten o'clock a seamstress sent for sewing-machine needles, size seven. Word was sent back that they were not in stock. The child ran home and came back to say that size eight would do. Don Leonardo was sorry, he had not size eight either, but he had size nine. The child came back once more and bought a needle, size nine, for three centavos. In the course of the day the needle was changed four times, until toward evening the parties to the transaction finally agreed on size five, and the sale was completed on the understanding that the seamstress might still change the needle again in the course of the week if she found that size five was not suitable.

Sometimes, of course, a pair of boots or twenty-five quinine pills or a length of cloth might be sold, or even a whole new dress—price twenty-three pesos. That is to say, don Leonardo asked twenty-three pesos for it, because he had got it from New York. At the end of four hours, during which both don Leonardo and the purchaser wept or at least pretended to weep, the dress would be sold for fourteen pesos. Don Leonardo wept because he was selling below cost price and did so only because she was his neighbor and wanted the dress for a wedding, and he hoped that now she would be a faithful customer of his for the rest of her days; while she gave way to tears because she had wished to spend eight pesos only and now all her savings were gone by such scandalous extortion. But when it was all over, don Leonardo told his wife that he had made six pesos on the dress; and the purchaser of it told the whole town how cleverly she had cheated don Leonardo by getting a dress that was worth at least thirty pesos for the ridiculous sum of fourteen, and that she had never in her life bought such a lovely dress—so well made, so stylish—for so little money.

Don Leonardo would never have been rich, or even comfortably off, on the proceeds of the tienda—there was so much competition. Every fourth house in the town was a store. Of course, they were not so large or so well stocked as don Leonardo's. Most of them were hardly stores at all; as for a good half of them, you could buy up their whole stock for ten pesos and still be a loser.

But don Leonardo had other strings to his bow. He bought maize in large quantities from Indian peasants who cultivated their own land, then sold it again at a good profit in the larger towns—Jovel, Tuxtla, Yalanchén, Balún-Canán. He bought coffee in the Simojovel district and cocoa beans in the Pichucalco district and sold them to the large American importers at the railhead. He bought bales of tobacco by the thousand at Hucutsín and sold them to the dealers in the towns. He had not the capital to go in for these enterprises on a large scale, and there were plenty more buyers about, all doing their best to rob each other of a good thing. Besides this, the output was not large enough or constant enough to get rich on. Nevertheless, these sidelines were a great help; and he had reason to call himself better off than his father-in-law, don Arnulfo.

6

Up to his marriage an aunt of his had helped him in his business, but after that event she quarreled with him. Mothers and aunts have this in common, that they are apt to turn nasty and even vindictive when their charges marry and do not eagerly insist on sharing their married life with them.

Don Leonardo had no wish to see his wife constantly at the beck and call of the business, though this is the rule in the upcountry towns of Mexico and particularly among tradespeople of the lower middle class. The Mexican woman has a far better head for business than her husband. She is more industrious, more adroit, and quicker at grasping a situation. The Mexican woman has something that the Mexican man entirely lacks: foresight, and the patience to wait quietly on events.

It was because don Leonardo did not wish his wife to work in the store, at least not as a necessity, that he thought of having a boy whom he could train to take his place when he himself was away buying up merchandise. When she learned that it was Andrés whom her father was sending to Tenejapa doña Emilia described the boy to her husband and recommended him.

Andrés had been taken into don Arnulfo's home at the age of nine to wait at table. It is usually boys, not girls, who wait at table on the ranchos and haciendas of Mexico. They are nearly always the sons of peons on the hacienda, though sometimes they may be the children of the owner of the finca, or of his sons, by one or more of the Indian girls of the finca.

The work of a peon's son in the master's household counts as a duty, but the father gets some return. He may have a little more land allotted him; or he may be let off one or two days of the fortnight's labor he owes his master every month; or he may be given the right to pasture a few goats or even a cow on the master's grassland; or perhaps the boy works off a debt which his father contracted with his master when he wanted cloth for a shirt or purchased a small pig or a puppy from him.

Andrés did not only wait at table: he helped with the washing up and with the cleaning of the rooms; he watered the flowers in the garden, polished the master's saddle and bridle, helped to wash down the riding horses, helped to carry water from the river; and when there was nothing else to do, the overseer shouted for him to come and help in twisting ropes. But whatever the job might be there was no need to work himself to death. In fact, no one, not a single peon, serfs in a sense though they were, was required to kill himself with work—not on this finca, anyway. For nothing was done in too great a hurry. If Andrés was called by someone in the house and happened to be playing with the boys of the village, he would get a scolding and perhaps even a clout on the ear; but there it ended.

Meanwhile, Andrés benefited greatly by his service in the house. He picked up Spanish; and in fact by the time he went to Tenejapa he could speak it as well as any Mexican boy in the place. And as his native Tseltal was also the language of the Indians of Tenejapa and all the region around it, allowing for a difference in the dialect, he was naturally of great value to don Leonardo; for don Leonardo, particularly on market days, did more business with Indians than with Ladinos.

7

Don Leonardo soon came to have a very good opinion of the boy. Andrés was eager to learn and he was intelligent and quick. He soon learned to distinguish the various articles and to call them by their right names; and he knew their worth and whether they would last well, also their prices. He even got to know how much he could put on to them in making a sale, or how far to come down without depriving his master of a profit.

Nevertheless—not from any love of the boy, and still less for any thought of his future, but from purely self-interested motives—don Leonardo sent him to evening classes, so that he could learn reading, writing, and arithmetic. The boy had a very rudimentary knowledge of figures. If he was given a peso for a purchase costing eighty-six centavos, he had to ask don Leonardo or doña Emilia to do the sum for him; sometimes he had to go and find one of them, and this was annoying when don Leonardo had just sat down to a meal or to read the newspaper. It was annoying, too, that the boy could not read the labels on the cases and packages, and sometimes opened the wrong case and ran the risk of mixing up the price tickets and selling goods below their cost.

So don Leonardo came to the conclusion that the boy would be worth more to him if he could read and write and reckon figures. It was the same thing on a small scale as it is on a large scale all over the world. The manufacturer, the capitalist, the big landowner is at bottom opposed to the education of the worker. He feels, with reason, that an educated working class may endanger his privileged position. But economic life has become so complex that an industrialist whose workers are uneducated stands no chance against one whose workers are intelligent, alert, and well schooled.

The capitalist of today, if he wishes to remain one, must support the government, and even lead the way, in giving the children whom he may one day need on machines an education such as a hundred years ago very few children of manufacturers ever got. It goes against the grain with him, but he has no choice. Today, and still more is this true of the future, it is not the country which is most highly educated at the top, but the country which is most highly educated at the bottom that takes first place and decides the worth of the dollar.

So it was entirely out of consideration for his own interests that don Leonardo was induced to give the boy a little schooling. If he ever turned it to his own account in a way that was of no advantage to don Leonardo, don Leonardo was fully prepared to call him a thankless wretch, who repaid the kindness of a master who had made him what he was with black ingratitude; he should have known better and left the boy in his lousy Indian village and taken care not to spend good money on getting him taught anything.

8

The good money don Leonardo shelled out did not amount to very much. It was only sixty centavos a month. But don Leonardo made the most of it.

He had the right to; for he was certainly the only person in the whole town who sent an Indian boy in his employment to school and paid for it into the bargain. It never entered the head of any other Mexican in the place who had Indian servants to give them the slightest chance of bettering themselves. Girls or boys, they worked from five in the morning till ten at night. It was not always hard work, but they were never off their feet and had to be on the spot whenever they were called. They couldn't be spared for a single hour of the day; so, at least, their masters and mistresses believed. And to send them to school was not only a folly but a sin. It was a folly because the Indian might turn out to have more knowledge and ability than his master's own son—who, as far as schooling went, was left very much to his own devices; it was enough if he could just read and write. And it was a sin because the Church was not in favor of Indian children going to school. The Church wished the Indian children left in their innocence and ignorance, because of such is the Kingdom of Heaven; whereas once an Indian was educated you could not say where it might end. The case of the Indian Benito Juárez was very recent in those days and the memory of it is still fresh today. This Indian of Oaxaca, who had remained in blissful ignorance till his twelfth year, got the opportunity of being educated; and when at last by hard work he became an educated man he confiscated the wealth of the Church for the benefit of the people, and played havoc in a way that no one had ever dared to do before with the divine rights which God Himself conferred on the Catholic Church. No wonder, then, that the Church looked askance on education for the Indians.

Those sixty centavos that don Leonardo paid for Andrés's schooling were not so great an expense as they seemed—for Andrés received no wages. Who would dream of paying an Indian boy wages! He could believe himself lucky to have the honor of being allowed to work at all—that was wage enough. And the employer ought to be thanked for giving him something to do.

Andrés got his food. It was plentiful, certainly; but it was seldom anything but dry pancakes of corn flour, black beans, and hot peppers, or, to give them their names, tortillas, frijoles, and chiles. If the boy was not on the spot when he was wanted, or if he did anything amiss, he was told that he did not even earn his keep and that his master was losing on him every day.

He was also given his clothing. It consisted of one pair of white cotton trousers, a white cotton shirt, and a bast hat. He had neither boots nor shoes—not even huaraches, that is, the native sandals. He went barefoot, as he had all his life. He was used to it and knew no better.

Then on the day of the fiesta, the festival of the patron saint of Tenejapa, he was given five centavos, or even, if his master was in a generous mood, two reales (twenty-five centavos), with which to buy himself candies. This was once a year, because the fiesta came only once a year. On his día del santo, the day of his own patron saint, he received ten centavos and perhaps a new cinturón rojo de lana, a red woolen belt—or sash, rather—which served to hold up his white cotton trousers.

He had no bed, and he was not accustomed to one. He slept on a petate, a mat of bast, which he spread out in a corner of the kitchen or of the portico. He had brought this mat from home with him.

As he had never had wages during his service in his master's house on the finca and had never there possessed so much as a centavo, he had no idea what wages were. So now when he was given a few centavos twice a year he felt he had made a great stride forward in life. Such a system is enough to make any employer of labor burst with envy.

9

The schoolteacher was glad enough to give the boy his lessons for sixty centavos a month. His salary was twenty-five pesos a month. It was the lowest paid to any state employee. Public prosecutors and police chiefs were paid twenty times as much; and the reason why they were paid twenty times as much and held in a hundred times higher honor is because it is their duty to come down hard on the shortcomings of their neighbors. This task is laid upon them by the State for its own preservation and to remind people that respect for the law is a sign of civilization.

The jefe político, the district governor, received six hundred pesos a month, without counting the bribery and extortion by which he made a great deal more than that. The schoolteacher could not practice extortion. He had no right or power to do so. And it was to no one's interest to bribe him; for it was a matter of no importance, either to them or their parents, whether his pupils passed an examination or not.

The schoolteacher's only means of adding to his income was an evening school for grown-up people, or children who could not come to school during the day. Most of the children of the place and all the children of Indian parents had to work during the day, some in the fields, others in various home industries—molding candles, making cigarettes, casting pottery, weaving blankets, working leather, making sweets, plaiting hats.

The schoolteacher charged a peso a month for each student, whether grown up or not. Many families could not pay it, and so their children went without education. Don Leonardo, good man of business as he was, contrived to knock forty centavos off the peso he owed the schoolteacher for Andrés.

Andrés was supposed to attend the school every evening from seven to nine or half-past nine; and he would have liked to go every evening for the pleasure of learning. But if his master needed him in the store he was not permitted to go. The store came first.

Don Leonardo did not buy him any books. If he went so far as to give him a soiled notebook from his stock or a broken pencil or a bottle of stale ink, he made a great song of it and put on a wry face. But Andrés might take any old paper which could be used no longer for wrapping parcels, and when he was in the street he kept his eye open for stumps of pencils which had been lost or thrown away.

Rudimentary as this sort of schooling was, he learned a good deal. The most important thing he learned was the value of education; for until you can read and write you do not understand what the value of reading and writing is.

2

 When Andrés was fifteen he still went barefoot and still slept on a petate, which he spread out on the kitchen floor or in a dry corner of the portico and rolled up in the morning and put away beneath the rafters. The petate was not the one he had brought with him from home; nor was the woolen serape which covered him the same one. They had worn out at last, but don Leonardo had not given him new ones; for a petate of the kind don Leonardo sold cost one peso twenty-five centavos and a serape as much as five.

During this time doña Emilia had twice been to visit her father at the finca to let him see and marvel at the two children she had brought into the world. Andrés accompanied her on these journeys. He was by now a grown youth to whom don Leonardo could safely entrust his wife and children.

So Andrés saw his father and mother and his sisters and all his relatives again. And his father gave him a new petate and a new serape when he saw how worn out they both looked. He had to buy the serape from the master's warehouse—the patrón's bodega. It cost nine pesos, for it was a good one, made by the Indians of Chamula. He had to buy the petate from the patrón also, and this cost him one peso seventy-five; for everything in the finquero's bodega was fifty and even one hundred per cent higher than at a store in the town.

Criserio could not, of course, pay for them, because he got no wages; so he had to have them on credit and entered to his account.

Don Arnulfo said: "The serape is nine pesos."

"That is very dear, patrón," Criserio answered. "I can buy a serape at Simojovel for five."

"So you can, Criserio, if you have the money."

"But I haven't any money, patroncito," said Criserio.

"You've no obligation to buy it, Criserio, if it is too dear," said don Arnulfo, picking up the serape to put it back on the shelf.

"But I must have the serape for my hijito—my little son, he's frozen to death," said Criserio without moving a muscle of his face.

"The serape costs nine pesos, Criserio. I can't let you have it any cheaper. If it is too dear and you can get one cheaper somewhere else, you are free to do as you please. You're not forced to buy the serape from me. Do you think I want you to run up debts? I don't, I assure you. I would far rather my muchachos owed me nothing; then there's no bother and my boys are free and can go when they like. There is no slavery here."

"I know that, señor," said Criserio. "We are no esclavos. We are free and can go when we like and where we like."

"As long as you don't owe me anything, that is. You know that."

"I know that, patrón. As long as we don't owe the patrón anything." Criserio said all this by rote, exactly as a parrot might. He did not think of what it meant. The meaning was too remote.

Don Arnulfo, however, brought matters to a head. He had

no time to discuss the relation between freedom and freedom from debts with one of his peons. Such questions did not bother him any more than they did any other finquero. They were matters of hard fact. The State, the army, and the police stood behind his rights as a true son of the Church.

"Well," he said, "do you want the serape or not? If you do, say so; if you don't, you can go. The serape is nine pesos. You're not forced to take it if you don't want to run up a debt."

"I'll take the serape, and the petate too," Criserio said.

"Very well. Then I'll enter it against you in the book."

"Yes, señor, put it down. I want the serape and the petate for my boy, now he's so far away from home where it is very cold at night because of the mountains." Criserio picked up the articles and put them under his arm.

Don Arnulfo opened the heavy ledger with a bang and turned to Criserio Ugalde's account. "Now wait till we get this straight."

"Yes, patroncito, I'll wait."

Don Arnulfo scratched about with the pen to make the ink flow and made his calculations aloud: "The serape is nine pesos. Is that right, Criserio?"

"Yes, patrón, that is right. Nine pesos."

Don Arnulfo wrote it down and then said: "The petate is one seventy-five."

"Patrón," Criserio broke in, "but that is very dear. You can buy a good petate in Yajalón for seven reales."

"Por el diablo, the devil take it, do you want the petate or not? Make up your mind what you want and what you don't want. I've no time to waste."

Don Arnulfo was getting angry, and for fear of putting him in a still worse temper, Criserio said: "Yes, indeed, I'll take the petate—for my boy, Andrés."

"Bueno, all right, then that's one seventy-five. Is that right, Criserio?"

"That is right, señor."

"Muy bien, very well," said don Arnulfo as he wrote. "Then both together that is eleven pesos. Is that right, Criserio?"

"That is right, patrón."

"Eleven pesos, then; and as you can't pay me the eleven pesos, that makes another eleven pesos—twenty-two in all: eleven for the serape and the petate and eleven because you owe for them and can't pay. Is that right, Criserio?"

Criserio had no knowledge of figures. In any case, he could not have reckoned so quickly. And because he could not follow them, the figures only made him confused, and he did not want to question and make his master angry; and his master said all the figures in Spanish, and though he understood them well enough in Spanish he could not grasp them in his head. So it was very natural that he said: "That is right, patrón."

It must be right if the master said so; for he was a proud and rich gentleman who would never make money by cheating a poor Indian.

"Correcto, Criserio?"

"Correcto, patrón."

Don Arnulfo did not allow Criserio to disfigure the page by putting his clumsy cross to it. He would only have blotted this fine clear ledger which had "In the name of God" on its first page. There was no need, in any case; for if there was a dispute (as never in fact happened) the cross would never be required as evidence. It would have no value whatever, since neither Criserio nor any other peon on the finca could read what he had put his cross to. So it did not matter whether the cross was there or not. Don Arnulfo had asked "Correcto, Criserio?" and Criserio had answered "Correcto, patrón, that is right." Every judge in the Republic would accept this verbal confirmation between a finquero and a peon as binding. The peon had confirmed the transaction by word of mouth, and so he was responsible for the debt he had acknowledged.

Don Arnulfo was a decent, honorable man. He treated his peons better than many other finqueros of his acquaintance. Other landowners were a good deal less softhearted with their peons.

"The shirt is five pesos. Right? Very well. And as you can't pay for it, that's five pesos. And as you remain in my debt for the five pesos, that's five pesos. And as I shall never have the money from you, that's five pesos. So that makes five and five and five and five. That's twenty pesos. Agreed?"

"Yes, patrón, agreed."

The peon can buy a shirt nowhere else when he needs one. He can get credit nowhere but from his master, for whom he works and from whom he can never get away as long as he owes him a centavo.

2

It did not occur to Criserio to consider whether all this was just or not. It was altogether beyond his mental capacity to grasp the meaning of transactions of this kind. If anyone had tried to explain to him that he had been shamefully swindled, he would never have seen it however often it had been explained to him. He would have listened and listened and at the end he would have said: "The patrón is right. The patrón is an honest man and he would not deceive a poor Indian. And he reckoned it quite right, for I owe him eleven pesos and then that makes twenty-two. It's quite right."

Don Arnulfo might, of course, have gone about it another way to arrive at the twenty-two pesos. He might simply have said that the serape and the petate together came to twenty-two pesos and that Criserio could take them or leave them; but then Criserio would have known that the price was exorbitant. He would have refused to buy and would have found something else to serve his needs, such as animal skins, which he could get on his own. For he could understand the prices of things. He understood, too, that all goods were dearer on the finca than at the market in the town, for the finquero had the cost of transport, and there was no knowing what he had paid for them. The peon could get as far as the mere price of a thing; what defeated him was the finquero's rapid calculations and jugglery with figures.

Indeed, the peon had no comprehension whatever of figures beyond five. Fifteen or twenty-two or sixty-five pesos were all the same to him. Figures like that were so confusing to him that he fell into a kind of hypnosis, and this hypnosis would only become more profound if it ever actually came to an investigation of the finquero's accounts by a judge or any other official in order to ascertain whether an injustice had been done to the Indian peasants. They knew only one person in the whole world to whom they could bring a complaint, and that was their own master.

3

Criserio was delighted to be able to give his son the serape and the petate. He told him they had cost eleven pesos, but he did not say that he had on their account contracted a debt of twenty-two pesos.

It did not appear to him in that way. The articles cost him eleven pesos. That was correct. But it had nothing to do with them if he owed twenty-two, which was only because he could not pay the eleven pesos in cash. For this reason he did not consider it necessary to say anything to his son about the other eleven pesos.

But Andrés was very well aware what even eleven pesos meant to his father; for he knew how a peon lived on a finca. Perhaps he had not known this, or understood its economic significance, when he left home; but now he was older, and during his two visits to the finca he had heard these matters spoken about in his parents' hut and in the huts of other peons. They were never discussed in any critical spirit. Things were taken for what they were. They were regarded as an immutable decree of fate which no human power could alter— any more than water can flow uphill instead of down. The patrón was the patrón and the peon the peon. So it always was; so it will continue to be. The peon's son will be a peon in his turn; and if the patrón hands over the finca to his son or sells it, the name of the patrón changes, but everything else remains the same. If there was any criticism among them it was only because the land allotted to one or other of them by the patrón was poor or stony or hilly, or that he would have liked a little bit more, or that the price paid for pigs by the dealers ought to have been twenty-five or fifty centavos more—two-eighty for a well-grown pig was really too low.

Not a voice was raised against the patrón's right to purchase all pigs, goats, or sheep his peons had for sale, and to decide on the price of the pigs he chose to buy from his peons so as to sell them again, and to give or withhold his permission if they wanted to sell their animals to a passing dealer, and to take fifty or seventy-five centavos or even a peso out of the money the peons got for them. For all this was his right as patrón, and always had been. The pigs, sheep, and goats had been reared on his finca, even if the peons had had to buy them as suck-lings and feed them on maize they themselves cultivated.

It was the same with any maize or beans they had to spare; they could not sell them just as they liked to a passing dealer or in the market of the nearest town. Here too the patrón had a prior right, and his permission had to be asked before they might sell anything, and a part of the money they received had to be handed over. If they were in the patrón's debt—and they were all in his debt—they might not be permitted to sell at all but had to give him whatever they had to dispose of. And the patrón deducted what he chose from their debts.

All that was just: it was the law and the decree of heaven, and the Church confirmed it. For the gods were blood relations of the patrón, but they were not relations of the Indians.

It was so and it could not be altered. It had always been so, and so it would always remain. The peons knew no better. They knew only that it was the same all over the world; for wherever they might go, there was not a finca where it was otherwise. Therefore it must be the same all over the earth. Their earth, or what they knew as earth and world, was the region inhabited by Indians who spoke the same language as they themselves. A world where their tongue was not spoken was foreign to them and quite unknown. They had no idea what might go on there and they could never find out.

True, there were some independent villages in their district. They were mostly inhabited by Indians who had never been made peons on a finca. Either the land was so barren that no Spaniard had ever wanted to own it, or else the Indians there had always been so turbulent and rebellious that no Spaniard could survive there. The latter had always been the case with Bachajón and with several other villages. But when the peons went there they found that these independent Indians lived an even more wretched life than they. These free Indians were sometimes so desperate that they forsook their villages and of their own accord went as peons on a finca. There were a number of reasons for this, some of which were to be found in the temperament, habits, and customs of these Indians; but the chief reason was their ignorance and the cleverness of the big landowners, backed by the Church, in leaving them to their ignorance.

4

Andrés's father was in no way bound to buy his son a new serape and a new petate. He did it for love of his son and because he could not bear to see him suffer.

The man whose place it was to buy these things for Andrés was his master, don Leonardo. But to him it was a matter of utter indifference whether Andrés froze at night or slept on the bare floor and got a bad chill which might ruin his health. What did the health of an Indian boy matter to him? He might get inflammation of the lungs or a fever and die if it came to that—there were plenty more Indian boys. He would merely ask his wife to write to her father, who would then send another along. Where would it end if he began looking after barefooted Indian boys? Besides, it did not hurt them to sleep on the bare floor. They were used to it. He had better uses for his pesos.

Andrés still got no wages and don Leonardo never thought of giving him any. The only difference the last two years had made was that now, when there was a feast day at Tenejapa, Andrés was given, instead of five or ten centavos, a tostón—fifty centavos.

"See you don't spend it on trash—and no aguardiente either," don Leonardo warned him when he bestowed this largesse with an air that suggested a gold twenty-peso piece.

5

Don Leonardo now trusted Andrés sometimes with matters of considerable responsibility. He sent him with large sums of money to San Cristóbal, the nearest large town, where he had to make purchases and then bargain with arrieros—mule drivers—for the transport of the goods to Tenejapa, and accompany them and see that nothing was missing or damaged when the goods were delivered.

These tasks gave Andrés valuable experience. He got to know what a real town was like and saw the wealth and variety of goods which came from all over the world and heard of towns which were a hundred times larger than San Cristóbal, though when he saw it for the first time it seemed to him that there could not be a larger and finer town on earth. There were streets half a mile long, house touching house, and all of stone and many with windows. He had never till then known that there were houses with windows. He had never seen such a thing. In Tenejapa, some had latticed apertures, but that was all. And now he saw windows with glass panes, and even shop windows with huge sheets of plate glass behind which the goods were piled up and it looked as if you could put out your hand and take them.

He saw bullock carts—carretas—for the first time. Until then he never knew there were such things as carts and wagons and that they could be drawn by animals. He had never seen them before. The fields on the finca were not plowed; a hole was simply dibbled in the ground with a stick and then the maize or beans were dropped in. With plants like tomatoes or peppers, where shallow plowing was necessary, it was done with a plow that was little more than a wooden stick pulled by a peon. So how could Andrés have known anything about draft animals? There was not in all that vast area a road on which wheeled vehicles could have gone. There were only narrow paths, called veredas, frequently so narrow and stony and so loose and crumbling that even a pack mule was barely safe on them.

Andrés was told by a carreta driver that the carretas made journeys fifteen times as long as the journey from Tenejapa to

San Cristóbal—and from Tenejapa to San Cristóbal was a good day's journey for a pack mule. The boy looked incredulously at the carretero when he told him this. But other carreteros said the same. And an Indian dealer in salt, who was selling in the street, told him that it was all true; and he knew it because he had once accompanied a carreta with a load of salt as far as Arriaga.

This was how Andrés got his first idea of the size of the earth on which he lived. So far he had not had the faintest notion of it. When he heard Tuxtla, Tonalá, Tapachula, San Gerónimo, Veracruz, Mexico City mentioned in don Leonardo's house or store he supposed these places were much the same as Tenejapa, the only town he knew. And when they were spoken of as far away, it only meant to him that they were twice, or at most three or four times, as far away as his native finca, Lumbojvil, was from Tenejapa. In any case they must be within the horizon, for there, as everybody knew, the world came to an end.

Another carretero whom he encountered beneath the portico of the cabildo—the town hall—told him, while he ate his tortillas and frijoles which an Indian woman warmed upon a little tin stove, that Arriaga was the end of his journey with his carreta and that Arriaga was the railroad station. When Andrés asked what that meant, the carretero explained to him that gigantic wagons brought goods to that place from distant lands so that they could be loaded on the carretas and taken upcountry. He told him more: that the wagons were as large as a stone house, and that one wagonload was enough to fill forty and even fifty carretas to their utmost capacity. These wagons ran on roads made of iron, and forty or more—sometimes many more—were pulled by another big wagon which made a lot of smoke and puffed and sweated like a great beast. And the name of this was ferrocarril, railroad.

Andrés knew the word; he had been taught to write it in school. But the schoolteacher could not explain the thing, because he had never seen it, or a picture of it, and so was unable to form any idea of it. He had to be satisfied with giving them the word and teaching them to write it correctly. The word was in the spelling book. Because Andrés knew the word and could write it correctly he now felt that he was in some peculiar way familiar with the thing itself. When the carretero described what it looked like and how it puffed and sweated, coughed and bellowed and snorted, the boy almost felt that he had actually seen a ferrocarril somewhere. It did not seem to him like something strange and new and unexpected, for he knew its name, by which it was called and described, and not only knew it but could write it. In spite of its puffing and roaring the monster aroused no fear in him. On the contrary, he wished to see it with his own eyes. And he made the discovery, without being aware whence it came, that if you know of an unfamiliar thing and can call it by its name, this unfamiliar thing loses its power to strike you with fear. To be able to write this name inspired him with unbounded confidence and gave him a sense of his own identity such as he had never had before.

In these few minutes he had an inward experience, trivial in itself, which suddenly opened his mind to the real meaning of education—for here was this terrifying monster (which the carretero to increase his own importance had represented as being far more terrifying and frightful than it actually was) reduced to sober proportions by the mere fact that he knew its name and could write this name down in visible and intelligible characters. He would not have been able to explain to anyone how this came about. He could only feel that it was so.

And the more he thought about it, the clearer it became— and not only it but the whole world too. The word, with which he was already acquainted, explained and dissected the thing so that there was no mystery left in it: ferrocarril—quite simple. "Fierro" meant "iron," "carro" meant "wagon," "riel" meant "rail": a wagon, then, of iron that ran on rails. All this was only slightly obscured in the word itself: each syllable was shortened so that the whole word should not be too long.

From this insight he arrived at the perception that all words were alike in this: every word explained a thing and a process and brought their secrets to light. He thought of other words and found that this sudden revelation was borne out.

His attitude toward education altered completely. He no longer thought of education as being useful only for success and quickness in business. He felt that it had a further value, greater perhaps than its mere business utility. This set him off thinking.

6

It was the same with Andrés as with anyone who reasons out a philosophic theory from a strictly limited relation to economic or social life, and does not know that the same theory has already been enunciated by a multitude of men before him, and that among these there were some twenty or so to whom the groundwork of his little theory was familiar when philosophers sold sandal thongs in the streets of Athens to make a living. For even in those days a philosopher could not live on his world-shattering theories alone; he needed a sideline which guaranteed him bread and a roof over his head. And so it was the same with Andrés as with all who believe they have struck on a new idea. He believed that education might weaken the threatening and fear-inspiring power of finqueros, priests, and all those dread phantoms of superstition which play off their fooleries on mankind. He thought that if education could render harmless such unknown monsters as the railroad, if education could throw down superstition and menacing phantoms, it must also be able to set his father and all the peons at home on the finca free from the apparently unending oppression of serfdom.

He had education and he was free.

But Lucio, the mule driver who was going to transport the goods to Tenejapa next morning, broke into the wild turmoil of his thoughts.

"Where are you sleeping then?" Lucio asked.

"I can sleep here under the portico of the cabildo," said Andrés, spreading out his petate only three feet from the Indian woman who all night long kept the simple food of the drivers hot for them.

"Stop that and come along with me," said Lucio. "We'll sleep in don Ambrosio's gateway where the goods are. The mules are near to hand in the back yard. We'll load up at three and be well on our way by four."

Thus Andrés was reminded that he was not free, that he could not do as he wished, that he was not even free to sleep here under the portico, where all night there was a lively coming and going of men on horseback, of carreteros and mule drivers, of troops of earthenware sellers and basket-makers, where there was so much to see and hear. He had to sleep where Lucio would have him under his hand without the need to go and look for him. For Lucio was to be in command during the journey back with the goods; he had been put in charge of the transport by his master. And Andrés too had his master, who had ordered him to accompany the goods whether he liked it or not—for his master fed him and allowed him to spread his mat in a corner of his house.

Andrés had made the discovery, as his thoughts whirled through his brain, that education, which he believed he pos-sessed, could destroy all fear of monsters and idols; but as soon as Lucio spoke soberly and practically of daily tasks and reminded him of his master, he felt afraid again. He knew by experience how hard and furious don Leonardo could become if anything did not go as he thought it ought to go, knew that don Leonardo didn't think twice about seizing a board or the iron band of a packing case and hitting him over the head with it when he lost his temper.

What good was education to him then? thought Andrés as he went with Lucio through the dark streets to don Ambrosio's house. It was of no advantage to anyone but don Leonardo if he could read and write and reckon figures. He remembered what he was: a peon, who got no wages, who had to do as he was told, who had to be on the spot all through the twenty-four hours of the day in case he was wanted.

But he was free, for he knew what freedom was. The peon was free when he was not shut up in the dirty hole called calabozo, or prison. His patrón could send him there when he liked. And it was freedom when during a Sunday your hands and feet were not tied together behind your back for idleness during the week or for disobedience or because a calf had run away.

So Andrés could not say he was not free. He was not in prison, nor was he lying bound in the harness room of the finca. He was free. If next day with the loaded mules he wanted to go over to the right because the way to the left was too marshy or soft, he could go to the right for the safety of the mules. And he was free to give the yellow mule a few more kilos than the gray one. And he was free to smoke cigarettes if he had any. What more freedom can a peon expect? Perhaps the freedom to marry when he grew up, if another peon gave him his daughter for a wife. And then he had at last the great freedom to beget plenty of children and to rear them on the produce of the patch the patrón assigned him and so supply the patrón with more peons.

He had all the freedom he could think of. And if he had been asked he would have rattled off in a loud voice that article of faith which was drummed into every child at school: "I am a free citizen of an independent republic. Viva la república! Viva la patria! Viva!"

And not only rattled it off but believed it.

3

 Don Leonardo had bought thirty mules at Chilón very cheap from a finquero who was hard up for cash. With Andrés as convoy they were brought to Tenejapa, where don Leonardo saw to them well so that they should look their best.

He made inquiries and found out that mules were bringing a better price at La Concordia than anywhere else at the moment, as there were coffee planters there who were in the market for hundreds of them. So he decided to take the mules to La Concordia.

Don Leonardo rode ahead on his best horse to negotiate a deal, leaving the mules to follow with Andrés in charge and a few Tenejapa boys to help him; for a patache of mules cannot on a long journey keep pace with a good horse mounted by a good rider.

Thus don Leonardo sold the mules two days before they arrived. Buyer and seller were equally pleased with the transaction. Don Leonardo made a handsome profit, and the planter had got the mules much cheaper than he had expected. Had he had to buy them in Tabasco he would have paid half as much again.

2

There were a great many people at La Concordia that week. The town was holding its annual fiesta and there was a large fair—a feria—in connection with it.

There were horse dealers, cattle dealers, donkey dealers from Comitán; there were agents recruiting Indian labor from the independent villages for the coffee and cocoa plantations; buyers of coffee, maize, timber; agents for the sale of machinery; agents for ironware and agricultural implements; land speculators; dealers in goods and necessities of all kinds. All these people had a lot of money on them, so as to do business on the spot; and they also made a lot of money. This year they hoped to make more than usual.

The evenings were long and drink was plentiful; and as a change from talking business all day they played cards.

Don Leonardo did not return home immediately after selling his mules. He took the opportunity of doing more business with the money he had made, hoping to make a good profit. But he was no more able than any of the rest of the men to bring his business to a speedy conclusion. No one was in a hurry; there was plenty of time, and everyone hung on for a better bargain. So it was very natural that don Leonardo, like the others, should sit down and play cards.

He was acquainted with every one of the caballeros with whom he played. They were all, as he was himself, known to be men of honor when it came to cards; though all, not excepting himself, did their utmost often enough to get the better of another in business by any ruse they could hit upon. At cards a man had to play fair; it was a point of honor with the caballero, even though in business he might stretch a point and still remain a man of honor. They were playing Siete y Medio (Seven and a Half). The game is a very fast one, and by two o'clock in the morning don Leonardo had lost every penny he had got for the mules. The game went on, but he had not even a peso to stake in the hope of winning back his money; and no caballero borrowed money during play. That was an old and well-tested rule.

They were playing in a large room in the house of a citizen of La Concordia whom they all knew. All had their muchachos—their boys—with them. These boys were always in attendance on their masters. On this occasion they were lying close by, asleep on their mats. Some were under the portico, others in the room where their masters played. Their presence did not interfere with their masters at all.

Now and again his master would give one of the boys a push with his foot: "Oye, Lázaro—listen, Lázaro, get up and run across to the cantina and knock at the door. Here are twelve reales for a liter of comiteco añejo—good and aged, the real stuff. Don't let them pass off a cheap tequila. Well, off with you, don't stand there, we're dry."

3

It was not Lázaro but Andrés who was kicked up by one of the caballeros. On these social occasions all the boys were common property and nobody noticed which boy it was who was sent on an errand or who sent him.

Andrés returned with the bottle of comiteco and put it on the table.

"Here, have a drink, muchacho," said don Laureano, who had sent Andrés out for it. He filled a glass and pushed it toward Andrés, who drank it off, and then with a toothpick helped himself from a plate of cheese cut up into cubes.

The relation between a master and his boy in Mexico is not that of master and slave. Particularly on journeys the master is not too proud to drink from the same bottle as his boy, whether it contains water, coffee, brandy, or some soft drink; the same with food. The master is scrupulous in sharing his roast turkey fairly with his boy; the boy breaks off with his fingers as much as he wants of the lump of posol or the chunk of meat. But he will never touch his master's provisions, even though he is dying of hunger, unless his master eats at the same time or has eaten already. And yet, although the muchacho may have just drunk from the same bottle as his master, the master does not think twice about giving him a kick if he does not jump up quick enough to catch a straying horse before it has gone too far.

Andrés was just squatting down in his corner again when don Leonardo noticed him.

"Listen, don Laureano," he said. "I'll stake my muchacho. How much will you stake against him?"

Don Laureano held the bank.

He looked Andrés up and down as though examining a horse he had to bid for then and there.

"Does he speak Castellano or just dialect?" don Laureano asked while he shuffled the cards.

"He speaks both and he can read and write a little too," answered don Leonardo.

"Twenty-five pesos," don Laureano rapped out, to show that it was the most he would offer.

"Aceptado—agreed," answered don Leonardo.

The game went on and don Leonardo lost. He pulled out his revolver and balanced it in his hand.

Had it been anywhere else the men would have sprung to their feet to prevent don Leonardo from a rash suicide. But though each had seen his movement, not one of them stirred or so much as thought of falling upon him. Each of them was a good enough philosopher to be able to say to himself: "If he wants to shoot himself it's his own concern and no business of ours. We'll bury him decently and there ends our duty as friends and caballeros."

But these gentlemen were far too good judges not to know that no one is in such a hurry to shoot himself. As long as a man still has his rancho and his house or the house of his father-in-law and his best horse to gamble away, there is no danger of his killing himself. Mexico is too fine a country for that, and it is by no means certain that in another life a man will land in Mexico again. So it is better to stay where you are and not tempt the gods.

Don Leonardo stroked his revolver caressingly and then set it down in front of don Laureano, who put down the cards he was shuffling, picked up the revolver and examined it as one might a work of art. He tried its balance, weighed it in his hand, looked down the barrel, tested its action, and said: "Caliber 38. Bueno, my bueno. All right. Fifty pesos."

One of the other players shouted: "I'll give sixty for it."

"So will I," don Laureano said dryly. "Does anyone bid more?" he asked, looking around the table.

No one bid.

"Right. Sixty pesos," don Laureano said with a jerk of his head at don Leonardo.

"Aceptado," answered don Leonardo.

"Will you stake the sixty, or what is your stake, don Leonardo?" asked don Laureano.

"I'll see the first card and then call my stake."

"Bueno; as you like, amigo."

Don Leonardo picked up the card dealt him. It was a seven. "I lay the sixty," he said.

"Good," replied don Laureano. "Otra—another? Or are you content?"

Don Leonardo thought for a moment. A seven was a good card and no one but a fool would ask for another. If he lost his revolver there was only his saddle left and finally his horse. Then he would have to ride home on a borrowed horse, and that for a caballero is nearly as bad as having to go on foot like an Indian. A Mexican caballero will never be seen on foot unless his horse has foundered.

Don Leonardo thought it over for a second longer while he fixed the card, which don Laureano had half drawn from the pack, with such intensity that he might have been hoping to read its value from the back. He made up his mind to say "Enough, gracias—thanks," but quite against his will blurted out: "Otra."

The card was dealt him. For a moment he held it as he had received it—face down—afraid to look at it. All the players watched him in order to relish his suspense to the full. That is the great charm of the game: you live in suspense twice over—in your own and that of the other players.

Cautiously, don Leonardo turned up the card. Everyone at the table of course knew already that his first card must have been a six or a seven, for if it had been less he would never have hesitated to ask for another.

He saw that he had got a king. Putting the two cards down, he released his pent-up breath: "Siete y medio, caballeros—seven and a half, gentlemen."

He took up his revolver and quietly pushed it back into its holster, as though no other issue had been possible. He raked in a few hundred pesos, and besides that he now held the bank. Whoever holds the bank is always half a point to the good above all the other players.

4

The game went on.

At five o'clock on the following afternoon they agreed to stop after three more deals. After this no revenge was to be asked for or taken. Fatigue was the reason: they could scarcely hold their cards or count right.

Don Leonardo had won back his losses and two thousand and some hundred pesos in addition.

A rough calculation of gains and losses showed that no one had been too hard hit. The two or three thousand that one or other of them had lost were not taken tragically. The losers, half asleep, calculated how much they would need to put onto the goods they hoped to sell in order to balance their losses at cards. On a final count it will usually be found that it is not the gambler who pays for his losses. Someone else who has had no share in the game has to bleed for them.

5

The men rose unsteadily to their feet and went out onto the portico. The boys who were lounging about there waiting for their masters ran up at once and brought out chairs from the room where the game had gone on. The men dropped wearily into the chairs. Some dozed off; others talked drowsily, more to keep themselves awake than because they had anything to say. Half an hour later their host summoned them to supper in the dining room.

The meal over, they stood up, stretched themselves, and got ready to go out into the streets to see how the world had gone on since they last saw it and what prospects there were of bringing their businesses to a conclusion and who was out and about to be talked to.

Don Laureano left with don Leonardo. They were both putting up at the same fonda, or inn. As they came through the gateway they found Andrés leaning against the gatepost, chatting with another boy who was also waiting for his master.

Don Laureano tapped Andrés on the shoulder and asked him: "What's your name, hijito?"

"Andrés Ugalde, su servidor—at your service, señor," he replied.

"Andrés, eh?" said don Laureano. "Ever worked with oxen?"

"No, señor," the boy replied.

"There's no difficulty in it," don Laureano went on. "You'll soon learn. You're a strong young fellow and you look intelligent. You'll get on. We'll know more about you presently. You know, of course, you're my muchacho now."

Andrés looked up at don Leonardo.

"Your pardon, patrón, but I belong to don Leonardo."

Don Laureano turned his head and looked at don Leonardo. "Don Leonardo, haven't you told the boy?" he asked.

Don Leonardo remembered, as if it had been a dream, that he had staked the boy and lost. When he had staked his revolver and won, he had wasted no time in taking it back and shoving it into place at his belt; in fact, he had done so before raking in the money he won in the same game. In this game, as he now remembered, he had won the bank too; and from that moment had thought only of the money he had lost and meant to win back. But he utterly forgot having lost the boy; otherwise, when at about midday don Laureano too got short of money and began to stake personal belongings, he would have asked him to stake the boy first of all, so that he might have had the chance of winning him back.

But the game was now over. Don Laureano was in no way bound to return the boy, not even if it were possible to offer the twenty-five pesos staked for him.

In Mexico there is no longer traffic in human beings as there was in colonial times; no man can be bought, no man sold. It is forbidden by the Constitution, which, further, solemnly declares that every subject of the Republic is a free, independent, and inviolable human being on whom only his own father or the police or the public prosecutor or the State has the right, in stated circumstances, to lay hands. For this reason it was now out of don Leonardo's power to undo his blunder. He could not offer don Laureano twenty-five, or even fifty pesos for the boy. That would have meant the purchase of a human being, and he, as well as don Laureano, might have got a long term of imprisonment for it. Besides, they were both good and believing Catholics, for whom it would be a sin to sell a man, even though an Indian. They would have felt ashamed of themselves, both as caballeros and as Mexicans, if they had offered or received money for a fellow citizen of the Republic and treated one of their own fellow countrymen as merchandise. In any case, it would be a breach of every code and custom.

But morality is so complicated, and not only in Mexico, that it is not considered unfitting or impermissible or discreditable if men stake at cards the property of their wives or their children or their parents if they are short of money with which to continue to gamble.

In this case, however, the moral question was very little involved. Andrés was a peon who belonged to a finca as part of the property. The Constitution might forbid his sale, but he could be given and taken in an exchange between property owners. A peon was not asked whether he wished to go to a new master or not. He was too well brought up by the Church and the landed gentry to think of discussing such a thing or to make the slightest hint of an objection to the exchange. That would be disobedience, and no peon has the right to be disobedient.

The caballero is much more attached to his favorite horses than to his muchachos. Don Leonardo was not likely to think twice about the loss of Andrés. As soon as he got home he would send off a request to his father-in-law for another boy from the finca.

"Yes, that's right, Andrés," he said sleepily. "You are now don Laureano's muchacho."

With that the affair was ended. He resumed his talk with don Laureano at the point where it had been interrupted. One doesn't think again about losses at cards; they are nothing to weep over. It is bad manners to be niggardly. A caballero is always openhanded.

6

A week later don Leonardo was home again at Tenejapa. He had hired a boy in La Concordia to accompany him. He paid him off on his arrival and sent him back.

Doña Emilia did not at once ask about Andrés. She supposed he was occupied with something or other and would arrive later. And when a husband and wife who are not yet tired of one another meet again after three or four weeks' separation, they usually have more important and pleasanter things to talk of than the whereabouts of an Indian muchacho.

But when two days passed and still nothing was to be seen of Andrés, doña Emilia said to her husband: "What is keeping Andrés? Why didn't he return with you?"

It had been don Leonardo's first intention to say that the boy had met with an accident—kicked by a mule and they had had to bury him. He had made up his mind on the way home to say this, but now he thought it would sound too absurd. Instead he said with indifference: "The boy? Oh, him. He lost three mules on the way—cost me days and money too to catch them again; and then they were good for nothing. Don't know what's come over the boy. He was no further use—insubordinate and impudent. When we got to La Concordia he ran off. He told some of the other boys he was going to Tapachula, where he could earn good money. I didn't go after him. If he wants to go, let him. That's all I get for the trouble I took with him. We'll write to your father to send a good boy from the finca."

His wife had no wish to argue the matter. It would have disturbed the joy of reunion, just when she was finding her husband's embraces particularly pleasing, as is usually the case after a separation which has interrupted the routine of a happy marriage. So she said no more about it.

Andrés was forgotten. The new boy whom don Arnulfo sent soon settled down. And since he came straight from the finca and was very obedient and submissive and timidly kissed his master's and mistress's hands morning and night, as was the custom on the finca, doña Emilia and don Leonardo agreed that the new boy was better, more industrious, more agreeable, more obedient, more loyal and honest and reliable than Andrés had ever been.

4

Don Laureano Figueróa was a comisionista—a commission agent—who lived at Chiapa de Corso. He was the representative of two or three hundred firms in Mexico City, Puebla, Monterrey, U.S.A., Spain, France, and other places besides, of which he knew no more than the names.

He united all the agencies in his district for sewing machines, maize, porcelainware, roofing material, hardware, petroleum, typewriters, Spanish muzzle-loaders, flower seeds, barbed wire, newspapers, bottled beer, wines, cigarettes. He undertook the forwarding of goods to all parts of the world, as stated on his letterheads. He bought and sold land, houses, and securities. He was better known in every little town of the state than the governor or his ministers. There was no place in the state, however small it might be, where you did not see hanging up in every shop, fonda, hotel, and office a calendar on which was depicted a gaudy landscape of a kind that could never be found anywhere in Mexico. Above the landscape his name was printed in bold type, and the landscape was framed by a list of all the articles for which he was the general agent.

There is no cause to smile at don Laureano for combining so many agencies in his own person; for if he had represented only one large firm he would soon have starved. He was agent for a world-famous piano manufacturer in New York. In three years he had succeeded in selling one whole piano. But—as he wrote them—he was justified in hoping that within two years he would be able to sell another, for there was a newly wedded couple who had been contemplating the purchase of one for several months. Sewing machines were brisker, though even they left much to be desired. He reposed great confidence in typewriters, for the business people of the state were just making their acquaintance and might take them up. Also, he was on good terms with the secretaries and hoped to provide all government offices of the state with typewriters.

His mainstay, certainly, was the forwarding of goods. It was as a carrier that he earned his daily bread and kept his business going.

He had forty carretas working between Arriaga and Balún-Canán. As he and all his family were well known throughout the state, and as he himself had the reputation for strict reliability and honesty, he was never without a freight. His caravans were entrusted not only with the transport of valuable goods and money, but also carried women who were traveling alone or a child who was being sent to relations somewhere or to school. It was well known that his carreteros would give their lives in the defense of the goods entrusted to them, whether against bandits or any catastrophe of nature.

2

Andrés did not wonder why he was passed on by one master to another without ceremony or without his being asked what he thought about it. In any case, it would have made no difference. Horses, donkeys, and mules were sold and exchanged by their owners, and no one asked a horse whether it wished to go to a new master; so why should they ask him?

It did not even occur to Andrés to make any remark at all, and still less to think he had any right to say yes or no in a matter that the gentlemen arranged between themselves. He did not know that a man as such had rights or anything of that sort. He knew one thing only and had known it since childhood: a peon must obey. There is not a soldier anywhere on earth who is allowed to say a word if in wartime or peacetime he is left to rot up to his neck in water. Obedience is the first duty of a soldier; and it is the first and last duty of a peon. The soldier is sent to Flanders whether he likes it or not. And his masters swap him about: today he fights and bleeds for the well-being of the British, tomorrow for the French, and the day after for democracy. When the obedience of the workers and soldiers begins to be shaken, the foundations of the State tremble and rebellion crouches for another spring. Every law of nature would be thrown into tumult and confusion if it ever occurred to a finquero to say to his peon: "Hijito mío, cómo te gusta—well, my son, how do you like it?"

Andrés had never expected his patrón to ask him what he thought. He did what he was told—no more and no less. He might have resisted if his master had ordered him to hang himself from the nearest tree; for that would have been against the commandments of the Church. On the other hand, it was breaking no commandment to permit himself to be whipped or placed in the stocks. The Church had taught him that disobedience to him whom God had made his master might end in disobedience to God and the Holy Father. Only when obedience is established—and firmly established—on all sides, can obedience to God and the Church rest on a firm foundation. That has to be got into the blood from the very beginning.

Perhaps what affected Andrés in the whole affair was simply that he was being thrust out of a life he was used to and into a new one. And there is generally something painful in being removed unexpectedly and against your will from your accustomed life.

3

However, even before they had reached don Laureano's home, Andrés realized that his new master was a far easier man to serve than his previous one.

Don Laureano knew nothing of life on a finca from the inside. He knew that there were peons on a finca, but he did not know how harsh the discipline—the tyranny, in fact—was on the fincas. If he happened in the course of business to stay as a guest on a finca, he had no opportunity of gaining any insight into the conditions of the laborers; nor did he bother his head about such matters. It was none of his business to study them. He was there to do business and for that purpose wished to make the finquero his lifelong friend.

Don Laureano was a businessman. His attitude to all his carreteros and muchachos was governed by the plain rule of all good men of business: Live and let live. Experience had proved to him over and over again that if this rule were observed by all businessmen the results upon business, commerce, and trade of all kinds could only be beneficial. It is true that all his men lived hard and penurious lives, but when they compared them with the life of a peon they found theirs far from intolerable.

The men employed by don Laureano were free men. When one of them returned with his carreta to his employer's yard he could say: "Listen, patrón, I want to quit and look for something else." And if he was a good and reliable carretero don Laureano would say: "Why do you want to go, Julio?

You've been with me four years now. We've always got along. Bueno, you can have a half-real more a day."

The carretero perhaps stayed on, took half a real more per day and was contented; or else he left and went his way. Don Laureano did not insist on his staying if he wanted to go. The man was free.

Of course, he very soon found out that in reality he had very little freedom. The next man paid him less, worked him harder, and treated him like a dog. But since he could not fill his belly by holding his mouth open when it rained, he had to work for any man who paid him, so that he could buy tortillas and frijoles. In this way, the free carretero learned the great lesson that freedom and the liberty to go where he pleased were fine words which were used merely to veil the hard countenance of economic conditions.

So it really came to this when you saw it through to the bottom, that the loyalty and reliability of the carreteros in the service of their employer were no more voluntary than the compulsory service of the peons on a finca. The carreteros knew that they were free and could go when and where they pleased. The peons knew that they were not free and had no right to go when and where they pleased. But when you fully understand the economic conditions in which they both lived, it becomes clear that both were in the same hole; only it was called by different names. The finqueros made a higher profit by maintaining the peonage system, and the others made more by having free men to work for them.

The peon did only what he was told. He left it to the patrón to do the thinking and to bear all responsibility for the results of his orders. The carretero, on the other hand, had to think for himself and take the responsibility for what he did. For if he only did strictly what he was told and never thought from one kilometer's end to the next how he could best and most

safely get his carreta forward, no carreta would ever deliver a
load to its appointed destination.

4

Andrés rode along beside don Laureano. They had just left
the fonda, where they had spent the night.

"So you haven't yet worked with oxen?" don Laureano
asked, while he lit a cigarette and offered one to Andrés.

"No, patrón. Don Leonardo had no carretas. Carretas cannot
go on the roads from Tenejapa to Jovel, or on the road to
Simojovel and up to Bilja. The tracks are too narrow, boggy,
and hilly, and often full of stones. We could only use mule
transport, and on many of them not even a mule could go,
where the track had broken away and fallen into ravines.
There we could only use porters."

"I know some of those roads up there," said don Laureano.
"Been there on business. For miles you have to lead your
horse, unless you want to lose him and break your neck as
well. Were there no oxen on the finca either?"

"Only in the herds, señor, to sell. And they were driven
loose in droves to Juan Bautista and Frontera when the patrón
sent them to Tabasco to market."

"Never mind, muchacho," said don Laureano. "You'll soon
pick it up. There's not much to it. You seem a smart boy and
ready to learn. You'll soon learn to yoke an ox and put it in.
And once you've been on a trip or two with the old carreteros,
you'll know the road and the tricks of the trade."

"I'm sure I shall, patrón."

"It's not such hard work as it looks, my boy," his new
employer told him. "After you're loaded there's little more to
do. The beasts know the road better than any muchacho.
They find their own way however black the night. Of course,
when the roads are bad there's sometimes plenty to do. You

have to take a hand then. You have to throw your weight on the spokes. And sometimes a carreta has to be lifted out of a hole, and stones and stakes have to be put down to level up the bad spots. As long as you keep your eyes open and don't go to sleep you'll very seldom have a broken axle. That makes work—but it's your own fault. You pay the penalty for going to sleep and not keeping a good lookout."

"I'll take good care."

"You'll like it, I can tell you. You get to know the roads, see lots of different places and towns. Often you go down to the railroad. And you have company all the time. Sometimes you'll have a family in the carreta. Then there'll be half a peso for yourself if you make yourself agreeable and do what's wanted."

"Muchas gracias, señor."

"And now about your wages, Andrés. We'd best go into that, so we know where we are. What did don Leonardo pay you by the day?"

"Don Leonardo paid me no wages," Andrés said truthfully.

"That's not my way," don Laureano declared. "Every man who does his work deserves his pay. That is my motto. No one works for me for nothing. Every job is paid for. There are no peons and no slaves with me. A man, as well as his master, must live and have something to look to. There's an encargado—a head driver—of mine. He worked for me for over eighteen years and now he has a nice little store at Suchiapa. Another who was with me fifteen years has a fine ranchito in Acala. Fellows who didn't drink worked well and saved their money. I like my muchachos to get on and not to work for others all their lives. Anastasio, who has the store at Suchiapa, gets all his stock from me on credit and always pays punctually. Muchachos who have worked for me and proved themselves loyal and reliable never lack my help and support for the rest of their lives. I don't forget one of my men."

What don Laureano said was quite correct. He did not exaggerate by a syllable. When the men were past their peak and of no further use as carreteros—and the life of a carretero is a hard one, as Andrés was soon to learn—don Laureano helped them to set up for themselves in a small way. They were then his best customers and at the same time acted as subagents in the districts where they settled down. They did him good service, too, by keeping him informed about other traders in their neighborhoods and giving him many a good tip on new property owners and their requirements in the way of machinery and goods. He was no fool at organizing and extending his business.

"As I say, Andrés, nobody need work for me to no purpose. As for your wages, this is what I'll do. I'll give you a real and two-thirds a day—twenty centavos. That makes six pesos a month. That's a good wage."

"Muchas gracias, patrón."

To Andrés it certainly seemed a good wage; for so far he had had none at all, and six pesos was a very big sum for one whose needs were so small.

"But first there's a debt to deduct, Andrés."

"What debt, patrón?" asked Andrés. "I have bought nothing."

"That's true, muchacho. You have bought nothing. But I must tell you that don Leonardo lost twenty-five pesos to me at cards, and you naturally have those twenty-five pesos to pay."

"Sí, señor."

"That makes—let me see." Don Laureano reckoned it aloud to himself. "Yes, that makes twenty centavos in a peso, that's five, and in twenty-five there's a hundred and twenty-five. So that's a hundred and twenty-five days. So you have to work a hundred and twenty-five days before I can pay out your wages in cash. I'm not a tyrant, of course. If you're in need of anything, tell me and I'll give you an advance of three or four pesos which we can count against your wages later on."

"Sí, señor."

"You understand that, Andrés?"

"Sí, señor."

"Then that's a bargain."

"Sí, señor."

"Of course, you get your keep. On the road you have your rations—beans, salt, sugar, coffee, rice, dried fish, dried meat, and now and then a can of sardines; and you get money for the road to buy tortillas with. Not a carretero of mine has ever gone hungry. And if you don't spend your wages on drinking tequila, you can always put money by and set yourself up in life."

"Sí, patrón."

"You understand, of course, that you cannot quit my employment until your debt of twenty-five pesos is paid in full, and if I pay you any money in advance of wages, that is also a debt which you must pay before you can think of looking for another patrón or running off to Guatemala. Muchachos have a far worse time of it in Guatemala, I may tell you. Don't you believe it when vagabond muchachos in Arriaga tell you what a lot you can earn on the plantations in Guatemala. It's nothing but damned lies these loafers at Arriaga, Tonalá, and Tapachula tell you. Stay in your own place, Andrés, and serve your master well and you'll want for nothing. La patria, tu país propio—in your own country, there you're among your own folk and never starve; that's the best and safest thing in life. I'm convinced from the look of you that you'll make a good and loyal carretero."

"I will do my best, patrón."

"I hope you will, Andrés. As a carretero you have a great responsibility. If any goods should be missing from your carreta, whether stolen or burned or fallen down a ravine, you naturally have to replace them. It has to be reckoned against your wages. It's a debt against you. But if you take good care, nothing of the kind can happen."

"I will take good care, patrón, that no goods are lost."

"I am sure of it—you're a very reliable boy, Andrés."

They went on at a walk for a little longer. Then don Laureano threw away his cigarette butt.

"We'll have to trot a bit now if we want to get on."

5

 Lurching and rattling, the caravan of carretas painfully made its way up the fifteen kilometers from Chiapa de Corso to the high pass of El Calvario. This pass led over the Cerro de Chiapa. The Cerro de Chiapa is the highest point of the Sierra—that precipitous and rocky mountain range running all the way from Chiapa de Corso to Ixtapa and parting the tropical lowland of Tuxtla Gutiérrez from the cool upland, La Mesa de Las Casas.

This high pass, El Calvario, had, in spite of its pious Catholic name, a very ugly reputation. It was in every possible respect a veritable tribulation, a tribulation for travelers of every sort and description: for travelers on foot, on horseback, or on mules. It was no less a tribulation for Indian porters who carried up heavy loads of goods or basketwork litters in which sat a female traveler or a man unable to ride. Not least, this mountain pass was a tribulation to the drivers of carretas and strings of pack animals.

These drivers, less stoical than the Indian porters who tripped along silently and indefatigably with a nimble rolling step, began to curse as soon as the little town of Chiapa de

Corso, nestling pleasantly in the unfading greenery of its palms and banana groves, was an hour behind them. The steeper and more arduous the road became, the more thorough and violent grew their curses. The drivers cursed their own souls and the souls of those who begot them. They cursed the day on which they were born, and did not forget to curse the day which had made them drivers of carretas. They cursed at the tops of their voices God in heaven and the Holy Virgin and consigned into the bargain all the saints of the Church to hell. As each bend of the road came in sight, they offered up their souls and the souls of all their children to the devil if he would get them safely past before a wheel or an axle broke or the oxen fell down a precipice or a pack mule slid backward into a ravine. For the men had to get up the pass, and whether it was God or the Holy Virgin or the devil who helped them in their tribulation was to them a matter of indifference as long as they got there with their carts, their beasts, their loads, and their goods intact.

At the summit of this mountainous Calvary stood a large weatherworn wooden cross, set up on a high cairn on which withered wreaths and flowers lay in heaps. As soon as the carreteros and mule drivers reached the cross they all removed their large weather-beaten bast hats, made three genuflections, and crossed themselves. With this they were received once more into the company of true believers and the devil had no more power over them or their souls; for God and the Blessed Virgin are quick to forgive the sinner who turns again in repentance to songs of praise and consecrated candles, while He who made mountains, ravines, rivers, bogs, and lakes took the responsibility for all that happened or was done because of these creations of His.

Not that after reaching the cross their tribulations were by any means at an end—as might be supposed, since there stood the cross which promises relief to all men. Things are not so easy as that for men on earth; if they were, men would soon wax fat.

For many travelers, particularly for those on horseback who traveled singly or in twos with a boy or two boys in attendance, the real tribulation only began after this.

El Calvario had a double meaning. When the first meaning had been grasped in a torrent of curses, imprecations, lamentations, groans, and sweat, there was still the second to solve; and the answer to the second meaning frequently enough ended with the swift, businesslike, and merciless death of the travelers.

2

The pass was notorious and dreaded on account of the bandits who lay in wait there for travelers and caravans. These bandits were smart men of business who knew their job and went about it with sense and discretion. Under a dictatorship where governors, generals, police chiefs, councilmen, mayors, and customs officers robbed land and people whenever they had the chance, there was often nothing left for hundreds of unofficial persons but to rob in their turn. When officials steal it is called corruption; when stealing is unofficial it is banditry. But you never find bandits except where officials are thieves; and as soon as robbery ceases at the top, the bandits all die out in a week at the bottom.

The bandits of the Hill of Calvary did not lie in ambush every day. Their wives would have had no patience with them; for a wife wants more of her husband than daily bread and an occasional new rag. Besides, these footpads could not live on banditry alone: they had faces to save. So they all had small, in some cases large, farms, to which they devoted the greater part of their time—firstly, in order to remain respected citizens; secondly, to divert unnecessary suspicion;

and thirdly, to have an assured income for their children, who were to grow up into worthy citizens.

For all these reasons they did not go hunting every day. Besides, it would have scared people from ever traveling that way; or they would have made certain to travel only in large companies and spoiled the game. For another thing, the government would have established a military post there, which, again, would have been a nuisance to the bandits. So weeks and months often went by without a single robbery taking place. And then suddenly for three days every traveler and every caravan on the road was looted. Or again, it might happen that only two or three travelers were held up and only a small pack-mule train robbed, while all the rest who passed that day or that week were unmolested.

It was this very irregularity of the bandits' onslaughts that made this road a road of terror. It was like running a gantlet. You could never say beforehand whether you would get through with your money or your life. No one could be certain of conveying from one place to the next money needed for or acquired in commerce, and the same with valuables of any sort. Even if he had neither money nor valuables, he might be stripped and killed. Only horses and mules and saddles were safe, for the animals were branded and the saddles had so many little marks and features of their own that with their help the bandits could have been traced.

The travelers, of course, might have traveled in large companies. But that is not as easy to arrange as it is with a company of soldiers, who fall in and march off at the word of command. The day that suits one party of five does not suit another five who had thought of joining forces with it. One has a child sick, another a wife brought to bed, the third has bought a house and must go see to it, the fourth's stomach is out of order, and the fifth has come to the conclusion overnight that his journey is not urgent. The first party of five also melts away. The first has a summons to attend the courts; another's house burned down early in the morning. And thus there remain only three, or even two, who have to go at all costs because their business compels them to be at Tuxtla or Arriaga by a certain day. Trusting to their luck and to the charms and blessings of the Church, to the prayers of all their relations and to a good revolver, they ride off; and two days or two weeks later they are found at the foot of a precipice, shot or struck down. Some of the bandits, innocent, industrious, and simple countrymen on whom no reproach can be cast, help in the search and blame the government and the irreligion of the bandits who are a scourge to the country just because they have no belief in the retribution of the life to come.

3

Whatever was responsible for the creation of the pass of El Calvario, whether it was the good God in heaven above or an earthquake or a slow contraction of the earth's crust—whoever or whatever it may have been was not niggardly. He or it made one of the marvels of nature.

The road wound up in over fifty hairpin bends to the rocky summit. Perhaps there were eighty or a hundred and twenty. Quién sabe? Who knows? Nobody counted them. Or if he started to, he soon lost count; for there were more important things to concentrate his attention on at the moment than topographical observations.

The climb began before you were out of Chiapa de Corso. The last church of the town was already on such high ground that those of the pious who were short of breath could not get there. The streets of the town were well paved with rough cobblestones. But as soon as the last paved street was left behind, the torments began which never ceased until, after nearly a hundred kilometers, the next town with paved streets was reached.

Leaving the tropical plain where streets and squares were bordered by tall palms, where fields, gardens, and large cultivated estates were luxuriant with the plants and flowers, bushes and trees of the torrid zone, the road wound up to the cool highlands of the Sierra where the conifers grew as tall and straight as in northern Ohio.

On the left hand the sheer drop to ravine and precipice increased step by step in height; on the right, for nearly the whole distance, there was the steep cliff face of the Sierra, diversified only by the various plants and thorny scrub which clothed it.

Once up on the pass you saw spread out at your feet the whole expanse of the tropical plain. Far away in the greenish-blue shimmer of the horizon rose the long mountain chain of another arm of the Sierra with its high peaks touching the clouds. Like a silver thread woven in a gigantic carpet, which has no shape or pattern or design of any sort, the Grijalva River lay apparently motionless and apparently meaningless across the flickering expanse.

The irony of it was that just at this spot, where a man could forget himself altogether in the contemplation of the extravagant generosity of nature, the bandits with revolvers, rifles, and knives were likely to be closest at hand. For it was just at these places that travelers and caravans could neither give ground nor turn and flee. On the left hand there was the sheer descent of two or three hundred meters; on the right the abrupt face of the cliff, so steep and rugged and so dense with thorns and finger-long spikes that even a goat would have hesitated to attempt an escape there.

It was easy to see why many travelers on reaching the pass called out: "Ayúdame Purísima—help me, Holy Virgin." But since the bandits too were good Catholics and also invoked the Purísima, so that they might have a good catch that day, the prospects for both parties were fifty-fifty.

4

Knowing well the countless dangers of the road, the carreteros were in the habit of waiting at a camping place outside Chiapa de Corso until enough carretas had collected to form a long train.

A long train of carretas could be held up for a time by the bandits, but it could not be successfully attacked and looted. As soon as they fell on the first carreta and a single shot was fired—or even at a shout from the carreteros who had been attacked—the whole train came to a standstill, and the drivers in the middle and at the rear, well covered by the carretas, advanced with their firearms, machetes, bludgeons, spokes, stones, and whatever else they could lay hands on. Then the bandits had short shrift unless they cleared off in good time. If they attacked the hindmost carreta, it was the same thing with only a change of front. It sometimes happened, when the bandits knew that carretas were loaded with specie, that a caravan was attacked simultaneously at the front and the rear. In the wild melee that ensued they would succeed in hurling some of the carretas over the precipice after rapidly cutting the oxen loose, and in looting a few of the carretas and throwing their contents into a ravine where they had some of their number posted. But by then it was high time for the bandits fighting above to take to their heels and convey their own skins into safety, for half of them were wounded, some lacking portions of their anatomy. They had to give up the fight, without having got possession of, or as much as set eyes on, the well-hidden and well-guarded coin the carretas were carrying.

If the carretas were laden with goods of no great value in themselves, such as salt, tiles, books, bottles, or with goods that the bandits could not easily sell, such as machine parts, tin plates, iron stakes, then the carretas went in small trains of five or six. The carreteros themselves had little money on them, perhaps sixty or seventy centavos apiece, and this they knew how to hide where no bandit could ever find them.

On the other hand, when they were transporting valuable goods, such as silks, clocks, clothing, articles of adornment, wines and liqueurs, revolvers, sporting rifles, ammunition, they went only in large trains of forty, sixty, and more.

But these large caravans, however good as a protection against bandits, had many disadvantages. Their pace was much slower and this made the freightage more costly, for every day there was the fodder for the oxen and the wages of the men; also, a day's delay could mean the loss of his market for a merchant. A large caravan, too, increased the difficulty of obtaining fodder for the oxen. In a large caravan there were more broken axles than in a small one, and the whole caravan was held up while an axle was mended. These large caravans were only for protection.

5

The carretas were stout, heavily built, two-wheeled carts. The wheels were very high on account of the rivers and marshes that had to be crossed. The body of the carreta was narrow— about twice as long as it was broad. It was provided with a rounded awning on a framework of hoops.

In a string of twenty carretas there would seldom be two with awnings of the same material. One might be covered with stout canvas, another with rush matting, another with plaited palm leaves, another with doe or antelope, lion or tiger skins, another with a patchwork of scraps—old shirts, cotton trousers, tattered blankets. Then there was perhaps a roof of basketwork and others of brown, well-tanned hides of cows, goats, or sheep.

Each carreta was drawn by a pair of oxen—big long-horned beasts. Many of them looked so heavy and powerful that they might have been taken for elephants in disguise.

The two oxen that made up the pair were stood side by side, and then a heavy tie beam was put over their heads, close behind their horns. This beam alone was so heavy that it was all a strong man could do to lift it. When the beam was in the required position, with the oxen at the proper distance from one another, it was lashed to their horns with thongs of tanned hide. Sometimes the horns were pierced, so that the thongs could be more securely lashed and thus not shift. When this yoke beam had been tightly lashed to the horns, it in turn was lashed to a pole. The pole was fixed rigidly to the carreta.

The oxen did not pull the yoke with their necks and shoulders but with their mighty foreheads. Neither beast could move its head on its own; each movement of the one necessitated a corresponding movement of the other. They could do nothing while on the road to protect their forequarters from the bites of the large flies and other insects which swarmed in thousands around the carretas. They could not lick themselves—could not even shake themselves. They had to bear the inflictions laid upon them by these ferocious insects. And so on days when rain threatened or when for any other reason the insects were peculiarly ravenous and bloodthirsty, blood trickled incessantly in innumerable thin streaks over the oxen's tortured forequarters.

With their large glazed protuberant eyes fixed on the road before them, with scarcely a movement of the eyeballs, they moved lumberingly along, step by step, drawing their carts behind them. Their tread was extremely slow but as regular as a machine.

The oxen were urged on by a long goad, not a whip. The goads, made of hardwood, were sharpened at the tip; some had a nail instead of the sharpened point. The carretero, when he had to quicken their pace, goaded the oxen in their hindquarters. What the insects could not do here because the oxen were able to swish them off with their tails was done by the carretero with his sharp goad. When the going was hard and the oxen too weary and hungry to get on as fast as the carreteros wished, the beasts' hindquarters too were streaked with trickle after trickle of blood.

The carreteros in their turn were pricked and goaded and cursed by their employers and threatened with the sack if they were too long on the road. So the oxen had at least the satisfaction of seeing that the world was a complete and ordered system and that God was just and evenhanded.

In the dry season the road was inches deep in a layer of very white, fine chalky dust, which burned in the eyes, nose, and mouth like a consuming poison. In the rainy season the road was a foot or more deep in a layer of stiff tenacious plaster, which gripped the wheels of the carretas and the feet of the oxen as in a vice. But whether in the dry or rainy season, the road was never anything but an unrelieved martyrdom, with its thousands of holes, ruts, and pits, with its millions of stones, boulders, and projecting spars of rock, with the thick roots of gigantic tropical and semitropical trees laid bare by floods, with the landslides along whole stretches of its course, and the crashing down of chunks of cliff and trunks of trees whose roots had rotted or been washed out of the ground. There was neither mercy nor pity for man or beast, no pause in the rain of sufferings that descended on carretero and oxen alike. In Suchiapa, Tuxtla, Chiapa de Corso, Ixtapa, Jovel, Balún-Canán,

Sapaluta lived thousands of people who wanted salt, clothes, boots, mandolins, locks, liqueurs, clocks, shoes, typewriters, phonographs, porcelain cups, silk shirts, earrings, photographic apparatus, perfumes, felt hats, matches, cinnamon, aspirin, oil paintings, crochet hooks, bottled beer, pencils, safety razors, spectacles, rubber teats, screws, tear-off calendars, buttons. Without transport there is no civilization.

6

A caravan of carretas on its way up to El Calvario moves with such an orchestration of noises as no composer could ever achieve; for, discordant as all the various notes are, they produce in combination a wonderful harmony.

The panting and sometimes the lowing of an ox, the grinding of wheels, the squeaking of axles, the wheezing of leather thongs, the creaking of the hooped awnings, the jingle and rattle of articles badly packed in boxes, the jarring and bumping over stones, the shriek of a wheel sliding off smooth rock, the lurch or collapse of one side of a carreta into a pit in the road, the collapse into trenches mined by water, the rattling over stretches of knobby rock, the rumbling over thick roots, the shouts of the carreteros cursing, quarreling, swearing, urging on the beasts, while one whistles a tune, another sings, another hums to himself. A carreta gets stuck in a hole and won't budge. The men from before and behind run up to give a hand and with much shouting and heaving the carreta is hoisted out. The whole caravan goes heavily forward again. By the sides of the road, in the bush and the grass, crickets and grasshoppers chirp shrilly, some birds are singing, bees hum through the quivering air, butterflies eddy to and fro in the wake of the caravan, waiting for the moist dung of the oxen.

If you look down from just below the head of the pass,

whence you can see many windings of the road at one view, you get the impression that some enormous and fabulous worm is crawling up the road. Each single carreta looks like one ring in the worm's long body. And the impression of a great crawling worm is all the more realistic because the carts sway and lurch to and fro; and from that height you cannot tell that they are carts. The distance and the heat vibrations of the air which hover over the earth like a trembling white veil make you take for real and true what sober consideration would tell you was not real at all. But beneath the oppression of the tropical sun, wrapped in eddying clouds of dust, climbing on and on without a moment's respite from the hardships and dangers of the road, even a man of normally clear mind loses all power to judge things soberly and see them as they really are.

7

As they emerge from the last gorge beneath the overhanging cliffs the carretas roll onto the wide plateau of El Calvario.

There were three ranchos on this plateau. The largest was the rancho El Calvario, looking with its numerous peons' huts like a village. Another smaller one at the farther side of the plateau made, with its whitewashed walls and pillared portico, a clean, almost idyllic impression and usually served as an inn for travelers on horseback; for it lay just about midway between Tulum and Jovel. Travelers from Jovel always tried to get as far as this rancho because the stage from there down to Tulum seemed shorter than when they spent the night at the little town of Ixtapa.

The plateau was covered all the year round with grass. At the end of the dry season, certainly, the grass was poor in nourishment; but hard-driven oxen, mules, and horses very quickly forget to be fastidious on treks like these. They show every sign of delight at having reached the resting place at last. The sight of the welcome expanse of grass, however thin and wiry it may look, makes the animals neigh and low. The oxen in particular, accustomed all through their working lives to make their halt here, could not be driven a kilometer beyond it by the most expert of carreteros. The stage from Chiapa de Corso to the plateau was the longest in the whole trip from Arriaga to Balún-Canán; for there was nowhere on the road where the carretas could possibly halt. The track was too narrow and there was no fodder and very little water all the way.

8

Once on level ground the carreteros would like best to fling themselves down and sleep where they fall. They are tired; their exertions have drained them to the last dregs; but there is more work still before them.

With shouts and commands, all the carretas are drawn up close to one another, aligned side by side. The carreteros, like all Indians, have an inborn instinct for beauty: no artillery regiment could wheel its guns into line with a more beautiful precision than the carreteros do their carretas.

The oxen are then taken out from the carts, but it happens often enough that the carreteros are so dog-tired they don't unyoke them. The beasts are left with the heavy yoke—the massive and ponderous yoke beam—behind their horns. They remain coupled two by two. Where one grazes, the other must graze. They can scarcely turn their heads from side to side, and if the one moves its head to the right the other must do the same.

There is sometimes a different reason for leaving the oxen yoked, in spite of the obvious and intolerable suffering it causes them. At certain halting places, where the grass is meager, the beasts may scatter far and wide in search of the best pasture. When they graze singly, they may stray as far as five kilometers from the camp. Then the carreteros have to go in search of them and sometimes have to bring them out of the bush into which they have penetrated in their preference for the foliage of certain trees. The search may cost the carreteros half a day, or even a whole one.

The carreteros are practiced hands at tracking runaway oxen. They can read every broken twig, every trodden-down shrub, every trampled tuft far more easily than many students can a spelling book. They know at once whether a hoof mark is a day or two weeks old and whether it was made by a free ranging animal from the herd of a neighboring rancho or by one of their own animals. Nevertheless, it sometimes happens that oxen are lost for a whole week, either because they are quick on their feet and try to make off for the rancho where they were reared or because they join a herd and go to the rancho where that herd belongs.

Time lost over runaway cattle has to be made up in some way or another. If they are too often late with their freight the men get badly told off by their employers and perhaps severely punished or fired. Then they have the reputation of unreliable carreteros and there is difficulty in finding another job.

One must not, then, be too hasty in accusing the carretero of cruelty to animals if he sometimes leaves his oxen yoked. Yoked oxen cannot go far; the heavy yoke beam across their necks collides with trees and holds them up.

Nevertheless, the carretero cannot risk leaving his oxen yoked at every stop, for they cannot feed sufficiently when they are not free. They stay hungry, fall out of condition, fail to pull properly, and perhaps even have to be left by the wayside. Nor is it practicable to take fodder along in the carretas and tether the animals at the halts. These are big animals who need a lot of fodder to keep them in working condition; and if the carreta is laden with it there will be no room for the freight. The maize which has to be taken along for the animals, because it cannot be bought at all places on the road, takes up enough room in any case and adds a lot of weight for its bulk.

So however much thought a good carretero may give to the task of doing equal justice to his employer, his beasts, and the merchant who requires his goods by a certain date, he is up against circumstances and conditions at every turn which are more powerful than he is and stronger than his best intentions.

6

 The caravan had made its ascent. The carretas were neatly dressed in line. The oxen were taken out and unyoked, and no sooner were they free than they sought out a place to lie down. They were too weary to graze.

Each man joined his own group. On the road the carretas kept the order in which they happened to fall, but at the halts the carreteros of each employer formed groups. Don Laureano's carreteros formed one group, don Nicasio's another, and so on; for they made their meals of the rations their employers gave them for the road.

The carreteros set about preparing their simple meals. A man from each group ran with a battered gasoline can to the stream for water. Others ran into the bush to get firewood. Others cut the branches from which the pots were suspended over the fire.

It had been an unusually long trek and the evening was well advanced. Soon the campfire of each group burned brightly. Over the fires hung anything and everything that might with some adjustment of the imagination have been called a pot or pan.

The men cooked black beans in quantities large enough to do for breakfast as well, for frijoles take a long time to cook. They boiled rice and heated their tortillas. At every fire coffee was made—the indispensable drink at every meal of all people on the road in these tropical regions. If coffee was scarce, pinol was sometimes used. Pinol is roasted maize ground to a fine powder. If there was no pinol either, then tea was made of lemon leaves picked on the way somewhere.

The beans were cooked until soft and then made palatable with lard, brought with them in bottles and as fluid as oil in that hot climate.

The rice was cooked differently than in other parts of the Republic. Lard was heated in a pan and when hot enough, the dry grains of rice were added and stirred to and fro until browned. Then very slowly, little by little, water was added. If it was done clumsily the flames leaped into the pan and there was a blaze which often burned up all the rice.

Coffee too was made in a special way. A conical-shaped tin can was filled with water and a handful of ground coffee and a good quantity of brown unrefined sugar put into it. This was then boiled together to a thick soup, which was not strained; the coffee grounds were swallowed with the coffee.

The carreteros had plenty of opportunities on the road to catch fowl and little pigs as an addition to their meals, but carreteros never rob a farmer and, least of all, Indian peasants.

One of the men might have caught a rabbit or an armadillo, or someone might have shot a wild turkey; another might have chased a tepescuintle out of a hollow tree with the help of his dog. If anyone had meat, it was game of this kind.

The dogs sat waiting around every fire for bones and other morsels. All the carreteros had dogs with them. An Indian and his dog go together as a carbine goes with a soldier.

2

There were many women with the caravan on this occasion—women traveling singly, women with their children, women with their maidservants. Some were bound for Jovel, others for Balún-Canán or even as far upcountry as Tabasco or Campeche. They were all women in humble circumstances whose husbands were not well enough off to enable them to travel on horseback. Even if the husband had a horse or two, he would have had either to accompany his wife himself, which would have meant sacrificing his time and leaving his business in other hands, or else to hire reliable men to accompany her, and this would have been costly; whereas if a woman traveled with a caravan she only paid a peso or even half a peso for her seat in the carreta. And since there were usually several other women, she felt more protected than if she had been the only woman among men hired to accompany her on horseback.

Sometimes it might happen in a small train of carretas that there was only one woman traveler, but on no account would a carretero molest her either by day or night.

Some of the carreteros took their wives with them. An Indian or half-breed could not do without his wife for long. Carreteros who had their wives with them often proved more reliable than those who were without them. If they left their wives at home, they sometimes had a wild longing and ran off to them, leaving the carreta wherever it happened to be on the road.

The carreteros' wives shared the rations given their husbands for the journey. The rations were plentiful, though they were only black beans and rice, commodities which were practically given away in that part of the country. Potatoes, on the other hand, were so scarce and expensive that a carretero seldom ate two in a lifetime. Even the patrón used them with the greatest economy in his own household.

It was nothing to the patrón how many shared his carreteros' rations. It did not concern him at all. He did not care whether a carretero took his wife along or not, and still less did he, or anyone else, care whether the carretero and his wife were legally married. It was a matter for themselves entirely on what terms they lived with one another.

The patrón had other reasons for not counting the few black beans which a carretero's wife ate. He had the extra labor for nothing; and though the women were not essential to the safe and punctual arrival of a train of carretas, they were useful all the same and helped in many ways.

They helped to find and catch strayed oxen; or if they didn't help in the search they stayed in the camp and kept an eye on the loads and so set all the carreteros free to go after the lost animals. They cooked for the men while the men were busy mending a damaged carreta; and by doing the cooking and by mending and washing their husbands' shirts and trousers, they gave the men more time to rest so that they worked better and didn't doze off on the road. And when there was an easy stretch of road the wife drove the oxen while her husband took a nap in the carreta. What more could the patrón ask in return for the handful of black beans which a carretero's wife shared with her husband.

3

Not all carreteros had wives; and of those who did, not a fifth took wives with them on the road.

Many of the women lived with their parents or with married brothers or sisters at some place on the road. Others lived in the house of the patrón when they were not on the road.

Others, again, had small children and the wife remained with them in the hut where they lived.

Some carreteros had had wives at one time who had since left them; or wives who had tired at last of the endless trekking on wretched roads night and day in tropical heat and torrential rains; or wives who were pregnant; or wives whose parents or husbands' parents wanted them to stay at home with them.

Again, there were carreteros who were bad husbands. They soon got tired of a wife and got rid of her—peaceably, or with blows and abuse. Others were inveterate woman hunters who wanted a woman occasionally, but otherwise, and particularly when on the road, could not bear a woman near them. They made merry over the domestic brawls of their married companions.

So now and then there was a train in which not one carretero had a wife with him. It was here they had the merriest, jolliest, and wildest time of it. The men could indulge their humor and gave themselves up to the pleasures of hearing and telling the broadest of tales and anecdotes. According to them, the worst thing about wives was their way of interfering and getting mixed up with their lives. The ideal wife was the kind that could be put in a drawer and taken out only when needed, then wrapped up carefully in tissue paper again and put away till next time. But such a wife is a blissful dream of male fantasy. She is rarer than the egg of the Phoenix.

Carreteros, certainly, had no time to go in search of such treasures of an ideal world. Like the rest who sigh and groan under the yoke of the flesh, they had to be content with what they could get and try to avoid the thorns on the rose-strewn way.

4

Besides the women who had to make a journey to see a doctor or to visit relations or the devil knows whither or wherefore, and besides the carreteros' wives, there were often women engaged in trade to be found traveling with the caravans, women who had bought goods in Arriaga or Tonalá and were now traveling upcountry to dispose of them at markets or places where fiestas were being held.

None of these women traders and except in rare cases none of the other women travelers shared the camp and campfires at the halting places. There were usually ranchos nearby, and as soon as the caravan came to a halt they went to the rancheros' houses.

There they found other women, the wives, daughters, mothers, aunts, and all the rest who make up a family in Mexico. Often they were even distant relatives; or if not acquainted they would usually have mutual acquaintances somewhere in the state. And so there was enough gossip to keep them up half the night. Women on lonely ranchos are always eager to hear news and scandal and gossip from other places.

These women travelers had their meals at the ranchero's table. Usually they paid nothing; and if they did it was only twenty or thirty centavos, more for form's sake than for profit.

When they had all talked themselves hoarse and had come to the end of their gossip and eyes began to close, they were offered a bedstead or else mats were spread out for them on the floor, which had been thickly strewn with pine needles. Here the women could lay out their bedding, which the carreteros had obligingly carried along for them.

If there were no ranchos or haciendas in the neighborhood,

the women had to be content with sleeping places in the carreta, on top of the loads. That was very uncomfortable. But what else could they do?

5

The wives of the carreteros, less tied to the habits of domestic life, slept wherever there was a spot. They were used to a hard life from childhood on. They could sleep wherever they lay down, no matter where. If there was room in the carreta, they slept in the carreta. If there was no room or if the bales and cases and packages were too lumpy and irregular to afford them a bed, they slept on the ground beneath the carreta; or just crouched, their backs against one of the wheels; or lay on the grass nearby. In some way or another they managed to spread the mosquito net over themselves at those stops along the road where insects abounded.

As for the carreteros, they did not know the meaning of the word discomfort. When they had their wives with them they did their best to find them as good and comfortable a sleeping place as they could. But for themselves it was only the sleep, wherever, that mattered. They were always so done in by their work that when they once dropped down beside the carreta it took a torrent of rain that soaked them through and through to wake them; and when they awakened it was not to crawl for cover under the carreta—not that it would have helped them very much to crawl under, for in a good tropical downpour the whole camp was soon turned into a lake and any planks or ropes lying about very quickly floated away. No, the carretero jumped up not to protect himself but to see to the goods in his charge. He fastened firmly the matting which curtained each end of the carreta against dust and weather, so that the rain would not whip in and damage the goods. He tied the awning down tighter and plugged its rents with grass or rags.

The dogs sought out dry places between bales and cases. The carretero was not a dog able to squeeze himself into crannies. He was a human being with a soul which, after the toils and cares of earthly life, would take flight one day for paradise. He was a human being who loved and wept and laughed. He was a human being, born of a mother who loved him and agonized for the well-being of her child.

He was a human being just as the patrón was; a human being quite as much as don Porfirio, the dictator president of his country, the great statesman, hung about with medals and orders.

But his employer could not spare the money to provide his carretero with a little tent and cot, which when the camp was a swamp would have ensured the man a dry sleeping place. The transport of goods did not run to that; the patrón had other expenses to meet which were more important than nonsense of that kind. And though don Porfirio, whose portrait hung in a large and glittering gold frame in the patrón's principal sitting room, decreed so many thousands of wonderful laws, there was not among them all a single one that put the carretero on a higher level than the oxen he harnessed to his patrón's carreta. Oxen can take their rest in the open in pouring rain, so why in the name of all the saints should laws be made to protect a carretero from it?

All the better if he sleeps out in heavy rain. He will not oversleep himself when he's not too comfortable. He will get up in the middle of the night in the pouring rain, put the oxen in, and continue his journey; and that will be half a day gained. The patrón then gets the name of a good carrier who keeps on schedule. This helps trade and increases the prosperity of the country.

6

After El Calvario and farther on into the interior of the state there was no more fear of bandits. There might be a slight risk in the neighborhood of Balún-Canán. There was an occasional holdup on the roads there, but there were only three or four bandits, who apparently were brothers. They never attempted more than two or at the utmost three carretas. The larger trains were safe. These lone wolves were more of a danger to single travelers on horseback. They had the repute throughout the state of being highwaymen who murdered their victims so as to lessen the chances of discovery.

As the next hundred and twenty kilometers were safe-going, and as, too, many of the carretas, more than three-quarters of the train, were bound only for Jovel, or perhaps for no further than Shimojol, the long caravan began here to break up again into small strings of from eight to ten carretas.

Each train had its own leader, or encargado, who was responsible for it and decided on the day's journey. There was no timetable laid down for the daily journeys of a train of carretas. The encargado arranged the timetable according to his judgment.

In the hot plains the carretas traveled only by night and rested by day. Oxen will not travel in great heat, or, if they do, they are utterly exhausted after two hours. They are beasts of the temperate zone, and such they remain even if they are reared on the grasslands of a tropical region. It is not only the heat that diminishes the oxen's capacity for work; there are the thousands of large horseflies which settle on them in swarms and drain their blood. These flies bite only in the sunshine. If there is even a cloud over the sun they vanish.

In the cool of the uplands the carretas traveled by day as well. They went for four or six hours at a stretch according to the difficulty of the road and the distance between one good camping place and the next. Then there was a halt of four or five hours before setting off once more.

A train of carretas needed from five to seven days for a journey of a hundred kilometers. The freight charges were reckoned by distance and weight; sometimes, too, by bulk. The weight of the goods was not ascertained by scales. It was judged by the encargado; so was the distance. And the units of measurement used were the old Spanish ones.

The measures of weight were the arroba and the quintal. An arroba is eleven and a half kilos; a quintal is forty-five kilos. The charge for an arroba for a distance of a hundred kilometers was usually one peso, although sometimes it was three-quarters or even a half. The distance was reckoned by the legua. A legua is about four kilometers, but the encargado estimated a legua by time. Many a distance which he computed as ten leguas may in actual measurement have been only eight-and-a-half or perhaps only seven leguas; while another bit of road which he estimated at twelve may really have been fifteen. But the distances on the main routes were settled for good. They remained unaltered even when the roads had been surveyed and measured accurately. The carreteros who first estimated them had died over two hundred years before and their names had been long forgotten, but all freightage was still reckoned by the estimates of the distances they handed down.

However inefficient and primitive this may seem to an outsider, it worked out in the long run without a hitch and with perfect harmony. Nobody cared very much whether the five leguas were a little less or more, or whether the weight was half an arroba less or more. The carrier came to terms with his clients either when he took on the goods or when they were delivered.

"Now listen to me, don Laureano, you have reckoned this case at ten arrobas. It's scarcely eight. How can you charge fifteen pesos carriage?" says the merchant.

To this don Laureano replies: "Don Miguel, whatever it weighs, you can't deny it's a good size and weighs a lot. I don't know what you can have inside it. Fifteen pesos is not a lot to charge. And I don't see where my profit is to come from. Maize gets no cheaper and the muchachos are always wanting more money. You know yourself, don Miguel, it's close on forty leguas and I've only reckoned you thirty-five. All the same, I don't want to be hard on you and this is not the last deal we shall make together. Give me thirteen-fifty. You can surely pay that, don Miguel."

They come to terms at twelve-eighty. Everyone is happy and the transaction leaves no rancor behind it.

When don Miguel forwards goods by rail he pays to a centavo what the waybill says, for the railroad does not care whether don Miguel remains its friend or not; and the clerks, who have no say in the charges, refuse to discuss the matter with don Miguel. They have their fixed hours of work, and when the time is up they go home whether don Miguel has received his case or not.

7

The campfire of one of the trains was already blazing up again at one o'clock in the morning. The encargado had observed that the oxen were in good shape, and as his carretas were not too heavily laden he had made up his mind to be at Ixtapa by the early morning. Ixtapa was only six kilometers from the pass and he had goods to deliver to shopkeepers there.

The carreteros gave their oxen the feed of maize. Then they ate some beans and drank their coffee; and when they had finished they began to yoke the oxen and put them in. Then a boy ran across to one of the ranchos and knocked on the door of the room in which he had been told the evening before that the women who traveled with the carretas were sleeping.

"Hola, señoras, vámonos, listo—we're off and all ready to start."

" 'Orita, muchacho, right away," a woman answered at once.

The women got up without wasting time to stretch and yawn. They quickly put their skirts over their heads and opened the door. The boy rushed in and swiftly grabbed hold of their bedding, rolled it all up in a bundle, and tied it together.

The women dipped the forefingers of both hands into a gourd of water and wiped their eyes. This is all the washing a carreta traveler, man or woman, undertakes on a journey as far as the face is concerned. After this they held out their cupped hands to the boy, who poured a little water into each. The gourd held only a third of a liter, but it did for the four of them and they did not bother their heads about its purity.

The women rubbed their moistened hands together and smoothed their hair. Then they combed it flat with four strokes of their pocket combs and were ready for the day's journey.

It was all done so quickly that scarcely two minutes had elapsed since the boy knocked at the door and the women were already swallowing a few mouthfuls of hot coffee which a girl of the rancho brought them. The knocking had roused the girl and the coffee had been kept hot on the red ashes of the hearth.

No traveler went to more trouble than this when he was on the road. It used to be the same with us—or our grand-fathers—before there were sleeping cars and railroads, and when rattling along in a coach was the quickest and preferred means of travel. An ox-drawn carreta is a clumsier affair than a well-sprung coach of the latter half of the nineteenth century, and therefore you cannot expect those who travel by it to be as smart and well-groomed as though they were to dine at the Ritz with the Emir of Afghanistan. A toilet unsuited to its surroundings disturbs the harmony of life—and anyone who traveled with a carreta had, unconsciously, a fine and cultivated instinct for the harmony of things with their surroundings.

Carreteros never washed their faces during their three- or four-week trips, or shaved or cut their hair. Although those of Indian blood commonly have no beard to speak of, some tribes do have strong beards; and carreteros who came from those tribes or whose ancestors intermarried with them began to look so frightful on the road that the devil himself would have thrown them out of hell.

This picturesque appearance of the carreteros might sometimes be disturbed by a false note. If they halted long enough near a river and were not too exhausted, they bathed; if there was time they bathed for two hours at a stretch. But the harmony of dirt was soon restored again.

The first thing a carretero did in the morning before he ate or took a drink of coffee was to rinse his mouth thoroughly and at great length. And night or morning or during the day's journey, before he put a bite of his meager provisions into his mouth, he washed his hands. If there was no water near and his gourd was empty, he would not eat rather than eat without washing his hands. Even though the washing was a mere symbolic act because he may have had only a drop of water to do it with, still he must have performed this act before he could eat.

Three minutes after being waked the women, a fourth part washed and an eighth part breakfasted, were seated in the carretas and the train was in motion.

8

Meanwhile other trains were getting ready for the start. One of them had to find their oxen from among the oxen of the other trains and bring them in; and this was not easy, as it was still dark. Another train was delayed by having a wheel to mend. With another the oxen had flesh wounds to be doctored.

The encargado of a fourth, after a careful inspection, found that it would be impossible to start until midday. The oxen were so exhausted that nothing would induce them to get to their feet. Owing to their exhausted condition they had scarcely grazed at all during the night. The carreteros carried maize to them and put it right under their noses to try to make them feed. These oxen had made four trips without having rested, and each trip had lasted three weeks. This was don Laureano's train in which Andrés drove a carreta.

Don Laureano's carreteros and oxen had particularly long and hard spells of work because he always had plenty of freight. Before one cargo was disposed of there was another waiting. There was a limit, however, beyond which the oxen could not be worked without a break. When they got too low and exhausted and were not given a rest out at grass, they finally refused to rise to their feet while on a journey, and then not the best of feeds or any other persuasion could urge them to go any farther. Blows had no effect. Oxen will very often act as mules do. They lie down, refuse food, and die.

Oxen and mules required a break of three or four weeks out at pasture in good grass three or four times a year; and they got them. Oxen and mules were costly, and therefore suicide on their parts was expensive for their masters. The carreteros never had a holiday. They worked day after day, Sundays and holidays, by day and by night, in rain or tropical glare, in sandstorms and thunderstorms of such violence that the sky seemed to burst. The carreteros too sometimes lay down by the way; but they did not commit suicide from exhaustion. That was the privilege of oxen and mules. And if a carretero actually perished by the way, or fell down a ravine while hoisting a caretta out of a hole, or got under the wheels, he was no loss to his employer. Carreteros did not mean the outlay of a centavo, unless it was that the employer took over a debt of a carretero to a previous master; and this debt would be little compared with the money an ox cost, even if the employer were left with it unredeemed due to the mishap of a carretero.

7

Andrés was now nearly nineteen. He had been working for don Laureano as carretero for more than three years. The debt of the twenty-five pesos which brought him into don Laureano's possession had long been paid off and he had for some time been getting his wages in cash.

Andrés had meanwhile become an excellent carretero. He knew the road from Arriaga to Balún-Canán so well that he could travel it on the darkest night and avoid any hole and every place where the road had given way. He knew every stone, every bend, every boggy patch, every ford. He knew to an inch the depth of every river which had to be crossed and the best place to cross in mid-June and mid-September. The fords shifted their position according to the rain that fell. In the rainy season a halt had to be made for a few hours or perhaps half a day on the riverbank till the water had run down and the carreta could cross without the load getting wet. He knew every halting place on the road by the name given it by the first carreteros who had halted there two hundred years before. He knew every patch of grass on the road and what its value was as feed and how many oxen it would carry. He knew every rancho and every Indian hut and all the people who lived on the road. He had learned how to load to the best advantage, how to handle the oxen properly so as to get the most out of them, and he could undertake the repair of a wheel or an axle as well as the most experienced man. Whatever happened on the road he was never at a loss, even if he was alone. He had already on several occasions acted as encargado of a small train. Don Laureano had not a criticism to make of him or his work. In every respect he had turned out even better than his patrón had expected.

Don Laureano had even raised his wages on the strength of all this and he now received forty centavos a day—twelve pesos a month. This was no mean sum when he compared it with the four or five pesos a month which the laborers earned who worked in the sugar mills, brandy distilleries, henequen processing factories, brick works, timber yards he passed on the road and who had to work sixteen hours a day and lived, often with families to keep, more wretchedly than beasts.

He worked hard enough, but he was not racked by the consuming and hectic toil of those half-starved men on the haciendas where the products of the soil were dealt with in factories. He and his fellow workers were not tied to hours. Once his load was well stowed away and his carreta in good going order, if his oxen were not overtired and overworked, and if the road offered no special difficulties, he could sit hour after hour in the carreta, dreaming or contemplating the beauty of the landscape around him.

The oxen knew the road, which they had traveled over and over again, every bit as well as the carreteros. That was only natural, since their eyes and noses were closer to it. Experienced oxen are not so stupid as may appear from the way people have of using the term "ox" to express contempt for a fellow man.

Their pace was slow, for it was all one to them whether the carreta reached its destination the following day or the following week. There was time; and they took their time both in feeding and working. Perhaps they knew that they would always remain oxen and draw a carreta as long as they remained on their legs, that their fate was the same whether they hurried or not. No, the oxen were not stupid. They knew the road, and they would not venture one step more than their strength allowed.

And they did not just plod blindly on. They carefully inspected each bit of road as they came to it, and so far as the encumbrance of the carreta allowed they avoided every large stone, every hole and broken piece of road, every gnarled tree root. This was not, certainly, from love of their drivers, but for their own advantage. It lightened their toil and brought them more quickly to the next halting place.

By lightening their own toil the oxen lightened the toil of their drivers. The carreteros who had experienced oxen in their carretas could dream and doze over long stretches of road. It was the aim of all hardened carreteros to know the worth of all the oxen of their respective trains and to get hold of the best ones at the start of each trip. The encargado of a train, who had to keep his eye on all the other carretas as well as on his own, had first pick. Then came the carretero who had been longest in the patrón's employment. The rest took what was left.

2

Andrés had the inborn cunning of the defeated and downtrodden races. And as the peons from youth up relied on their cunning for their existence, they did not cramp their cunning by petty considerations of morality. Strike before you are struck. And if you cannot strike because your master can shoot you down like a dog if you raise your hand against him, then you must turn and twist like a snake to avoid a blow or to ward it off if you cannot avoid it. The lead swinger among soldiers and other slaves is the clever man; the rest are the fools.

It was to little tricks that Andrés owed his raises in wages. The worker is rarely paid for what he really does, but only for what he seems to do in the eyes of the one who pays his wages.

Don Laureano once accompanied a very long train of carretas for a whole day, because his way happened to be the same. The oxen in one of the carretas refused to pull; they backed, and did all they could to shake off the yoke. The encargado and the drivers did everything to get the oxen to move on, but without success. Don Laureano came up, but he too was at a loss. The carreta was holding up the whole caravan. Don Laureano said he had a good mind to sell the oxen and plant them on a friend of his.

While the whole caravan was at a standstill because of this intractable pair of oxen, with the carreteros standing around and making suggestions which led to nothing, Andrés came up. He tried to urge the oxen on. They took a few steps forward and then jibbed again.

"I think I know what the trouble is with the bueyes—the oxen," he said.

"You!" the encargado broke in. "You're the one to tell me— an old stallion who's done his thirty years with carretas on the road. Run home to your mother and get a dry diaper."

But Andrés was not to be daunted. He said quietly: "The oxen are lashed too tight to the yoke—that's the trouble; or else a hard thong has got twisted and cuts into them." Without waiting to hear what the encargado had to say, he set to work unlacing the thongs.

Don Laureano sat down on a boulder by the roadside, lit a cigarette, and without taking much interest looked on at what Andrés was doing.

As soon as Andrés had got the straps loose he smoothed them out and softened them with plentiful applications of spit. "These two oxen won't stand being strapped too tight," he said. "Lucio has not been long with us and he doesn't know the animals. It's no fault of his."

By saying this he cleared his mate, Lucio, of all blame; otherwise Lucio might have been told off by don Laureano or the encargado for bad harnessing.

While he was loosening the oxen Andrés had stood in such a position that he was able by adroit movements of his arms and hands to divert attention from what he was actually doing, and neither don Laureano nor the encargado nor any of the carreteros who stood around in boredom had been able to see the trick he was engaged in.

The evening before he had made some little sharp pegs out of hardwood and early in the morning when the oxen were put in he had cunningly inserted them under the thongs. For the first half hour the oxen felt no discomfort from them and went along as usual. But when the sun came up and it got hot, the thongs hardened and contracted and the pegs pressed into the skin at the back of the oxen's heads. With every kilometer the pegs pressed deeper and became so unbearably painful that the oxen behaved as though they were going crazy.

Andrés knew very well that tricks of this sort were often played with thorns and prickles when a carretero wanted to have a little fun. But the thorns penetrated so quickly that the beasts refused to pull from the first. Then of course their driver knew at once what was wrong. He had to unharness and harness up again. It was a joke played on greenhorns to give them double work and to make fools of them.

But the trick with little cones of hardwood was Andrés's own invention. It had a delayed action and so was quite unsuspected. Even the oldest and most experienced carretero would never have been able to explain why the oxen should start by going well and then by degrees become recalcitrant until finally they refused to go on at all.

When Andrés had lashed the yoke to their horns again and then to the pole, he urged the oxen forward and they set off as willingly and cheerfully as a pair of thriving dray horses. The old encargado gaped and made up his mind to treat Andrés henceforth as a grown man and veteran carretero, whose friendship was worth cultivating.

Don Laureano opened his eyes wider than any, though it is true he knew very little at first hand about a carretero's job, and if he had had a train of carretas to take from Arriaga to Chiapa de Corso, it's doubtful whether the caravan would arrive before the end of this century.

When the train was in motion again he found an opportunity to take Andrés aside. "Listen to me, my boy," he said. "You can have three reales a day now. You know your job and you're worth your thirty-six centavos a day."

Andrés owed his second raise to another trick he played. During the time he had worked as carretero he had acquired enough wisdom to see that he would never get recognition or reward from his employer merely because he worked well and hard and efficiently. His work was not greatly valued. He had to draw attention to himself and arouse the fear in his employer's mind that he might lose a thoroughly efficient carretero, who knew more about the management of oxen than an old encargado, unless he gave him a raise in wages.

3

Andrés had had to work more than four months before he worked off the debt of twenty-five pesos which his previous master had lost to his present one.

During these four months Andrés had had to buy shirts, trousers, a bast hat, a new serape, a white cotton blouse. The work of a carretero was almost as hard on clothing as sulfuric acid. One packing case had a nail sticking out, another a long splinter of wood; and when he was loading up, they caught in his shirt or trousers and in a moment the thing was in shreds. On the road his clothing was wet through one hour and in the next dried so quickly in the tropical sun that in a few days the cloth was as brittle as tinder and fell to pieces if his carreta so much as lurched against the side of the cliff. The thorny scrub by the roadside tore bits right out or made a long tear. However careful he might be, something went every time he handled the goods, either to load up or to shift them while on the road.

A carretero during a journey stands himself a comiteco when it is cold and wet and he can't get his clothes dry. He buys a few lemons and makes lemonade, or a few mangoes or a piece of cheese to vary his rations. He may pass through a place where there is a feast day or a market day and he does not want to look on like an outsider—he wants to join in and enjoy himself for a change. He buys a mouth organ or a cheap guitar to cheer up the evenings around the fire, which are usually so dreary. Then he must have a piece of soap now and again, have his hair cut, and now and again he loses his wooden comb and must buy a new one. Then the bottle of creolin for doctoring the oxen gets broken and he has to buy some more and a new bottle. As for shoes to protect his feet against the stones and all the myriad thorns and prickles on the roads—he cannot think of them. He has no shoes and cannot afford them. He is thankful if he can get hold of untanned hide to patch up the Indian sandals he wears.

However carefully he might stint and save he was always in his employer's debt; for his employer was the only man on earth who would give him credit. Almost every article he needed had to be bought from his employer, and the employer fixed the price of everything he sold to his carreteros.

These advances on wages were debts, and as long as he had a debt with his patrón he could not leave his service. If he did, he was brought back by the police and the cost of apprehending him was added to the debit side of his account.

But the carretero was no peon—who was a fixture on a finca or hacienda. He was a free laborer. He only had to pay his employer what he owed and then he might go where he liked. The whole world was his and all it produced. No one forced him to run up debts; neither the law nor the State compelled him to. He was entirely free to choose whether he contracted debts or not. If he did not avail himself of his liberty, neither his employer nor the State nor the dictator, General Porfirio Díaz, could be held responsible. And if he did not amass capital in order one day to be a forwarding agent, a factory owner, or a finquero, it was only because he did not choose to save. The way was open to anyone who wanted to start a bank. If the laborer did not become a banker it was only because he blew all he got. The capitalist system is all a myth, trumped up by agitators and anarchists in order to fan the flames of a world revolution and take over the banks and perfumed daughters of the directors. Save, workingman, and then you can acquire the bank at the first corner you come to—without the bother of a world revolution.

4

By the time Andrés had worked out that debt of twenty-five pesos, he had run up a debt on his own account with don Laureano of forty-two pesos for goods he had bought from him and sixteen pesos in cash he had needed for other things.

Now that he had served his employer well and truly and

with a proper Christian humility and submission for over three years, his debt with don Laureano amounted to ninety-four pesos. A mathematician could have told him in two minutes, not as a guess but with precision, that if he continued serving him so well for forty years he would by that time have a debt of nine hundred and twenty-four pesos, thirty centavos with don Laureano or his son, after counting all raises which he might secure by true and loyal service or by ruses.

Andrés, like all carreteros, looked down with pity and compassion on the poor peons who had no liberty and were tied to the finca to which they belonged. And indeed there was a great difference between the social and economic liberties of a carretero and those of a peon on a finca.

If a carretero fell down a ravine on a journey or a carreta ran over him and crushed him, or a mad ox gored him, or a rattlesnake bit him on his bare foot, or malaria carried him off, then his debts were canceled. The patrón did not lament the death of a carretero who had died in his service; he lamented the bad debt. But at least the carretero was free and duly received into paradise.

When a peon died, the finquero did not lose a centavo of the peon's debt. It passed as a matter of course to his eldest son, or was shared among all his sons, or passed to the dead man's brother if there were no sons, or to the husbands of the daughters if he had daughters only. So the peon was not free even after his death. He had to live on as a peon in the persons of his sons, his daughters, or his brothers.

When the peon was buried, the finquero summoned his sons or brothers or sons-in-law and showed them his ledger and the dead man's debit account. "Is that right?" he asked. And the representatives of the dead man replied: "Yes, patrón, that is right."

Then the finquero turned up the account of the next of kin

and entered the dead man's debt and added the two together. He then said the total aloud and asked again: "Is that right, muchacho?" And the man replied: "Yes, that is right, patrón."

When this was disposed of, the finquero opened the little chapel of the finca and the wives of the peons were permitted to enter and place candles for the soul of the deceased on the altar of the patron saint of the finca and light them. For the patrón of the finca was a good Catholic who would have incurred a mortal sin if he had not allowed candles to be lighted for the salvation of a deceased Catholic, even though that Catholic was only a poor peon.

That was just. It was accounted just. And because it was just, it was, like all else which is just, supported by law and by the State. For what would be the use of the State if it did not with its police and its soldiers, its judges and its prisons, support what is just?

It was these little differences which gave the carreteros the right to consider that they stood one rung higher on the social ladder than the peons on a finca.

The world is full of justice. It is the fault of the carreteros and the peons and of all other workers in the world if they make no use of the justice which is theirs for the asking. Nobody puts a loaded revolver to a carretero's chest and forces him to run up bills; nobody forces anyone to do so; not even the most money-grubbing finquero forces a peon into his debt. To contract debts or not to contract debts is the greatest of all a worker's liberties.

If the carretero and the peon make an improper and even positively dangerous use of this great liberty, which forms the very core of every national anthem of every people, one must not blame the finquero or the cartage contractor. That is unjust and not at all fair.

All men without exception are equipped at birth with free

will. For every single one two ways lie open, the way to hell and the way to eternal joys and songs of praise in paradise. The inventor of the phrases "wage slave" and "slaves of economic conditions" is the Antichrist—the same Antichrist of whom the apostles said: Beware. It is the sacred duty of all good, just, and noble people to hang their false prophets, or to seat them in the electric chair, or to designate them as fanatics and destroyers of the State.

8

It was the last week in January. In the middle of February there was the fiesta of San Caralampio at Balún-Canán.

San Caralampio was the patron saint of the town of Balún-Canán. He was at the same time patron saint of Sapaluta, a small town lying in the wide plain of Balún-Canán, about twenty kilometers away.

San Caralampio would have been hard put to it to say how he became patron saint of Balún-Canán; nor was there anyone else who knew why San Caralampio was chosen to defend the town of Balún-Canán against the devil and all other hazards, or who had made him its champion. Even the curas—the priests of Balún-Canán—would have been in a fix if they had been called upon for a concise answer to the question why Caralampio was of such importance to the town as a saint. And nobody, all the curas included, could have said with any certainty who Caralampio was, when he lived, and what he had done to be made a saint. Everybody was content with the fact that his effigy in wood was in the cathedral church of Balún-Canán and in the church of Sapaluta, where anyone could see it as large as life if he wished to convince himself that such a personage as San Caralampio really existed.

The fiesta in honor of San Caralampio was nothing whatever but an unabashed excuse for promoting business. It lasted a full week; and as there were festivities in preparation and in conclusion it occupied in reality two weeks at least.

Whatever can be done under the sun was permitted by the civic authorities during this holy fiesta; for these two weeks brought tremendous business to the mayor, the revenue officials, and the chief of police. It was because of this great opportunity, not discounting the everyday ones during the year, that the elections for the civic offices and the post of chief of police were enlivened by hundreds of revolver shots and the shooting and wounding of rival candidates and voters.

All traders had high charges to pay for their stands. And as gambling was forbidden by law throughout the Republic and only the authorities could give special dispensations, every proprietor of a gambling table had to pay for one in hard cash. But it was the cantineros who had the heaviest charges to pay.

Business in the cantinas was encouraged by "barmaids" who arrived in troops with their "mothers" and "foster mothers." For the permission to employ "barmaids," the cantineros had to pay through the nose. And the "mothers" who acted as the business managers for the girls had to pay the mayor and the other dignitaries well for permission to send the girls off for an hour now and then with customers of the cantina. The good citizens too, who desired to let their good rooms and double beds by the hour to these "barmaids," had to buy "a permission to let" from the authorities, with money down.

Even the doctor who was authorized to examine the girls and give them a clean bill of health had to come to an understanding with the mayor, in case another doctor offered more and stole his privilege from him. Every girl had to have her certificate renewed three times a week—such were the regulations of the mayor and the chief of police—and each certificate cost three pesos. Thus the doctor too regarded the sacred fiesta in honor of the sainted Caralampio as the most lucrative time of the year. The good folk of the town who were his regular patients would only be cured on credit; and their bills often went unpaid for three or four years in a row. These "barmaids," on the other hand, were self-respecting clients who paid on the spot and made no grimaces about it.

The authorities gave some return for the money, lest anyone should say that it found its way into their individual pockets. They spent two hundred pesos or so on rockets and squibs and arranged firework displays to delight the populace. They had not studied Roman history, but their own intelligence was sufficient to direct them to the political philosophy of ancient Rome: bread and circuses.

They did not forget the bread. An ox and a few pigs were roasted in the square and all the poor received their piece of barbacoa. Even on the fireworks and the barbecue the authorities made a bit; for the men who wished to provide the fireworks and the barbecue for the poor had to oil the official who disposed of these contracts, lest others who were also in the same line of business got the contract in their places. No one on earth expects anyone to fete the populace or feed the poor for nothing. Nobody does such things unless he wants to be called a fool. And since the contractors had to come out on the right side, they delivered only half what the authorities had paid them for, or else the quality was so poor that it was worth very much less than half.

As every official had his finger in the pie in some way or another, no inspection was made. What would be the point? Life is much more cheerful when things are not looked into too closely. The mayor, the assessor of taxes, and the chief of police all have cares enough on this earth; why should anyone further darken an already sad existence by submitting their accounts and ledgers and receipts and bills of delivery to a rigorous examination? And if an investigation were actually undertaken—the devil only knows by whom—the inspector appointed for the task would very well know the value of fifty pesos and could very easily earn them in the course of his duties. We are all brothers and none of us is perfect; so we stand by each other for our country's good. Viva la patria.

2

Andrés had conducted a small train of carretas from Chiapa de Corso to Sapaluta. Don Laureano entrusted it to him because he could not spare any of the older carreteros that week, as he had an exceptionally heavy freight on the road from Arriaga to Tulum, and the goods were of a kind that required handling by experienced carreteros if they were to arrive undamaged.

It was the dry season, and Andrés's responsibility had been further lightened because the caravan had been accompanied by a number of small traders, male and female, who were conveying their goods to Sapaluta in the carretas, and who all had a personal interest in the safe arrival of their wares. When anything occurred on the way—a broken wheel, a broken bit of road which had to be hurriedly made passable—they all turned to with a will in order to save their goods and get them to market in good time.

Sapaluta, which probably had the same patron saint Caralampio as Balún-Canán because they could not think of or did not know of any other, held its fiesta two weeks earlier than Balún-Canán. A sound business instinct had dissuaded the good people of Sapaluta from holding it at the same time, for they would then have had to share the proceeds with the much larger Balún-Canán. As it was, they had things all to themselves and could skim the thickest of the cream.

Hundreds of people from Balún-Canán went to Sapaluta for the occasion. They took advantage of the fiesta to visit friends and relations whom they had not seen for so long and yet loved so dearly. In this way they had free board and lodging and saved the expense of a hotel. What was said about the infliction behind their backs did not worry them, because they never heard it; and the good people of Sapaluta got their own back when two weeks later they all arrived in Balún-Canán for the fiesta there and demanded and received free board and lodging from their friends and relations in turn.

All this helped trade. The interchange of visitors by the hundreds between one town and the other made a large increase in the number of consumers; and when consumers are numerous the outlook for business is bright.

The entire district, in a circle with a diameter of perhaps a hundred kilometers, lived in a constant tumult of excitement for the four weeks of these two fiestas, and only recovered when it was time to start on the preparations for the Semana Santa—Holy Week.

The Church too made a very good thing out of this double fiesta of San Caralampio. No one can blame the Church for that. It had made San Caralampio as well as the other forty-two thousand saints, and therefore it was only just and reasonable that it should not be left empty-handed.

The people of Balún-Canán who visited Sapaluta by the hundreds made it their first duty to pay their respects to San Caralampio in the church of Sapaluta and to give to the Church. And when the people of Sapaluta paid their return visit to the fiesta at Balún-Canán, it was equally necessary for the good of their souls that they should do honor to San Caralampio in the cathedral and give to the Church in their turn. All the pious of the whole neighborhood, even though they were not domiciled either in Sapaluta or Balún-Canán, made pilgrimage to both fiestas, lest they might by any chance fall short in adoration of San Caralampio. Better give twice to the Church than not at all. In matters of religion it is far better to err on the side of doing too well than not well enough. Not a centavito offered to the Church is ever forgotten in heaven, as you may read clearly enough on the poorboxes in the churches.

The churches of Sapaluta and Balún-Canán did not take money only from the pious. The Church is no respecter of persons and does not inquire into the whence and the wherefore of its takings.

Every trader and gambling-table proprietor, as soon as he had taken his spot and come to terms with the authorities for the rent and tax on it, went at once to the church to beseech San Caralampio, in whose honor and at whose invitation he was there, to bless his business and multiply his gains, since it was only for Caralampio's sake that he had made such a long and hard journey—when really he would rather have stayed at home with his wife and children. There they all offered candles and put good hard coin into San Caralampio's poorbox, because as experienced businessmen they knew that you get nothing for nothing in this world. You must give while you have a pocket left you. Once you're aloft on your journey up pockets are commonly absent and then it is too late.

The cantineros also opened business with an ardent prayer to San Caralampio accompanied by hard cash. They had to make sure of a handsome profit on the sale of their comiteco and other alcoholic drinks. Above all the "barmaids" knelt for hours before San Caralampio and offered up—or if they had nothing on them because they had not yet earned anything, they solemnly promised him a percentage of their takings.

And with quiet dignity knelt also their chaperons, who stood in the place of mothers to the poor innocent virgin girls. With a noble gesture they drew their black shawls right over their faces and reeled off dozens of rosaries on end. They prayed for the salvation of the poor girls entrusted to their care—innocents, their souls endangered by the snares of the evil one—who could not protect themselves, because they had pretty faces and yet did not want to starve. By their prayers and their generous offerings the "mothers" of these girls acquitted themselves of all guilt from the very start. Once this was done the way was clear for a thriving trade, for it had been said to them: Believe and pray and make offerings, and you will find forgiveness; whoever believes and has faith, to him the Kingdom of Heaven is open.

All the strolling peddlers and swindlers who came in droves from every corner of the state to relieve the good people in Sapaluta and Balún-Canán of money, goods, and chattels—pickpockets, thieves, card sharpers and dice jugglers, soothsayers, fire-eaters, sword swallowers, and snake charmers—these too came into the church to pay their respects and make offering.

The cripples and beggars gave their part, remembering that it was to San Caralampio they owed their prospects of a good haul. As soon as their prayers were at an end, they crept out of the church and sat at the door and on the steps and began business. They wrangled among themselves a good while at first for places nearest the door. But then they saw reason and came to an agreement that each should have the right to sit nearest the door for two hours, and they drew up a detailed roster of shifts and reliefs.

Once the preparation for the fiesta had been made to the general satisfaction of all the heavenly and earthly powers, the real business could begin. And it began with a solemn High

Mass at which no eye was dry, no heart untouched; all vowed from now on to keep themselves from evil on earth and prepare themselves exclusively for eternal life.

When High Mass was over and the pious congregation filed out of the church, the bands of musicians and the marimberos were already starting up on the square before the cathedral. From the gambling tables came shouts of "Se fué—gone!" and the roulette discs spun merrily. The stallkeepers bawled: "Soy el más barato del mundo—I give the best value in the world!" From the cantinas you heard: "Otra copita—another little one for a dry throat!" The cripples and beggars on the church steps whimpered: "Tengo hambre, caridad, por Dios, me muero—I'm hungry, charity, for the love of God, I'm dying!" The "barmaids" took out their lipsticks and colored their lips a hectic red.

Business had begun, to the glory of San Caralampio.

3

In pursuance of his duties Andrés had by this time brought his caravan from Sapaluta to Balún-Canán, for the traders had to be there with their wares for the fiesta. He was to wait until it was over and then take the people home again to Tulum and Suchiapa, or wherever it might be.

The loads diminished very little, because the traders, whether on the road or at the places where they plied their trade, always found opportunities for buying fresh wares in districts where they were made or produced. These might be tobacco, coffee, wool, blankets, skins, mats, bastwork, wickerwork, comiteco, clay figures, toys. They bought all these wares cheaply and took them along to sell either at small places on the road or else in the larger towns along the railroad, where they made a big profit on them.

Andrés's caravan had not lain idle during the preparations

for the fiesta at Sapaluta. The carretas were driven back to Tsobtajál, halfway between Balún-Canán and Jovel. Here they had taken on a full load of earthenware, made by the Indians of Tsobtajál, and delivered it to the agents of don Laureano in those towns.

Against this, don Laureano had given orders when the train left Chiapa de Corso, that the oxen were to be thoroughly rested on good grazing land during the fiesta at Balún-Canán, so that they would be in a condition to make the return journey in good time and without great fatigue. He had a lot of freight already booked and wanted the animals ready. The carreteros made use of this two weeks' rest to give themselves a thorough washing and put their personal gear in order, and to get drunk as often as they had the chance.

Whenever a man on the low rungs of the social and economic ladder does not have to work because it is a feast day or a day of rest, he gets drunk. And when he gets drunk he feels there is some sense in a feast day and persuades himself that now he is having a jolly time.

He knows no better. No one has taught him to use his time profitably. No one has told him to learn to think for himself instead of letting others think for him all his life long. He has only learned one thing and he has learned it well: to obey. He had that flogged into him in his childhood. His father began it.

It adds to the employer's prosperity when his men get drunk—provided their work does not suffer. And as they know of nothing better to do on their days off, they drink on every day off they have. Thus they play into the patrón's hands by remaining in his debt. As free men they have the right to get drunk and spend their money as they choose. But of course they must see to it that they get drunk at the proper time, so that when work begins again they are in a condition to get on with it.

Time off was a rarity in the life of a carretero. It was only when the oxen were in urgent need of rest that the carretero might perhaps get a day off, as long, that is, as there were no repairs to be seen to. The oxen had their days of rest undisturbed, and they had their feed as usual. They were paid their wages in full. But, then, they were oxen. They could have their sleep out, because they did not know how to repair broken carretas. When there was a heavy load and spare oxen could be driven with the caravan, there were no days off for the carretas—not the whole year through very often. The carretero got his days off when he was down with fever, cramped and writhing on his mat, or when he had got a leg under the wheel of his carreta and could not use it.

4

Andrés's caravan was camped outside the town on a wide prairie beside the road which led to El Puente. The carretas were neatly lined up and the carreteros had made a roomy camp for themselves.

The oxen pastured far and wide over the prairie. Now and again they were rounded up and driven to the little river, where they immersed themselves for hours at a time so as to kill the thousands of ticks which had burrowed into their skin. After this they were driven to the camp. The carreteros looked them carefully over for sores, which, when necessary, they doctored. Then the animals got their feed of maize, and when they had eaten their fill they were turned loose again to graze.

Cattle, horses, mules, and donkeys grazed in hundreds over the prairie. The cattle grazed apart from the other animals. All the native animals out at grass kept together in herds, mostly in herds belonging to the same owner; for though they were free they were used to each other's company through having been raised in the same corral, and also because they were occasionally rounded up and driven to their ranchos to be given salt.

But some herds came together out of sympathy; others of necessity, because they were neglected by their owners and no longer knew where they belonged. It was to these looser droves that the newly arrived animals attached themselves—the oxen, for example, of the carreteros, and the horses, mules, and donkeys of itinerant traders.

Although thousands of animals were grazing over the prairie only a few droves were visible. The prairie was so vast that most of the animals were lost to sight and could scarcely be seen even as dots in the distance. Nevertheless, it was not very difficult for the carreteros to find their oxen. On the road and at every halt the oxen are trained to keep together and not stray far from the carretas. These animals wander off only when they find no grass near at hand or when the grass is sour or when the ground has been fouled by animals grazing there before them.

The oxen of the carretas are so different, too, from other cattle that it is easy for experienced carreteros to distinguish their oxen even from a great distance. The carreta oxen are big powerful beasts with heavy, widespread horns, and they can hardly be compared with ordinary cattle.

But there were four other caravans resting here whose oxen were also grazing over the prairie, and so it often happened that the carreteros who went out to look for their oxen might go six or eight kilometers after a group of carreta oxen they had sighted, only to find when they came up with it that the animals were of another caravan. But as all the carreteros knew the brands of all cartage contractors in the state, they were able to tell each other where their oxen were to be found.

During the last three days of the fiesta a general scouring of the prairie would begin, in search of the animals out at grass.

Men on foot and on horseback could then be seen going off in all directions to recover their mounts and pack animals. It often happened that a traveler who had come to the fiesta on horseback spent a whole week searching for his animal, and even then could not find it, and had to ask a ranchero in the neighborhood to let him know when the animal turned up somewhere, as he could wait no longer.

Owners of herds which were at pasture on the prairie had now to send out their men to keep a watch over their horses and cattle, for this was the opportunity for thieves of horses and mules to go on the prowl and pick up a good animal. No one could say offhand, in the confusion of traders and others who were all leaving at once after the fiesta, whether this or that mount or pack animal belonged to the man who went off with it or whether it had been stolen.

It was only during these fiestas, when hundreds of strangers were about the place, that animals could be stolen from the prairie. At other times travelers were so few that every inhabitant knew exactly what each one looked like, how he was clothed, and what animals he had come with. If he had even a single horse with him which gave rise to a suspicion of his having stolen it on his way there or back, he would be caught before having been two days on his way, or even two hours.

For this reason the herds on the prairie were as safe in ordinary times as they were in their yards and stables. But when the two towns, which were separated by this wide prairie, held their great Church fiestas, the owners of the herds had to be in the saddle day and night during the last week, keeping their herds together.

5

Just as the seaman whose ship is in port loading or unloading a cargo cannot by any means take his ease, as the innocent landsman may think, but has rather to do more and heavier labor than when his ship is on the high seas, so it was with the carreteros.

As soon as they had bathed, doctored, and fed the oxen, it was the turn of the carretas. If there was a breakage of any kind over the next twelve weeks they would get it hot. "You goddamn loafers had two weeks at Balún-Canán and nothing to do but sleep and get drunk. This broken wheel will cost you a month's wages—to teach you to keep your carreta in repair," don Laureano would say. "What do you think I pay you thirty centavos a day for? I'd do better to break a stick on your thick skull, you lousy son-of-a-bitch."

And you should see what a carreta looks like after half a year or a whole year on the roads without one day off.

It was usually one of those built two hundred years before, though of all that was new in it two hundred years earlier not a plank or spar was left. First the left wheel was smashed, then the right; then the pole, then the body. The newest bit of it might be five weeks old, the oldest forty years.

And as all the parts of a carreta are of different ages, according to the dates when they were renewed, and therefore of different degrees of durability, a practiced eye and an accurate knowledge of a carreta's history are required before you can say which part of it is likely to break down on the next trip. It was the carreteros' task to renew these parts when they had any days off.

Don Laureano knew very well that something or other was bound to have given out on every journey, even though none of the carreteros said a word about it. A carretero never betrayed a fellow worker, either to get his own back at him or to stand well with his employer. That was against his nature. It would never enter his head to behave so shabbily.

True, they sometimes fought like devils among themselves, both on the road and when camping. They went for each other with knives, machetes, and cudgels. Blood flowed freely and there were plenty of bruises and black eyes. Everywhere on earth the common people take a peculiar delight in cracking each other's heads. For this reason the heads of their masters escape attention. For the rage which accumulates under the influence of their wretched and aimless economic condition finds its vent in these fraternal whackings. This accounts for the lack of a proper impetus and healthy rage when the opportunity offers itself of throwing the whole economic system once and for all into a state of promising confusion. A new and healing order of things can never come into being through order, however admirable, but only through the boiling up of disorder.

No bad blood remained after these violent fights among the carreteros; none of them would dream of revenging himself by squealing on a fellow worker. It was against their code of honor.

All the same, don Laureano knew pretty well what went on during their journeys, and why. There were always travelers on horseback who passed a halted caravan and could naturally see what was up. Then when they arrived at Chiapa de Corso they met don Laureano in the street, or else they had to see him on business.

"I saw a train of yours halted on the road close to Santa Catarina, don Laureano. They were held up and hard at work on it."

"What was up then, don César?"

"Broken wheel—and an ox on the run. Lord knows how far the muchachos had to chase before they caught it."

Traders too, or their families traveling with the carretas, complained to don Laureano: "I tell you, don Laureano, your carretas are a scandal. Three times they broke down on the road, because your boys fell asleep. Your muchachos are lazy. Next time I'll do better to arrange for transport with don Mauricio."

Or else a merchant in Shimojol wrote don Laureano an angry letter because his goods had arrived two days late.

"Why were you two days behind time?" don Laureano shouted at the encargado.

Then it had to come out which carreta had broken down and whose fault it was, and the man whose carreta it had been that held up the train forfeited a month's or two months' wages. This meant that however hard he might work, however sparingly he lived, however he denied himself every little pleasure, the burden of debt never decreased but only mounted higher. So long as he had this debt he had to work for the man to whom he owed the debt. He could not seek other employment where he might earn more or have lighter work or a greater hope of achieving freedom and independence and doing what suited him and offered him a better life.

If a wheel broke or a carreta got off the road it meant not only the loss of half a day and consequent delay in the delivery of the goods, but also breakage or damage of the goods in that particular carreta. A packing case of china or medicines might easily be rendered worthless by a carretero's negligence. And if a breakdown happened when the carreta was crossing a river, his whole load might be written off if it consisted of goods which could not stand a wetting.

The loss was not borne by the sender who might have packed the goods badly. He took no responsibility whatever once the goods were dispatched. This was explicitly stated in the conditions of sale. The responsibility for the safe arrival of the goods was planted on the cartage contractor, who might certainly have refused to accept them if they were badly packed; but then another man would have taken the risk and don Laureano lost the deal.

And what did he have experienced carreteros for? And pay them good wages? Why had he taken over the debts they owed their previous masters when they came to him to better themselves? Why did he treat them as free men and not flog them and put them in the stocks as was done with enslaved peons? Why all this consideration on the part of a civilized employer for his men if they took not the slightest trouble to protect him from loss?

It was only just that any breakdown on the road should be set down against them in his books as a debt. If they looked after their carretas properly, if they knew the roads well and did not go to sleep but kept their eyes open, these losses and damages and accidents would never happen. It was only negligence on the part of the carreteros if they got behind on a day's journey or if wheels broke or goods were spoiled.

Negligence should never be tolerated; and it would simply be condoning negligence and carelessness if he did not make his carreteros responsible for all losses which arose through their fault. He did not pay his carreteros to sleep and drink, but to work—and work for his advantage. Every worker has been given a head to think with. He did not expect oxen to make good any losses they occasioned. That would be foolish, for a reasonable man knows that an ox cannot think. That is why oxen are paid no wages. A carretero is paid wages precisely because he can think. And as he did pay his carreteros wages he had the right to expect them to use their heads for his advantage.

6

Taking into account the actual condition of the carretas, there was only one way of avoiding breakdowns, and this was to replace them by new ones. But as some parts of each carreta were as good as new, because it was only a month or two since these parts had been patched up, to replace the old carretas would have been a senseless waste of capital which no business-man could tolerate.

If don Laureano had to add to the number of his carretas owing to the increase of freight to be carried, he always tried first to pick up old ones. It was only when he could nowhere find an old one that he ordered a new one to be made.

There was nothing left, then, for the carreteros to do but to patch up the carretas whenever they had an hour's spare time. This would have been simple enough if don Laureano had supplied them with material or given them money to buy it with when it was required.

It was true that when the carretas stood in their own yard a supply of good timber was there to freshen them up with. Besides this, each train of carretas was supplied with a few spare wheels, yokes, and poles for the journey. But it often happened that the carretas never saw their home for two or three months, but were continually on the road between Arriaga and Tuxtla or between Jovel and Balún-Canán, or wherever else the traffic in freight kept them occupied.

The carreteros were not given money to buy material with.

"I am not such a fool as that," said don Laureano. "The muchachos would drink up the lot at the first tienda they came to, or gamble it away at dice or spinning pesos. I know them."

Perhaps he had had experiences of the kind, but the fact remained that carreteros were never given money. He gave them only vouchers with which to buy maize for their beasts on the road. These vouchers, signed and stamped by himself, were accepted throughout the state. They were as good as hard cash.

The oxen had to be fed well. He could not hold a carretero responsible if an ox gave out on a journey, for it might have eaten the leaves of a poisonous plant or tree, or a snake might have bitten it. Oxen that refused to get up could not be patched up by putting in new bits, and so there was nothing a carretero could do in that case. Whatever happened to an ox was the will of God, Who watches over every sparrow to see that no feather falls from its tail without His express command.

As the carreteros had to keep the carretas in going order and had neither money nor vouchers they had to pick up material wherever they could find it. Not even the belief in a terrible retribution in the other world, which they had had thrashed into them, was enough to deter them from getting hold of it in ways that were irreconcilable with the laws of heaven and earth, not to mention the laws of the State. They had to think first and foremost of avoiding a breakdown at any cost; for the first duty of a good and loyal and obedient servant is to serve his master, to further his interests, and to protect him from loss of any kind. All other duties may wait.

7

Just as the several parts of a carreta did not come together at any one time, so too they were not all of one kind of wood. Some parts were mahogany, others ebony, still others cedar, oak, or pine. Every kind of timber to be met with on the roads the caravans traveled was to be found in a carreta.

A few kilometers from Balún-Canán on the way to El Puente there was a magnificent forest of pines with the finest trees it is possible to imagine. It was probably the beauty of this forest that moved the Indians of ancient times to offer the forest as a home to their gods. In the midst of it they built a group of pyramids and erected altars for the delectation of these gods. It is not to be supposed that the Indian gods live there still, but the pyramids are all there.

The carreteros had no time to go and look at the pyramids; they did not interest them. Their interest was focused on the state of their carretas. It does no good when the worker has any interests outside his work. He has his work to occupy him and he can leave pyramids and history to those whom the State selects for the task of arranging the history of the world to suit its own immediate requirements. The well-being of every State is furthered and its peace and good order assured when the shoemaker sticks to his last, when the workman is an obedient servant, and when it is left to experts to smooth over the problems of economic life.

Also, the pyramids were too far away for the carreteros, who only went far enough into the forest to find the trees they required for hacking out their poles, their yokes, and spokes. Then they brought oxen along and dragged their handiwork to their camp.

This forest belonged neither to don Laureano nor to his carreteros, nor to any other carreteros who camped on the prairie nearby and mended their carretas. The owner of the forest was all this time in the toils of a "barmaid" to the glory of San Caralampio; so he did not care very much who stole his timber.

There was, in addition, something else the carreteros were badly in need of, if they were to keep their employers' carretas in good order; so they crept by night out onto the prairie and slaughtered cattle. They required the hides from which to cut new thongs, because the old ones were rotten.

The carreteros never stole on their own account. They could easily have stolen poultry and pigs on the road and enjoyed the good meals they were so sorely in need of. However, once the cattle were slaughtered, it added little to the burden on their consciences if they took a few good cuts of the meat back to camp with them.

All the trains of carretas which had halted on the prairie were in the same condition and each needed a new hide. So, in the interests of the different cartage contractors, quite a large bag of cattle was made.

Stealing timber was a painful matter for a carretero if he was caught at it. There was a scene of fury and often a rain of heavy blows from a riding whip on the head of the culprit. But the slaughter of cattle was more serious—if a cowboy happened to see. That meant jail. It was true that don Laureano would not let his carreteros go to prison. They had debts to work off and he wanted their labor. If they had owed him nothing, perhaps he would not have minded so much; but as things stood he had to go to the rescue of his capital. So when there was trouble he paid the owner of the cattle the value of the slaughtered beasts, and he paid the mayor and the chief of police twenty pesos each as a mark of his friendship, and then the carreteros were released from the municipal jail. All these expenses were debited to the carreteros—and quite rightly. Don Laureano had never told his carreteros to steal timber, to slaughter cattle, to draw the nails from houses, to steal iron from blacksmiths by night. Don Laureano could not conceivably issue such orders even if one of his trains were to be held up on the road for a whole week. He was a highly respected and most estimable member of the community. He lived in awe of the Holy Church, and though the law of the land might in some instances require strengthening in favor of property owners, it had as a whole his ardent support; for it protected him in the enjoyment of his justly acquired possessions and kept those who possessed nothing in their proper places.

In spite of all this, the carreteros who were camping on the prairie contrived to get their carretas into a state of repair. The problem of getting hold of the necessary material had been more easily and quickly dealt with than they had dared to hope, because all those who might have interfered with their activities were devoting themselves to San Caralampio's wild doings.

So they had plenty of time left over for finally taking a closer look at the fiesta themselves, instead of spending every day as outsiders on the wind-swept prairie, where they could only hear the chimes of the bells and the racket of the fireworks.

Like everyone else who goes to a fiesta, they had the unfounded expectation that something of extraordinary interest was sure to happen to them or that something would fall into their hands from the sky. But on these occasions nothing surprising ever happens if you expect it to.

In any case the carreteros were desperately eager to see and hear and smell something else for a change than the everlasting carretas and oxen. Even an intelligent person turns very rapidly into an ox if he sees nothing but oxen day in and day out.

9

 The fiesta of San Caralampio was at its height. There was a surging, heaving mass of people within the narrow confines of the square in front of the cathedral. They cackled like flocks of geese, they cried and bawled and shouted in a confused uproar. Drunken men bellowed and sang at the tops of their voices.

Here and there bands of musicians were performing. The musicians went barefoot in patched trousers and torn cotton shirts. A marimba was playing in front of a circus which had pitched its tent in the roomy patio of a substantial house in a side street close by. Another played on the plaza in front of the cabildo. Every ten minutes policemen hauled a drunken man into the cabildo and put him in the lockup.

These drunks were mostly peons or Indian peasants. They could pay no fines. They had to work instead. In the morning when they had slept off their debauch they were given mugs of hot, sweetened black coffee. As soon as they had drunk it they had to go out and clean the streets and squares under the eye of a policeman armed with a loaded rifle, and on their return they were given coffee, two spoonfuls of black beans, and a few tortillas.

The cleansing of the streets was entered in the municipal accounts with an excellent precision at so much a day for wages. But there were always enough arrests for drunkenness every day, or, if not, there were always stray Indians who could be charged whether drunk or not, and so there was no need for the mayor and the treasurer actually to pay out the wages which were so clearly entered in the books.

The cost for maintenance of arrested persons was naturally entered also; and to judge by the entries you lived far better in jail than any substantial and respected citizen in his own house. The prisoners received meat, eggs, fruit, and cigarettes—according to the expenses charged. It is really surprising that Indian farm laborers did not get themselves taken in every day, for a look at the books showed that nowhere on earth could they hope to live so well as in the town jail.

2

The square in front of the cathedral was on very low ground. During the rainy season it was frequently under water for days on end.

Now, however, it was flooded only by stalls, refreshment booths, shooting galleries, gambling tables, and dice tables. The lanes between booths and stalls were so narrow that the people who crowded them could scarcely elbow their way along. There was a continual barging and pushing and squeezing. This gave the impression of tens of thousands; though, if they had been counted, there were probably three thousand at most.

What these surging and shoving, pushing and barging people really wanted they had no idea whatever. There was nothing to buy they could not have bought as well, and better and cheaper and far more reliably, whenever they chose at any shop in the town. But on every face there was the look of a man who hopes to find twenty-peso gold pieces at a peso a chance.

Whatever they bought, they bought not because they had any need of it, but because it was there under their eyes; because they were in the spending mood; because a knowing salesman persuaded them that only from him and from no one else in the world was a particular article to be bought, and that it was lucky for them he was there, and even though they did not want it at the moment they were sure to want it tomorrow, and then it would be too late and they would have let slip the greatest opportunity of their whole lives.

Thus people got into a kind of intoxication. The outcry, the noise, the music, the shouts of the vendors crying their wares went to their heads, and they bought and bought as though the end of the world was at hand; they lost all control over themselves and their actions. They were dazed and the power of calm reflection deserted them. So they bought and bought without sense or discretion, bought things that were hideous and had no value whatever. They bought and bought because all around them they saw people who were buying and buying too.

It was the same with the shooting galleries and the booths where black cats of pasteboard were knocked down with balls. For ten centavos you had three shots at a target with an air gun. If a marksman got three bull's-eyes he won a gilded flower vase of tortuous design. Such vases were sold for twenty centavos apiece in the larger towns and no one with any taste would buy them. Even here, in this little place where things were in fashion which in the larger towns had been written off thirty years ago, scarcely a shop could have hoped to sell these vases to its customers, or any other of the articles offered as prizes in the shooting galleries and other booths. But if you won such trash in a shooting gallery it was like a present. It was taken home and displayed in the house. It was entirely out of place, but no one had the courage to throw such a beautiful gilded vase on the rubbish heap. Attempts were made to use it as a flower vase, but as soon as flowers were put in it, it toppled over, water and all, because the Czechoslovakian manufacturer had thought less of true proportion than of giving it a costly appearance. So there it remained on show in the marksman's home because there was no other purpose it could serve. And so it never got broken but descended from one generation to another, and in this way the taste of the people was so misled that each generation strove to win a similar vase by paying for three shots twenty times over at ten centavos a time.

It was certainly by no means easy to win anything in the shooting gallery. It was pure chance, which could arise only when you aimed your three shots somewhere else than at the target. The air guns were sighted in such a way that even lucky hits were very rare. The proprietor could carry his vases and shaving mugs, his Japanese fans from Halle-an-der-Saale, his alarm clocks and his Virgin Marys around with him for two years to forty different fairs and fiestas; and when you saw him again he still had the same vases and alarm clocks displayed. And the people went on paying ten centavos for three shots to win an alarm clock which was rusty with long service and dented by all the packing and unpacking of its many journeys.

But the man was good-natured. If anyone had shot and shot and tried hard and made some good shots which just missed winning him a vase, the showman would call out with an encouraging smile: "Otra vez, caballero, más buena suerte— better luck next time, sir," and pin a medal on this fine marksman, which distinguished him among all the rest of the crowd as a man of great importance.

You could also shoot at packages of cigarettes stood up on end. These packages cost three pesos a hundred, and you could buy one in any shop for six centavos, but when the fiesta was on people went to great pains to secure such a package at the cost of three shots for ten centavos ten times over.

When they had shot their money away too recklessly and wanted to replenish their supply they went to the gambling booths and roulette tables. It was so simple to get five pesos at a blow for twenty-five centavos. It was an opportunity not to be let slip, and everyone was grateful to the roulette man for coming to the fiesta and giving people the chance of getting rich overnight without needing to work.

3

Everyone who attended the fiesta knew that the shooting galleries and the dice tables and the rest were run by crooks. The air guns did not shoot true and had not sufficient force to knock a package of cigarettes over unless the showman tipped it backward on purpose, so that the least touch upset it—for he had to lose a package now and then to encourage the rest. Even the man with the black cats put a bean here and there under their wooden stands, so that the cat fell down and the thrower got six more throws for nothing to try his luck once more for a gold watch.

But the man with the roulette table was different; he was an honorable man. Everyone knew that. Anyone who had put money on it had the right to spin the roulette, and if he thought it stood askew it was trimmed for him. There was no foul play here; nor would the police have put up with it. The remarkable thing was that the only man who won consistently and made money was the roulette man. How else could he have paid the high taxes levied on him? And he had to live. Nevertheless all the people who staked their pesos were firmly convinced that he only brought his roulette along to make them rich; and when the players, however hard they kept at it, instead of getting rich, lost all they had, they only blamed themselves and said they had no luck and that it had always been their fate to have no luck.

It was true that the knowing gamblers did not for a moment hope to win so much as a peso from the roulette man. They knew that if there was any risk of it he would not be there. These knowing ones played only to win from their fellow gamblers and so share in the gains of the roulette man. They kept it up at the table for hours and played by a system. They frequently won and so helped to encourage new clients; for the man paid out their winnings with a flourish: "Here, caballero, another five pesos for your tostón. You'll ruin me. I'll have to shut up shop tomorrow. I've a family to keep. But I'm a man of my word. Now, caballeros, a new game begins. Your stakes, caballeros. Se fué. Rrrr. Quince negro. Who has the black fifteen? No one? Your stakes, caballeros. A new game begins."

The knowing ones were, in fact, ahead—twenty pesos, thirty pesos—but they wanted to win a hundred before they stopped. And when the table was closed to them at one in the morning, its owner was the only man to have won anything; the knowing ones were fleeced as bare as the fools. The only man who came out on the right side was the roulette man.

All the gambling tables, roulette included, at which hard cash was played for, were licensed until nine o'clock at night. They were licensed solely on that condition. But it was only after nine that business began in earnest, because the caballeros sent their wives to bed at that hour, and then they were their own masters.

At nine o'clock the chief of police sent a policeman to say that it was closing time for roulette. The proprietor left the table in charge of his cousin and went to a cantina where he met the chief of police.

"A copita, Jefe—have a drink, Chief?" he asked. Without waiting for the great man's reply he ordered two large glasses of comiteco añejo, and before they were half empty he called for two more. Then he took five pesos out of his pocket and placed them in the chief's unobtrusively opened palm, and said with a wink: "You're a family man, Jefe. That's for the children."

Until ten o'clock not a policeman came near the roulette table. Play went on merrily. According to the conditions of the license no one was allowed to stake more than five centavos at a time, but of course he could put five centavos on ten different numbers, or on as many as he chose. After seven in the evening the roulette man was already greeting anything less than a quarter of a peso with a severe look. By eight only half-pesos were seen. By ten, less than a peso was not accepted.

But now another policeman appeared. It would have to be the last game: further play was forbidden. The proprietor gave the policeman a peso and went once more to a cantina—a different one this time. But sure enough, there was the chief of police. It was remarkable how he always managed to find the chief without wasting time on the search. He always hit on the right cantina. Once again he stood two glasses of comiteco añejo; but now it was ten pesos for the family.

And that was not all this time. The chief jerked his head toward a man seated at a table with a bottle of beer in front of him.

"El presidente—the mayor," he said.

The roulette man understood at once. He went up to the table.

"Cómo está, señor Presidente? How are you?"

"Ah, don Claudio, qué tal—how goes it? How's business? By the way, I must tell you that we cannot on any account allow you to carry on play after nine. You know the terms of your license."

"I am closing at once, señor Presidente, only another game or two. There are some gentlemen there who insist on having their revenge. I can hardly refuse them. The gentlemen are excited and there might be a scene. It might come to a few pistol shots."

"You're right, don Claudio," the mayor agreed with a nod. "In those circumstances, of course—but not too long, you know. Will you have a bottle of beer with me?"

"You must excuse me, señor Presidente," said the roulette man, tactfully declining the invitation, which was not seriously meant. "By the way," he added, checking himself in midcareer as he was hurrying out to resume business, "I hear you are building a hospital here. Will you allow me, señor Presidente, to make a small contribution?"

"I thank you in the name of the town," the mayor replied.

The roulette man took five gold pieces out of his pocket and slipped them halfway under the mayor's arm, which was resting on the table. The gold pieces vanished before the man had time to return his hand to his pocket.

"With your permission, señor Presidente, I must hurry back now in case there's any trouble at my table."

"Bueno, don Claudio, but remember, not too long."

At one o'clock business was at its height. The finqueros were playing now. All those who could stake only a peso or so kept away. The cheapest stakes were five pesos. And as play now was carried on only by chips it was very simple for the proprietor to say, if by any chance the chief of police or the mayor took it into his head at last to enforce the letter of the law, that they were only five centavos apiece. Nobody, not even if he were gifted with second sight, could say by looking at them how much the chips stood for.

The chief of police, after three more interviews in a cantina, had instructed his men to get after drunks and rowdies and not to bother the finqueros at the roulette table.

The mayor too had been three times sought out—about the hospital. Then he retired to his bed and left the town in charge of the gambling finqueros. It was safe in their hands; for the finqueros stood for law and order and believed that God was in His heaven and that all was right with the world.

10

 Andrés got to the town late in the afternoon. The dense crowd was growing denser. The cries of vendors were louder now, even if hoarser. The uproar came from every direction. It is a human characteristic that when people get together they like to shout. Each man wants to shout down his neighbor, because each thinks that what he has to say is more important than what the other has to say.

"Aquí, aquí, la seda legítima de Francia y la más barata—only from me can you get it so cheap."

This genuine French silk, which the shouting salesman held aloft and unfurled to show its undulating sheen, was made of henequen in Yucatán. But since it was so loudly proclaimed as French silk the women standing around believed it must be. Otherwise, a man who lied so loudly would be choked by his lies.

This dealer in silk was an Arab from Tabasco, who had been long enough in the country to know in Spanish how best to cajole and bamboozle Mexicans of small towns.

Next to him was a Cuban selling medicine. There was no

human ailment for which he had not the right remedy—roots, herbs, pills, extracts, waters.

A Spaniard stood at a table selling Peruvian toothpowder. This powder, he affirmed, had been used by the Incas. He had come upon it in the vaults of ruins in Peru and Bolivia. There was not a great deal of this wonderful toothpowder left, only a few hundred kilos. And when once he had sold out, those who wished to keep their teeth sound would be left to vain regrets. His advice was that they buy five packages right off rather than one. It was the best investment they could make.

When he had reached this point in his oration he caught hold of a little Indian boy who was hanging around. He forced the boy's mouth open, all the while talking hard and gesticulating and making passes like a conjurer, and then rubbed a little powder on his teeth.

"With this powder, ladies and gentlemen, no toothbrush is required. With this miraculous powder of the old Incas you need only use your forefinger as the old Incas themselves did," he said while he polished the boy's teeth with his finger.

When, still talking and extolling, he had done with the polishing, he poured a mouthful of water into the boy's mouth and told him to rinse and spit. After this he levered his mouth open again, far wider than it normally would go, and turned his face this way and that as though he were a doll. The boy's enforced grin revealed teeth of a blinding whiteness. All the people standing around were now convinced that this Peruvian toothpowder was what they had always lacked and that to this lack alone they owed their bad teeth. They bought the five packages held out to them, because one would certainly not last their lifetime, and were now perfectly sure that they would never have a toothache again. They had been promised as much.

The four little Indian boys who were the powder man's exhibits each got two centavos an appearance. For this they were required to smear their teeth with a greenish-yellow paste of maize which the powder man's helper prepared for them behind the stalls. Then they had to hang around within the powder man's reach so that when the moment came he could pluck them apparently at random from the crowd.

Near the powder man a gap between two stalls was occupied by two men and a woman. One of the men had a guitar and the other a fiddle and the woman had printed leaflets, red and green and yellow and blue, in her hands.

"Now the next song, ladies and gentlemen!" the man with the guitar shouted. "We will now give you 'Soy Virgencita'— I am a virgin still, a spotless virgin. Now then——"

And he bent over the guitar on his knee, tuned up, moved the bridge, and struck the key. The man joined in with the violin and the woman began to sing. After the first verse the men sang as well.

They sang softly and rather plaintively, but musically, and their voices were good. The woman pretended to sing the song from one of the leaflets in her hands, but she knew it by heart. She, and the men too, had sung this song and their whole repertoire a good ten thousand times before. They were cantadores de corridos, Mexican ballad singers who go from place to place and never miss a fiesta.

When the song came to an end they turned to the crowd standing around them in a ring. "This beautiful ballad which we have just sung for your benefit and with great pleasure, in sweet and melting tones, is now, together with other songs, at the disposal of our kind and valued patrons. Dos surtidos cinco centavos, cinco surtidos diez—nada más. Quién? Cuáles?" they asked. A selection of two went for five centavos, a collection of five for ten centavos—no more. Who would have them and which would he have?

The leaflets were handed around and picked over and twenty or twenty-five centavos collected.

As soon as business flagged, the singers called out: "No one else for the Virgin? Oigan, oigan, amigos, hear, hear. Then a fresh, an entirely new song: 'The Life, Exploits, and Death of General Santana.' Or shall we sing: 'The Gringos at Churubusco'? Say the word. We sing at your command."

The fiddler tuned up and another corrido was sung.

It was here that Andrés came to a stop. It was the cheapest entertainment. You could stand and listen to the ballad singers hour after hour. You were not compelled to buy a ballad.

Two of the corridos pleased Andrés and he bought them—one red and one green. He read them through, folded them, and put them in his shirt pocket with his package of cigarettes.

Then he thought it his duty to go into the church.

2

The church doors stood wide open. Now and then a few notes of the little organ mingled with the mundane cries and tumult of the square outside, but what could more often be heard was the monotonous chant in which the congregation gave the responses to the adjurations of the priests.

Andrés knew little of the Catholic and still less of the Christian religion; and what he knew was somewhat confused. The only things he knew well were the ceremonies connected with religious services. He could cross himself and sprinkle himself with holy water, and he knew when he had to kneel and how many times to cross himself at certain moments in the litany.

He knew neither less nor more of the Catholic religion than that which his mother had been able to teach him, what his neighbors in the huts on the finca knew, and what he had picked up without comprehending it when he was in service in his master's house at home.

Don Arnulfo and his family themselves had only the most

rudimentary knowledge of religion. It did not go a step beyond the ceremonial and the usual prayers and Ave Marias. Like all half-educated persons they stopped short at the surface and at a mere observance of the ritual, which in this country occupies so prominent a place that the reality behind it is forgotten and ritual is confounded with religion itself.

3

The church was built high above the square. Its foundations rose more than three meters above the level of the square. Thus the building was spared the frequent floods which in the rainy season turned the square into a lake.

It was not, however, the Spanish monks who had first discovered this excellent site for their church. They had merely erected it on the foundations of the Indian temple-pyramid which had stood there for thousands of years. With few exceptions all the churches in Mexico are built on the foundations of the old Indian temples or pyramids.

A broad flight of stone steps led up to the church—so broad that it extended a long way on either side of the main entrance. Crowds of men, women, and children—Ladinos and Indians—ascended and descended the steps.

This broad flight of steps was crowded not only with the pious as they entered and left the building. There were just as many beggars seated there day and night. The Church teaches charity, so the churchgoers give to the first who crouches at their feet with outstretched palm. The pious man distributes here a centavito and there a centavito, and with that his conscience is clear.

On the top steps and right up to the doors were crowded the stands of the dealers in consecrated and unconsecrated candles, prayersheets, amulets, crosses, rosaries, silver hearts, images of the saints, dried bits of their bones, fingers, pickled hearts in gold bottles, and brains in ebony boxes. About the doorway inside the church there were even more of these stands, and they stretched on and on along the walls. The fair inside the church was as extensive as outside in the square, with the difference that inside the church business was carried on in whispers and bargains made in undertones with vehement gestures of arms and hands.

4

Andrés climbed the steps, took off his battered bast hat, and entered the church. Dipping his hand in the stone basin he sprinkled his forehead, knelt down, and, prostrating himself at the very entrance before the altar at the far end of the building, crossed himself again and again.

With this he had acquitted himself of all that he knew of the Catholic religion. There was nothing more to be done. Thousands of others, even Ladinos, knew no more and did no more than this.

But Andrés was inquisitive and thirsty for knowledge. He wanted to see what it was all about that went on in the church. He had been in other churches often enough—at Tenejapa and Chiapa de Corso—but he had been younger then and had known less about the life he lived and all that went on around him. Everything had been new and strange. Now he was older, and the company of carreteros from various places, as well as the ideas and opinions he had picked up from time to time here and there, had added to his knowledge. The life he had lived for some years past had no secrets left for him, and now that things had lost their strangeness he saw them more plainly and clearly. He was already beginning to compare one event and one circumstance with another, and hence to criticize them. He was no longer taken in by words and opinions. He listened and considered a matter, compared it with other similar things he had heard and seen, and began to accept and endorse only what he himself was sure about in the light of the experience he daily acquired.

He had begun to think for himself. His thoughts sometimes went askew and jostled about, and by this he knew that they were on the wrong track. Then he went back to the starting point and began afresh on a new track. Work had become lighter because he now knew it from top to bottom and did not need to think it out; so his mind was more at liberty. He could sit for hours in the carreta, when the road was good and the carreta in good order, and do nothing but think and think. His thoughts took a free and independent course. He had the great advantage of which millions are deprived, that his thoughts had not been schooled to take one definite direction. His thoughts had no bias. He could attack anything without prejudice and without being hindered by what others before him had said or thought about it. He drew his conclusions from naked circumstance and from his own experience. He saw things and happenings not as someone else had described them, but as they were or seemed to him to be.

As he knew very little, or, to be exact, nothing about religion, he looked on it too and its ritual with an unbiased mind. He was quite free of the superstitious belief in miracles such as the virgin birth, the rising from the dead, the walking on water, the feeding of five thousand hungry people with two ordinary fishes, the turning of water into wine, the ascension into heaven, and the rest. If anyone had tried to persuade him to believe in all these things as being true he would have thought him a brazen liar. Only one of all these miraculous stories he might perhaps have believed—the story of Christ's appearing to the disciples after His death on the road to Emmaus. He would have believed it, not on the authority of the Church, but because in his father's hut and in the huts of other Indians he had heard much talk of such appearances. To some an uncle had appeared after his death, to others a long-buried grandmother, and to others a murdered son. None of his own relations or friends had as yet appeared to him after their deaths, but as he had grown up with such tales he might perhaps have believed that the dead Christ had appeared to several persons who had known Him.

From all this it is clear enough that Andrés was a wicked heathen who should have been burned for his sins. He was an example of the wisdom of the Church in gathering its flock together while the child is still a child and takes everything literally, without the faculty of thinking for himself and separating the possible from the probable and the impossible from the symbolical. Whatever is put into a child's mind before he can think and judge remains implanted there and entwines itself as years go on with the romance of adolescence; and since the grown man does not like to vex his mother who taught him all these fairy tales, he gives his assent to them all; and growing up to become a useful member of society he looks on with all the satisfaction of sentimental reminiscence when his wife tells his own children the same stories and teaches the children to believe them. The Church thrives and prospers because, like Communism, it makes sure of the new generation in good time.

5

After Andrés had finished kneeling and crossing himself he looked about him at the people herded together in the cathedral. It seemed that people outside, who pursued their customary lives and occupations, were never in harmony nor ever could be in harmony, whereas inside here they found the unity which as a herd they needed.

Hundreds of candles smoldered and flickered. There were candles not only on the altar, where they were most numerous, but in every corner of the church. They were alight in every niche that supported a plaster figure, whether in cotton frock or plush mantle. Candles were burning before every plinth—and these were endless—on which stood hideous wooden dolls with glazed protruding eyes and moldering human hair. People by the dozen who were too poor to have anything but splinters of pine to give light in their own homes sacrificed their last peso to buy beautiful painted spiral candles to set up in the church.

Many women and children knelt with their candles in their hands. They did this so that the figures of plaster and wood might know whose offerings the candles were. For, when a candle was set up among so many hundreds more, the saint—so they believed—could not possibly tell to whom he owed it, and perhaps might even forget to fulfill the prayer addressed to him.

The church had very few benches and these were all at the front. The seats on them were sold or rented to those who had money to pay for them and who did not wish to pray to the same God as a lousy Indian woman unless at a safe distance. That is more than you could expect of a family who has money; and it is nowhere said in the Bible that a man who has learned to use a handkerchief should sit down in church next to one who has not. Therefore it is no reproach to millionaires if they occupy mahogany-paneled boxes in the churches they patronize.

Several hundreds of people were on their knees, but scarcely twenty among them were men. When men submit to the influence of the Church and its apostles it is nearly always from motives of business and politics. They want to be shining examples and to pass as virtuous and honorable men in their public or commercial life. They like to inspire confidence in the sheep whom they design to fleece. They have observed over and over again how well it pays to be a zealous churchgoer. A woman, on the other hand, as a rule submits her whole being to the influence of the Church, even to the point of deserting her husband's bed at the bidding of the priests.

6

The floor of the church, made up of stone slabs, was thickly strewn with fresh pine needles whose aromatic scent mingled with the smoke of the candles and the censers that were swung to and fro by small boys who aspired to the priesthood. Owing to these fumigations the church was shrouded in a thick haze. Nothing could be clearly distinguished. Everything swam in a mist.

The women were so disguised by the long black cotton shawls over their heads that from behind they looked like rows of black ninepins. Many of these muffled women had consecrated images of the saints hanging down their backs from blue ribbons around their necks. Instead of an image some had a medal dangling. Those who had these objects hanging down their backs were particularly pious and holy; even a back view showed that earthly things had been put away and that no temptation of the evil one could touch them.

When there was nothing enjoined upon them from the altar and nothing was happening there, the women sang: "Al cielo quiero ir, al cielo quiero ir—to heaven will I go, to heaven will I go." They sang this indefatigably and without the slightest variation, so that the church was filled with a weird, monotonous chanting, like that in the Buddhist temples of India and China. Unless you knew the words beforehand you would never have been able to make sense of this unvarying singsong. It might have been Chinese or Japanese or Malay. No one could possibly have told. But it chimed in remarkably well with what was now happening in front of the altar.

A man stood there—though really Andrés was not very sure whether it was a man or a woman; for he wore a skirt to distinguish him from the very start from all other men around and to declare to all that he was something out of the common. Andrés got the impression at once that he was a magician or something of that kind.

He was enveloped in a wide and heavy mantle of gold brocade which entirely shrouded his human form. This garment probably cost more than all the women kneeling there put together could earn in their lifetimes.

Andrés saw only the gold-brocaded back, and the mantle was so wide that he could not see what the man did with his hands. But from the movements made by the mantle it was to be concluded that the man was engaged in all kinds of mysterious doings. He took a silver candlestick that was standing at his right and moved it across to his left. After a time, during which he kept on muttering, he moved the candlestick back to his right again. Then he muttered from a thick book which was lying open at his left, and again from another thick book which he had lying open on his right. Every few moments he inclined himself before the books and toward the little holy boys swinging their censers.

Then a man stepped forward out of a dense cloud of smoke. He was just a simple man, a half-breed Indian, clothed only in cotton shirt and trousers and with sandals on his feet. He bowed three times toward the altar and then he placed another golden mantle over the shoulders of the personage who was busied there. This new mantle was even more costly and splendid than the other; it was plentifully adorned with large and brilliant gems and there were gold and silver ornaments sewn into it. The man was now hung about with riches which the yearly budget of the whole district could never have bought.

Now he inclined himself several times. Then he produced from somewhere a gold vessel over which was a lady's handkerchief. He removed the handkerchief and waved the vessel to and fro. He then replaced the handkerchief and put the vessel down wherever he might have found room for it on his magic table.

After this he bowed again, and then produced from nowhere a golden stand on which there was a large golden-rayed nimbus. He waved this stand to and fro. Then at last he turned around and you could see that he had a face disfigured by pockmarks.

He held the rayed nimbus aloft in both hands. At this the whole multitude fell into a frenzy of ecstasy. All who were standing fell to their knees; and all who were kneeling—particularly the muffled women—pressed their foreheads to the stone. The man waved the nimbus nine times, three times in each direction. Each time he waved it, some of the acolytes, who wore red tunics with white lace capes, shook bunches of little bells; and each time the bells jingled the muffled women pressed their heads to the floor and tapped their foreheads with their fingers. It was exactly the same as in front of any Buddhist temple in southeastern Asia. There, when the priests beat the gong, the crowd of worshipers fall on their knees and, with the palms of their hands flat on the ground, strike the earth with their foreheads over and over again.

The man in the gold-brocaded mantle turned again to the altar and waved the gold stand with the golden-rayed nimbus three times up and down. Then he set it down in front of him and bowed.

When all this was over, he began once more moving the

candlestick from right to left and back again. Then he started to speak.

The worshipers replied in a singsong, but not a soul in the church understood a word of what the gentleman said to himself. About a third of those present spoke only Spanish, a third Spanish and Indian, and of the remaining third perhaps half spoke Tseltal, the rest Tojolaval. The gentleman, however, did not seem to worry whether anyone understood or not. He spoke in Latin.

Andrés did his utmost to find some rhyme or reason in these proceedings, but never for a moment could he get away from the impression that no one in the whole place knew why the man behaved as he did. It all seemed meaningless, nothing whatever but empty mummery.

It was not Andrés's fault if nothing he saw or heard here meant any more to him than what he saw and heard when he went with his father to the old Indian religious ceremonies, at which the gods were implored to make the fields fruitful and to protect the peons' huts from harm and bad luck and pestilence and evil spirits. The educated Catholic who sees a highly educated priest perform the office feels no taint of magic and masquerade. He knows that all this misplaced magic and masquerade is merely symbolic and possibly decorative.

But Andrés, like all Indians, like the vast majority of uneducated persons, saw nothing in it but magic and mummery and dressing up: just the dance of a witch doctor, and the muttering of incomprehensible formulas of enchantment and imprecation. It was not his fault if he saw nothing but sorcery, heard nothing but incantations, and if the people around him were nothing but a crazed herd gesticulating meaninglessly in a haze of smoke.

All the stallkeepers who had their goods for sale in the church broke off their haggling as soon as the bells jingled.

Like everyone else they fell on their knees beside their stands and touched the floor with their foreheads, in humble prostration before their gods. But their genius for business was such that even at these moments they did not forget their trade. They kept an eye on their stalls in case anyone might make off with a candle or an image or lay hands on the till. Some of them even had the presence of mind to glance covertly at the women with whom a bargain had been broken off when the nimbus was waved to and fro and to signal to them with their fingers in the hope of even now coming to an agreement over the unconcluded bargain.

When the great ceremony was finally at an end, the haggling at the stalls was resumed immediately, in louder tones and with more vehement gesticulations, at the point where it had been interrupted. The Church too now began to do business.

7

On the left-hand side of the church, about midway between the altar and the door, San Caralampio stood on a pedestal—that is, he did not actually stand on it: he was kneeling. He was made of wood with a halo around his head and had staring glass eyes and a beard. He was clothed in a dark-blue velvet cloak. He knelt with his face turned to an altar; whether it was his own altar was not clear. His palms were together and raised in prayer. Why, and to whom he prayed, no one could say; nor did anyone bother to ask. It was enough that he was there in person for all to see.

Very few of the people in the church regarded him as they would a photograph or a piece of sculpture. Most of them—all the Indians and nine-tenths of the Mexican poor—were firmly convinced that this figure was the actual saint in person, turned to wood or mummied, to whom they had come to offer prayers. But whether they believed or not that this figure was the real San Caralampio, they all without exception were utterly convinced that the soul of San Caralampio had crept into this figure and chosen it for its eternal habitation. If a wafer by a simple ceremony can become the flesh of God, surely a real saint could turn into a wooden figure, whether of his own accord or with the help of a ceremony. The ceremony had probably taken place centuries ago, and since then the figure and the real Caralampio had been one and the same.

When High Mass was over the whole congregation lined up, so that each singly might pay due honor to San Caralampio. The dark-blue cloak enveloped the saint completely and fell far below the feet whose soles were turned toward the people present. Each, when his turn came, walked up close to the soles of the saint's feet, muttered a prayer or a magic formula or a vow, and then, lifting the cloak up high above the saint's naked legs, kissed the naked soles three times. Then the worshiper crossed himself several times, muttered a few more formulas, and passed on, while the next advanced to kiss the soles of the saint.

No one, however, was permitted to kiss the soles of these feet for nothing. His retreat was barred by a barrier where a man stood with a box, which he held out on a level with the worshiper's chest. Anyone who wanted to kiss the saint's feet had to pay for it. "Plata, por favor" ("Silver, please"), the man whispered into the ears of everybody passing by.

Andrés had seen the mummery and masquerading and capering of his own witch doctors and sorcerers, and now he had witnessed the ceremonial of a Catholic church at a great fiesta. It was not his fault if he drew a comparison which was so apt. It was the fault of those whose duty it had been to give him a proper education. But the gentry of the Catholic Church regarded the Indians as children, and they regarded it as their sacred task to see to it that the Indians and all members of the lower classes remained children for ever and ever, with the Holy Father in Rome as their father and the priests as their uncles and guardians.

Though he did not know it, Andrés was certainly the only person in the church whose intelligence, owing to its rapid development during the recent months, was able to make comparisons which none other of all those present was able to make, because they were children and obviously content to remain children. It was so comfortable not to think. But influenced by the crowd around him, which behaved just like a herd of animals, he was carried away as all the rest were by the force of suggestion. Since all were doing the same thing and since among them there were many who, to judge from their dress, were cleverer than himself, he thought there must be some hidden reason of which he was ignorant that induced them all to act alike. He decided that some inward change might take place, even though it might not be outwardly discernible. So finally he lined up with the rest in order to discover whether this was the case and whether he might learn something by it. He did not want to feel shut out from the herd, and so he did as the herd did. He too went up to San Caralampio and kissed the lacquered soles on the places which a hundred other wet mouths had already moistened. And he too paid the man with the money box what he owed.

When at last he left the church he was not aware that any alteration had taken place in him, as he had hoped must happen if he did all that it was proper to do.

With this discovery he ceased to be a child. He thought of his father, of his uncles and grandfathers and all the men of his tribe, and also of the medicine man of whom he had lived in constant fear, and then and there he felt, as he stood outside the door and looked down on the square and its tumult of shouting traders, that a change had taken place in him after all.

It was clear to him that he had left his father behind; yes, and even the medicine man too. He knew now that he would never again be afraid of the medicine men of his people, and with that he lost all fear of gods of every sort, Indian or other. He had the impression that all gods drove a trade, each after his own fashion. Their secrets were laid bare to him. They had lost their terrors, for he saw how vulnerable they were—made of wax, of wood, of clay. They had no thunders, lightnings, and earthquakes at their disposal. Such things were merely used—so he concluded—by those who wanted to trade on the gods as the supposed authors of them.

From this he realized that the Church and all that had to do with it was only of interest and importance to people who had nothing better to think about.

So ended Andrés's approach to Christianity before it had really begun. He knew in his heart and mind that he was done and well done with the Church for the rest of his life.

8

On the second step from the bottom sat Luis. Luis was a carretero like Andrés, but with a different cartage contractor. He too was an Indian, though not from a finca; he came from the Indian town Yalanchén, which lies to the west of Balún-Canán.

Luis was eating enchiladas, which he had just bought and which were still hot. The grease ran over his hands, and at every moment he transferred the enchiladas from one hand to the other and licked the grease from his fingers.

Andrés and Luis had known one another for a long time. They had often traveled together in the same caravan. All carreteros recognized a sort of brotherhood among themselves.

They were constantly meeting on the road, some on their way down to the railroad, others on their way upcountry again. They helped each other when it came to repairing broken-down carretas or hauling out carretas stuck in the mud, and in many another contingency which threatened delays on the road or loss of wages.

"You been in church?" asked Luis as he chewed.

"Yes," Andrés replied, sitting down on the stone step beside Luis.

"You're a good Catholic then, are you?" Luis asked with a sidewise glance.

"I don't think so," Andrés answered. "It's all such a mix-up. You can't understand a word of it, and I don't know what that man's up to in the gold cloak."

"I know him well," said Luis, passing his enchiladas to the other hand and licking the grease from his fingers. "That man in the golden mantle who waves the golden vessels and the halo in the air is don Eusebio. He has only called himself Eusebio since he got the job in the church here. His name is really Nicolás. His father was a tailor in Tonalá. Then one day they won a prize in the lottery—I don't know how much. So his father sent Nicolás to a school to learn the magic—to a seminary, you know. Nicolás learned it there properly. He turns little cakes of flour into human flesh, and Spanish red wine into human blood. I heard that from Felipe, who was in the seminary too for a while, but they sent him away because he wanted to marry. They don't allow that."

"Then Nicolás can do magic now?" asked Andrés.

"Not much," Luis replied. "He did not learn it really well. Antonio—you know the fellow, one of don Ambrosio's carreteros—went to church here one day and Nicolás gave him one of those little cakes to eat. But Antonio told me it did not taste of human flesh at all, but only of flour, and so he knew

Nicolás had not learned the magic well. But he earns good money here, you know. They pay him a good round peso or two for christenings, marriages, and burials and for prayers to save you from hell. Felipe told me that the masters at the seminary tell them that the curas have to make the people in the church afraid by saying that they will all be roasted and nipped with tongs when they are dead. But if they come to church regularly and always do as the cura says, then they will not be roasted, but only washed in warm water to make them clean. Felipe says it isn't true, but only a tale to frighten people. You see, people are all such fools. When once you're dead, it's quite clear you feel nothing, not even though you are roasted and pinched with tongs. But there you are—the people believe it and it makes their flesh creep to believe it, and that's why they do believe it. The curas only want money out of the people, so that they can live well without needing to work hard. Our brujo at Yalanchén, the medicine man, was always telling us horrible tales of caves into which we were going to be thrown after we were dead—caves full of snakes and tigers. But as soon as my father or my uncle gave him a sheep or a young pig, he said he'd talk to the santitos, the gods, about it, so that we shouldn't be thrown into the caves full of snakes and tigers."

"Our brujo said the same thing," Andrés put in. "He told us we'd be put in a deep black pit when we died, if we didn't do as he said. And at the bottom of the black pit was a lake of mud, and we'd stick in it up to the chin and then we'd not be able either to die or to live, but simply freeze horribly in the mud. And there was no chance of getting out, because the sides were steep and slimy and thick with little snakes and great toads. We always had to give our brujo tequila and maize; then he danced and prayed, and the santitos told him in the night that we would not sink in the mud as long as we did all he told us. But if any of us told the finquero who the brujo was, then we would all without any doubt sink in the morass and no tequila and no little pigs for the brujo could save us any more."

"I'll tell you something," said Luis, who was nearly twice Andrés's age. "As long as you pay no attention to anything the brujo or the cura say, as long as you believe nothing of the roasting or the caves and pits, you'll live a peaceable contented life and always be in good spirits, as I am. Have you ever seen me with a long face? Never in your life. If the oxen anger me or a carreta breaks down, well then I may curse as loud as the next man—but that is only for a moment. Live, and when you've done, then let the others get on with it. When your life's done, nobody's going to bother any more about you. Who's going to take the trouble to play the fool with you year after year once you're dead? There are plenty more left alive and it's much wiser to bother them. Do we ourselves waste time on the road to whip an ox, once it's down and done with, because it once overturned a carreta in a ditch? And now I'm going to have a comiteco to wash down those enchiladas."

"What did you pay for them?" asked Andrés.

"One real for six, and they couldn't be better."

"Where?"

Luis pointed to a stall embowered in greenery.

11

    Luis went off to a bar for his comiteco and Andrés strolled across to the restaurant, which consisted of a stall set up within a very primitive pergola.

Behind the stall was a small tin stove in which charcoal was glowing. On top of the stove lay a tin sheet with a shallow depression in its center. Fat was frizzling in this hollow.

An old Indian woman crouched beside the stove, fanning the charcoal to a glow with a fan of bast. She was the restaurant's proprietor as well as its cook.

She baked tortillas on the flat surface of the tin sheet, then filled them, according to her customers' desires, with barbacoa, guajolote, pollo, res, ternera, or queso, folded them over, and dropped them into the hot grease. Barbacoa is mutton roasted in a special Indian way; guajolote is turkey; pollo, chicken; res, beef; ternera, veal; and queso is cheese.

It was all one to the cook in what language her enchiladas and their contents were ordered. She took the orders in Spanish, Tsotsil, Tojolaval, Tseltal. A Spaniard who had a stall opposite maintained that this Indian woman could equally understand English and Arabic, as long as the customer

143

pointed at the same time to the food he desired. For everyone, without exception, who bought her enchiladas pointed to what he wanted inside them, and so it was not easy to say with certainty whether she understood any language but Tojolaval.

On the ground beside her the Indian had more than a dozen earthenware dishes and pots; for besides the varieties of meat, she put onions, tomatoes, red chiles, green chiles, green salad, citron leaves, calabaza flowers, and twenty other herbs, leaves, and roots into her enchiladas.

She used only an iron spoon to turn and brown the enchiladas in the fat. Spatulas, knives, forks, and other such implements were foreign to her. She pulled off the flesh from a fowl or a joint of veal with her fingers. It was much quicker than slicing and she detached the right amount for an enchilada with an astonishing accuracy.

It was a joy just to see how she managed the tiny space at her disposal, without ever getting muddled among so many kinds of meat and vegetables.

Her two daughters, Indian girls with long hair hanging down their backs, served at the little stall. They handed the enchiladas to the customer on a small plate. He was given neither knife, fork, nor spoon—nothing of that kind was supplied by the restaurant. But when he had eaten he was offered a gray, greasy cloth with which to wipe his fingers and mouth, and after this a small earthenware bowl of water to rinse his mouth.

Plates and pots were never properly washed. To say they were dirty is to say next to nothing. And yet in these surroundings nobody found the dirt either disgusting or vexatious. It belonged—as the clouds belong to the sky. The harmony of the world around was in nowise disturbed by it.

It was impossible, certainly, to see or to find out whether or where or how and with what the dishes were washed. The plate was snatched from each customer even as he ate, and he had to pick up what was left of his enchiladas and make room for someone else. Meanwhile, fresh enchiladas were ready, the plates emerged again from behind the scenes, and before you could say whether they had been washed or not the next dripping enchiladas were already being served up; and you could not say whether the greasy brown marks belonged to the new enchiladas or had been left behind by earlier ones. It was the same thing with the cups of coffee, which were always filled to the brim and over, and so the grounds on the sides of the cup might either have belonged to a present or to a previous pouring. If anything seemed not quite in order, the daughter who was serving wiped the edge of the cup or platter clean with an adroit flick of her hand and then licked her fingers or wiped them on her apron, which was so marked and spotted that you could not say whether the girl had made a new mark that moment or whether she had made it three hours before.

However, those who frequented the place were not buying crockery, but enchiladas. Good and appetizing enchiladas were the chief thing, not the crockery—and the enchiladas were excellent.

Hence, business was brisk. People fought for their turn. Andrés had to wait a long time before he got his enchiladas.

2

Except that you could buy all the rubbish that was unsaleable in any of the bigger towns, there was scarcely any real distraction at the fair. There were no merry-go-rounds, swingboats, water-shoots or anything that gives life to a fair in other places. Such machinery could not be transported here; the transport would be so difficult and costly that the profit would be swallowed up by it.

You had to find what entertainment you could in the cries of the dealers and in the humorous back talk and discourses of knowing salesmen who offered gold nibs which bent but never broke, glass-cutters, knife-sharpeners, needle-threaders, lenses which could be used for detecting spurious silk or for reading or as telescopes, benzine, polishes, stomach waters, eye lotions, rheumatism salves, wart pencils, corn cures.

But Andrés found all this tedious after a while, for as soon as the man had got to the end of his pitch he began again with his quips and wisecracks in exactly the same words and with the same intonation.

The sword-swallowers, the snake charmers, and the strong men who freed themselves from ropes and chains became wearisome too; for each of them had only one trick, which he repeated from four in the evening until eleven at night, as long as there was even one spectator who looked as if he might have even five centavos in his pocket of which he might possibly be relieved.

The gambling tables also soon lost their attraction if you did not play yourself. Of course, there were always those people standing around and watching who did not play themselves but hit on a number and rejoiced when it lost, because it was not their money that had left its pocket.

For the majority the only pleasure lay in wandering around —standing a moment here, listening or looking on for a quarter of an hour there, and then elbowing their way on again.

The happiest of all were the girls and boys of the town, who made use of the crowding and squeezing to tease and come to terms with one another without being observed. In their ordinary lives they had few opportunities to do this, for even at dances mothers and aunts were always present, and the girls could go nowhere unattended. But now this chaperoning was impracticable. They might have come with their mothers to the plaza, but it was easy to be lost sight of for half an hour. It could not be helped—you got held up or separated in the crowd.

And so it happened sometimes that these carefully watched and tended girls of the place enjoyed a stolen kiss—or even closer embraces if they were quick—under cover of the crowd or in the shadow of a house; and these delights were not to be taken too seriously, because they were all part of the fiesta which was held in honor of San Caralampio. Many a daughter of highly reputed citizens was lost for much longer than half an hour in the crowd. She was not lost for good. She returned to her anxious parents, whom she had sought everywhere in vain, with ruffled hair and a little ruffled altogether, which only showed how she had had to fight her way through the crowd in the effort to rejoin her parents.

When the people were tired of wandering around and had seen every stand and stall three hundred and eighty times over, they put in another quarter of an hour in the church, through whose open doors could be heard the sound of the organ and the singing of the muffled women.

At intervals the church bells began to peal. Not the hardiest stallkeeper or roulette banker could shout them down; and so the crowd was continually reminded not to waste all their money at the stalls, on roulette, on enchiladas and comiteco, but to leave some over for eternal life.

The Catholic Church in Mexico is second to none when it comes to advertising. Again and again you will see on the poorboxes the following very attractive announcement: "Every centavito you give will be repaid in gold in heaven." A banker who put such a notice in his window would be arrested immediately for obtaining deposits on false pretenses. He would be asked by the judge for positive proof that the deposits would be paid back in heaven and whether and where this heaven was to be found. The Church is not asked for proof. It relies on faith. And he who refuses faith blasphemes God.

What is an Indian to make of it?

3

Andrés too, after he had been up and down the rows between the stalls a score of times, did not know what to do next. He heard the whining from the church and the moaning organ, which put your mind so comfortably and irresistibly to sleep that you said yes to everything. But he had not the slightest desire to enter the church a second time, all the less because a band of musicians had begun to play and sing on the side of the square near the fountain.

The fountain was the town's daily newspaper. The town had no newspaper, but the fountain took the place of this asset, or drawback, whichever you like to call it.

As they had no piped water, the inhabitants were forced to get all their water from the fountain. In order to keep a supply on hand each household had several earthenware crocks, each of which held from eighty to a hundred liters. These large crocks had been made by Indians in exactly the same shape and style for two thousand years.

There were families who considered it beneath their dignity to send their maidservants to the fountain with jugs to fill and bring back on their heads; and the dignity of these middle-class families had called into being a special trade—the purveying of water. The purveyors were Indians who had become urbanized and lived on the outskirts of the town. They had two or three donkeys which were kept at work from six in the morning until late in the afternoon. The donkeys were furnished with a framework by means of which they could carry large earthenware jars filled with water. These dealers in water went from house to house with their loads, offering their ware.

Families who wished to be even more distinguished had a donkey of their own, and an Indian boy who served in the house fetched the water with it.

Next in rank came the families who regularly got their water in by the load, for which they paid a real, or even less.

Then there were the families who did not pay for water. They may have had two Indian girls and sent one of them to carry water, or only one Indian servant who had to do everything, water carrying included.

Last in rank were the families in which there were only the wife or the children to fetch water, because they could not afford to pay for anything they could possibly do for themselves.

Nobody, not even the professional water carriers, went to the fountain and filled his vessels at one or other of the pipes from which the water poured day and night, and then went straight away again. Everyone who came to the fountain rested for a moment and gossiped with the others who were there. The men rolled cigarettes and the girls saw to their hair or the fit of their skirts. It would have been in very bad taste to go there and get the water and then rush off again. Fetching water was a leisurely and contemplative proceeding.

In the evenings all the girls, even from households which were too distinguished to send them to fetch water, found some excuse for going to the fountain, if only for ten minutes. They would explain in the house that the water in the large household crocks was tepid and flat, and that the health and good appetite of the master would suffer if they did not hasten out to fetch some fresh cold water from the fountain for the supper table.

When a girl got back, particularly in the evening, her mistress was waiting for her in the kitchen—not for the water, but to hear whether it was really true that don Jorge had been three times that week to doña Amalia's house and had not left by one in the morning; and how the quarrel of the day before yesterday between señor Osorio and his señora had gone off, and whether he had actually beaten the señora until she could not see out of her eyes; and whether it was a fact that doña Ana, the partera—the midwife—had said that señora Zavala's baby had come a month too soon, or whether it really was a seven months' child—for she was married only eight months ago. These matters were of far greater importance than such trivial facts as that, at the last re-election of President don Porfirio, only three per cent of the entire Mexican people had gone to the polls, because every Mexican, whether he had any sense or not, knew six months before the presidential election who was elected—and that there had been talk of revolution throughout the length and breadth of the Republic, so as to put an end to this tyranny.

The girls who came to the fountain had so much to say, too, about their love affairs and their comedies and tragedies of jealousy that it was no wonder if they were to be found there until late at night with the jugs of fresh water for their masters' suppers. And since the young fellows of the place knew that the girls they had their eyes on were sure to be found there, the fountain presented a scene of much animation every night.

During the fair, however, the idyl of the fountain was utterly broken up and scattered. It was too noisy with the cries of dealers and the chatter of people passing to and fro. Then, too, on ordinary evenings the fountain was in dark shadow, unless there was a moon, but now not a kiss could pass unseen. The whole square was illuminated by the lights from the stalls and booths.

4

The musicians had taken up their stand in front of the fountain and now began to strike up with spirit. A free space had been left there which the authorities would not hire out to the traders because there had to be room for the water carriers and their donkeys. On this free space Indian boys and girls of the town now began to dance. At the end of every dance one of the boys gave the musicians five centavos, and then they began at once to play another dance.

Once the musicians started they were pretty sure to keep it up until two or three in the morning, for as soon as the news got around Indian girls and boys from the farthest corners of the town quickly arrived in large parties. They could not forgo the prospect of a dance. There was no other large-scale diversion open to the townspeople, whatever class they belonged to.

Even the prosperous citizens danced if they felt the need of distraction—one week in the house of the Suárez family, next week at the Cota's, and so on the whole year through. Either it was the cumpleaños—the birthday—of the master of the house, or else it was the wife's día de su santo—her saint's day—or else it was a christening or a wedding. Then there were the two weeks of the posadas—the Christmas celebrations—and then the New Year festival. And if there was no better excuse for a dance, then all the bachelors of the town invited all the ladies to a ball in a hotel simply for the sake of dancing. If a young unmarried doctor left the town to go to the United States to pursue his studies, a farewell ball was got up in his honor. Another young man of the town returned from Mexico City, after completing his studies, to set himself up as a dentist or a lawyer. There was a ball to welcome him.

What else was there for them to do? There were no cinemas, theaters, or concerts, and no lecturers undertook the toils of a journey to this remote spot. Even a starving circus troupe was a rarity.

The Indians were carried even further by their urge to seek and find distraction in dancing. They danced even at their funeral solemnities. The coffin was placed in the middle of the largest room in the house. If they had no money the occasion did not give rise to inviting a priest—they knew he did nothing for nothing. But if the family had a few pesos to spare, they paid a priest to bless the corpse and sprinkle it with holy water. As soon as the priest had finished his murmuring, the music struck up and the couples, including the nearest relations of the dead person or persons, danced merrily around the corpse. They danced till daylight. Then the coffin was taken up, and with howling and lamentation the procession started for the cemetery.

The Mexicans—the Ladinos—did not of course do anything like this. They regarded such behavior as heathen barbarity. They lacked the maturity of tradition, and still more they lacked a sound natural philosophy. After submitting for centuries to the influence of a Church which puts the tinsel of ceremonial in the place of a straightforward rule of life, whose aim is to be that and nothing more, these people have become mere hypocrites, and so have destroyed in themselves everything that could minister to the development of a straightforward and honest human being. For if it is considered proper to dance at the birth and christening of a child, who is thrust into the pains and sorrows of life, why, in heaven's name, should it be improper and heathenish to dance when a person has taken leave of life's persecutions and oppressions and returns to the land of eternal peace? But there—they are worthless hypocrites; for if they believed what their religion preaches they would have to rejoice and dance from excess of joy at the thought of the songs of praise and twanging harps which await the departed in the realm of eternity.

The Indian, however, is too dense to appreciate the mysteries of the Catholic Church, and so he does nothing as we do it, and we are horrified at his barbarisms.

5

But the Indian boys and girls who danced by the fountain did not look in the least like barbarians. The girls were clothed in cheap—very cheap—but very clean dresses. They had all washed themselves well, and their long black hair had been combed more thoroughly than it could ever have been in a New York beauty parlor.

The boys wore white trousers and white shirtlike jackets. Some of them had sandals, but most were barefoot. Most of the girls too were barefoot, though some had patent-leather shoes with very high heels.

The girls stood or squatted on the ground on one side, and the boys stood in loose groups in a row on the other side. The Indian boy did not go up to the girl he wished to dance with, nor did he bow to her and ask in a set formula whether he might have the honor and so forth.

The boy, as soon as the music began, advanced half a step, pulled a red handkerchief out of the pocket of his shirt, and threw it to the girl he wished to dance with—in her lap if she squatted, toward her if she was standing. If the girl accepted the handkerchief, that meant she would dance with its owner; if she threw it back it meant she refused to dance with him. She never threw it back unless the fellow was very drunk, or unless she saw that another whom she preferred was making ready to throw his handkerchief to her. It was considered bad manners to return a dancer's handkerchief. Most girls accepted it even when the fellow was drunk, rather than offend him; and in such cases they danced for a while with him before returning to their places. The man was thus saved the shame of a refusal and was quite content.

The boys danced in a row with the girls opposite them. The partners did not say a word while they danced, or when the dance was at an end. They did not hold each other, but danced singly, facing one another. When they changed position they danced past each other to opposite sides, so that all the boys were still on one side and the girls on the other.

The girl held her partner's handkerchief in her right hand during the dance. When the dance was over she gave it to him, and without a word of thanks she turned her back and re-joined the other girls to stand or squat among them.

If the dance was too long, or the girl felt tired, or wanted for any reason to stop dancing, she went up to her partner, returned his handkerchief, and retired to her place. A girl had the right to stop whenever she wished; she had only to return the handkerchief. The boy had not the right to stop until he had recovered his handkerchief.

It happened at times that the music went on for half an hour without a pause. If the girl was an indefatigable dancer—as Indian girls are—and if her partner was not her equal in toughness—as is usually the case—she would dance him to a standstill. The girls did this sometimes if they wanted to pay a boy back for any reason. They danced till he dropped and was out for the rest of the night. Women have a fine instinct for a sound and well-aimed revenge on a man. The Indian women in particular are accomplished in thinking out ways and means to this end, when it serves their purpose and affords them amusement.

There were, it is true, many couples on the square who danced together as the Ladinos did in their ballrooms, for a good half of the boys and girls were town Indians who had been born and brought up in the town or its outskirts.

6

Andrés took up his position in the boys' row. He wanted to dance but felt shy because he knew no girl. Some of the other carreteros from the camp on the prairie were there too. They dug each other in the ribs and tried to urge one or another of their number to dance so that they could then follow suit. But not one of them found the courage. They felt strange and awkward.

Andrés, not liking to stand there foolishly like a little boy, backed by degrees out of the line of youths and strolled away toward the side of a house, where he sat down against the wall, his knees to his chin and his arms around his shins. From here the music was less strident and more harmonious, the notes blending together better because of the distance. He could dream in peace.

As he sat there dreaming to the sound of the music, through which he caught the suppressed laughter of the girls, he was overcome by a strange feeling of not knowing what he was there for, or what anything at all was for—he might as well be dead, for all the difference it would make.

Three girls passed close by him, smoothing and pulling at their dresses. After a while they came back, and, talking together and hugging the corner in the deep shadow of the wall, all three spoke at once in cooing voices which rose and fell in short snatches, now caught in with the breath they drew, now issuing with it on a louder, fuller note. For the first time in his life, Andrés was aware of sex.

These three Indian girls spoke in Spanish, but whenever they were at a loss for a word they fell into Tseltal, their mother tongue; for they were too eager to wait for the adopted word. They did not know Andrés was there in the deep shadow, so absorbed were they in their talk.

He could not gather what they were talking about, for their voices often sank into a whisper. He heard only the subdued murmur and the melody of the voices mingling with one another. It was this cooing, gurgling music that excited him. It set him longing. At first he thought it was a longing for his mother, but knew at once and felt with vehemence that it was for something else: a longing for something—something beautiful. He could not clearly make out what this beauty was. Again he thought it was homesickness—but no, it was not that. It was a glow of warmth that rose and surged up in him. He began to feel infinitely sad—and utterly alone.

Nothing of this had ever occurred to him before. He had heard women and girls talking hundreds of times, but he had never before been aware of anything in a woman's voice that excited him. Dozens of times women had been with the caravan—young, old, pretty, married and unmarried women. Sometimes the wives of carreteros had been with the caravan for weeks on end.

On all such occasions he had been in close touch with women again and again, but he had never felt anything particular in their presence. He had lifted women down from the carreta or helped them up into it. Time and time again he had carried women across rivers. He had waked women in the early morning at the ranchos and come upon them half dressed or even, owing to the heat, lying entirely naked on their beds. He had by accident surprised women who were traveling with the caravan in every sort of situation among the bushes by the roadside. Often in the night when there was a sudden flash of lightning or when the campfire broke unexpectedly into flame, he had seen men embracing their wives under a carreta or elsewhere. Hundreds of times he had seen women naked up to their waists when they were fording rivers, streams, and floods, and had come on girls bathing with nothing on at all. But he had never felt concerned with any of this, nor had it aroused desire of any kind.

A woman was made rather differently, otherwise she was the same to him as a man. In his home men and women alike worked hard. There was no distinction except in the kind of work, and that was because women were weaker and bore children and looked after them. To his feelings married women were the same as his mother or his aunts; and a girl was the same as his sisters.

The hut in which he had been brought up had only one room. As a child he had seen that his father had no other place to sleep except by his mother's side on the thin petate. The tropical moon shone brightly in through the thin slats of the walls, and he had seen all his father and mother did as they lay together. The children held the parents in boundless honor and this honor and love could never be shaken, least of all by what was as natural as the rising and setting of the sun or the springing up of the corn and the flowers.

Andrés knew nothing of the lies and deceits and treacheries of novels, poems, and films. And he had not been brought up in a land where preachers and paragraph-writers force young and old alike to know what uncleanness is and where it is to be found and how to avail themselves of it, in order to earn the right to be counted among citizens of repute.

He had no means for discovering the deep, hidden cause of this sudden glow of longing. He tried to explain it to himself, because nothing of the sort had ever occurred to him before. For half a minute he thought it might be a fever coming on, which he had caught somewhere, but almost at once he knew that it was not fever. A fever—calentura—did not begin like that. He had no headache and no heaviness in his limbs.

Rather the opposite—his head had never been so clear as now, even if perplexed. He was filled with a desire to walk and walk, all night and all the next day, anywhere, just to keep moving. So his limbs could not be afflicted with heaviness.

Round about him were people laughing, talking, aimlessly strolling to and fro on the plaza. There was the monotonous chanting and the bumbling of the organ from the church, which ever and again mingled with the dance music. And there was the dance music, meaningless and yet gay. There were the excited youths in white trousers. There were the giggling and chattering girls and their long, black, well-combed hair with flowers threaded in it; and their flashing white teeth and full lips and eager coal-black eyes, which sometimes fixed him with a sudden gleam. And all the girls were well washed and smelled of strong soap and their dresses were as clean as new pins. And when they moved you sometimes had a glimpse of their petal-white chemises.

But when those three girls passed so close and then stood for a time so near him, he had caught the smell of their light sweat, which reached him all the more distinctly because it was fresh and exuded from well-washed bodies. It affected him with the sweetness of a scent.

Above all, though, it was their voices that cast the spell. Their voices were not music and yet they acted on him like music—only it was music of another kind. It was not like the music made by instruments.

It was the softness in their voices. It was the deep womanly goodness, which can be at the same time the beloved and the mother, welling out on the warm, cooing, and voluptuous tide of their voices without their knowing it. It seemed they had discovered that very evening who was the man among all men on earth who alone held the power to present them with the whole world wreathed in roses.

Even though Andrés did not know the causes of his strange awakening, he knew he was no longer the man he had been an hour before. A change had come over him and he felt that it would take complete possession of him.

It was nothing new to him that women had not the same voices as men; but it was a new and hitherto unsuspected discovery that the music in a woman's voice could distinguish it so entirely from a man's, and that by the mere tone and color of her voice, and by the revelation of her soul in it, she could place a whole world between herself and him.

This discovery shook him so deeply that for a time he felt afraid. He began to feel uncertain of himself. He suddenly doubted his power to carry on his life in the world. His longing for something unknown yet beautiful was linked with this onset of uncertainty and fear.

He had a sudden fear of women. There was something about them he no longer understood. Nothing was left in him but the mere, simple feeling that he could understand only his mother and that she was the only woman, now and always, of whom he had no fear.

But at the same time, even while he was overwhelmed by the strangeness of women, he felt the longing to listen to them and to be stroked and caressed by the caress in their voices.

He fell into a deep melancholy and felt a vehement desire to cry. The way the girls had so carelessly walked away without noticing him told him that now, in spite of all the crowd of people in the square, he was utterly forsaken and alone. He had not a friend—no one to speak kindly to him, no one to whom he could tell what he felt and what had come over him.

He felt himself growing weary. He hoped he might die then

and there without pain or trouble, and without ever needing to get up again.

It was out of this prostration of mind that the longing, which until now had been so vague and wavering, became full and clear.

12

It was certainly a pity that he had never penetrated far enough into the mysteries of religion. In that case he would now have entered the church and offered up two good fat candles, encased in colored paper, to the King of Heaven and implored Him earnestly to grant him his heart's desire. It is much simpler to pray to the gods and goddesses for help than to labor to attain one's desire, either by hard work or by an adroit and intelligent manipulation of the circumstances which promise its fulfillment. The things a man deeply desires rarely arise of themselves, and very seldom in the way he hopes of them. But things that are earnestly coveted do come closer and, once close, are more easily grasped and held on to than things that are only halfheartedly coveted or not coveted at all. That is only natural and not by any means hard to understand. Persons of little education and little intelligence have to pray before they can concentrate on what they wish. And therefore it is of no importance to what one prays, since it is not the prayer but the strength of one's desire that brings the object of desire nearer.

Andrés was well aware from long experience that prayer

would not cause a single hole in the road to vanish—unless he or his fellow workers filled the hole with stones and, even then, kept a sharp lookout to prevent the carreta from coming to grief. He knew that his patrón would not raise his wage by so much as half a real however long he might kneel to the Holy Virgin. He had to fight that out with the patrón for himself, whether outright or by guile. And if an ox fell over a precipice, the most earnest prayers would never pull it up again. It meant hours of backbreaking toil before the carreteros could hoist the animal onto the road again—with lassos and tree trunks after digging out steps and excavating a way for it.

Although the church called to him so persistently through its open doorway it never for a second entered his head to beseech the Holy Virgin for the companion he desired.

2

Andrés was irresolute what to do next. Squatting there in his Indian fashion, he remained motionless as before. Seen from a little distance he looked, in the shadow of the wall behind him, like a statue put there as an ornament of the house. He did not even turn his head. He could see all he wished of what went on in the square without as much as moving his eyes. It was only within that the presence of the girls had made him restless.

He could not squat there forever, but he did not know where to go. There was nothing more to be seen. The boys and girls danced on and on, but dancing is wearisome to lookers-on.

Yet he did not want to return to the camp. The prairie was now wrapped in darkness. The carreteros were asleep, or, if not asleep, drunk and bawling senselessly to no one in particular. Carretas, oxen, and carreteros could be seen every day, but a fair—when he could sit idly looking on without a care—was a rare event in his life. There was no knowing when he would next have the chance to partake in a fiesta like this. It might be a year. It might be two.

And thinking how it might be years before another fiesta came his way, how his work might always keep him from it, owing to the long trips he might be on, he at last made up his mind to have another look around, among the stands and booths and roulette tables. There was always something of interest to be seen. He considered going to a bar and having a small comiteco. Perhaps he might meet a girl who had no boy friend and was wandering about alone like himself. His blood warmed at the thought of meeting a girl, a girl, perhaps, like one of those three who had aroused this new and strange excitement in him. It was possible he might find a girl who would be willing to talk to him, to dance with him, to stroll about the fair with him, and perhaps walk out with him beyond the last houses over the little bridge and as far as the last farms, after which there was the open prairie.

3

He stretched his legs and felt for his tall bast hat, which had slipped from his head. He was about to get on his feet when he heard a sound like a suppressed sigh.

He looked to his right. He had not once looked in that direction in all the time he had been squatting there. Everything worth looking at had been to the front of him; there could have been nothing much to see at his right.

When he now looked more closely into the darkness he could see, hunched in a corner of the house, a small bundle which appeared to be human. It was tightly rolled up as though afraid of claiming too much space from the world and other people. Indeed, this bundle did not seem to believe it had any right to any room whatever, so closely was it huddled together.

The bundle did not stir. Neither head nor feet were visible. It was entirely enveloped in a jorongo of black wool with narrow gray stripes.

4

Andrés could not make out how this bundle had come there— so close that he could almost touch it by stretching out his hand. No doubt his thoughts had been far away and he had not noticed when and how it had crouched down near him. Perhaps it had been there before he himself had sat down. In any case he had had no idea it was there, and owing to the unexpectedness of it, it seemed to him that this bundle had fallen from heaven.

He edged a little nearer, and as he did so he thought the bundle huddled itself closer together. Again he heard a gentle sigh, like the indrawn breath of a long sob.

"What are you crying for, little girl?" he asked softly.

There was no reply.

It occurred to him that perhaps she did not understand Spanish. So next he asked in Tseltal: "Why are you sad, little girl?"

The bundle stirred and sat up.

"Have you no mother?" he asked.

"Muquenal," the bundle said softly, and sighed again.

"In the cemetery, then," Andrés replied. "And your father?" he asked.

"Mee muquenal, tat milvil, nebahachisch, mucal aquil namal," said the bundle, meaning: "My mother in the cemetery, my father killed, I am an orphan now, my village is far from here."

In these few words her whole history was told.

5

Andrés moved a little closer.

"Can I help you, little girl?"

She said nothing for a time. She had to think it out. Then she said: "Bocon—I will go now."

"Where will you go, so late in the night? The wild dogs will bite you, and drunken men about on the roads will insult you."

"I'm not afraid," she answered to this. "I have sharp teeth and strong nails and I'll find two big stones and take them with me."

While she spoke she came further and further out of her jorongo. Her head was now free.

"How old are you?" he asked her.

"Jolajuneb—I am fifteen," she replied.

"Anelvaneg—a runaway?" he asked.

"Yes, anesvil—I've run away from a finca," she said.

Her hair was tangled, matted and long uncombed—dirty and, Andrés supposed, full of lice. Her face had not been washed for days. Her skin was a dark bronze. Her eyes were black like her straggly hair, and very large and bright.

"Have you nowhere to sleep?" he asked.

"I am going out onto the prairie," she said.

He laughed at her, and when he saw that she answered with a hesitating smile he said: "I'll take you with me to the carretas and I'll fix you a warm soft bed in a carreta. Will you come?"

"You are good to me, Binash Yutsil—you fine boy," she said simply. And with this the invitation was accepted.

6

"We'll go first to the fountain," he suggested.

"Why?"

"Suquel—to wash ourselves."

This was polite and gallant, for he had meant that she needed washing. As it was now a question of both of them she did not mind being told that she needed a wash.

He pulled a small piece of soap out of his pocket and gave it to her. She washed at the outer edge of the fountain, where the water ran into troughs for the cattle that were brought there to be watered.

"Stay where you are," he said and ran off. In a moment he was back with a wooden comb he had bought at a stall for five centavos.

"And now we'll go and give your hair a good combing."

He took her by the hand and they went back into the shadow of the house where they had first met. She began to give her hair a thorough combing. It took a long time. It was by nature thick hair and now it was a mop.

He watched and laughed and talked with her as though he had known her for years. It seemed to do her all the good in the world to have found someone to talk to freely, and she relied on him as she would on a brother.

The confidence she had in him filled him with tenderness. He felt his heart bathed in warm sunshine. Indeed, it ran all through his veins. The longing, which had made him sad because it had no object and was only longing for longing's sake, was now released in a great and quiet joy. There was no name for it; for it was a joy that was new to him and was not connected with anything he had known before. He wished the night might never end and the girl talk on and on and never stop.

When she tossed back her hair to shake it clear and then lowered her head again and looked at him with a smile which showed the beauty of her white teeth, he felt a new world open. He felt boundlessly rich to have bought her a comb, and richer still to be able to offer her a carreta in the camp for her home.

At last she had finished with her hair. She shook it back from her face and turned to him with a smile. Then she pulled the loose hair from the teeth of the comb, tapped it against the wall, and gave it back to him.

"It is your comb," he said, "a present from the fair."

"But I've no pocket to keep it in," she said, smiling. "Won't you keep it in your pocket for me?"

He took it and put it in his pocket. "I'm very pleased to keep it for you. Now you'll have to come to me when you want to comb your hair."

"I'll do that gladly," she replied.

He stood up. "And now, vehel ta hacabaltic—we will go and have supper. Would you like to? Are you hungry?"

She threw back her head so as to look up at his face, for she was sitting on her heels.

"I have never been so hungry, Binash Yutsil. It's two days since I ate."

7

They went to the little Indian kitchen where Andrés had bought his enchiladas earlier in the evening.

"Now what will you have for your supper, tujom ants?" he asked her.

Her face went dark as he said this and she looked down in shame, for "tujom ants" means "beautiful lady," and in the way he said it, and in his smile as he said it, there was not only admiration of her—but more. Then she raised her eyes and looked at him with a sidelong smile and half-shut eyes.

"Well?" he asked again. "What will the little girl have for supper?"

"Tibal," she replied, "meat, real meat—I'm very hungry."

He ordered the enchiladas. While they watched them being prepared she said: "But I am not a little girl, you know. I am big now. I have been a woman for over a year. You can take my word for that, Binash Yutsil huinic." She laughed.

Andrés looked at her. She had taken off her jorongo—which is worn like a poncho and like it has a hole in the center for the head—and now stood before him in a mud-spattered shirt and skirt.

The skirt was of coarse black wool, gathered into a thick tuck at the waistline because, following the Indian custom, it had to be wide enough to serve when the wearer was with child. It was torn, and smeared with dried mud. The cotton shirt, once white, was gray with dust and ingrained with dirt. It was embroidered along the border in lines and stars of red wool.

She was barefoot. Her feet were very small, and the toes were spread out in their natural form. No shoe had ever hindered their growth. The dense mass of her hair, still matted in spite of the combing, hung down below her waist. She was small, and thin.

8

When the enchiladas were ready Andrés asked the girls for a little salt, which was given to him in a banana leaf. A small lemon was also added.

Then he said: "We'll go over to the church steps to eat them and later come back and have a cup of coffee."

"Hutsil," she said laughing, "that will be fine."

"Aren't you going to eat too?" she asked when they sat down on the steps and he handed her the enchiladas.

"I've eaten already and I'm not hungry now," he said.

"Then you must just take a bite of each of my enchiladas or

I won't enjoy them and they won't do me any good," she said, holding one to his mouth.

"What is your name, little girl?" he asked.

"I have no name. My mother and father never called me anything but huntic—child—and the mistress of the finca, when she summoned me, said anstil vinic—girl. José, the master's son, always called me mejayel."

"Why did he call you mejayel?" Andrés asked angrily. "What a horrible name for a little girl like you. What a swine he must be. Over there in that cantina every painted girl who serves the men with comiteco and sits on their knees and lets them handle her as they like for money—every one of those girls is a mejayel."

She did not understand what he meant. It was as incomprehensible to her as the fable of original sin is to any normal person, but she realized that a strange and unknown world was opening before her. She could see no sense in what went on in that world. So, at the first glance at least, she believed there was no sense to be seen. But when she took another look at the cantina, and watched from where they sat what went on there, and tried to see what connection it had with what Andrés had told her, she began to understand by degrees. Indeed, she began to get it straight in her mind much more quickly than Andrés expected; for, after thinking over what she saw, she recognized that what went on in the cantina was the same thing she had seen on the finca. It was only that in that cantina next to the cathedral the dresses and lighting were different— that was all.

"José lied," she said. "I know now what a mejayel is, and José lied. I am not a mejayel, but he wanted to make me one. I see it now, and it is why I ran away from the finca. I will tell you all about it, Binash Yutsil," she said as she finished the last enchilada.

"First we'll go and drink coffee. You must be thirsty," Andrés suggested.

9

After the coffee they sat down again on the church steps. The eternal murmur of praying women came through the doorway and every now and again the monotonous chanting.

The shouts and cries of the merchants in the square died down. There were still plenty of people wandering to and fro, but no one was buying anything. Only at the gambling tables, at the shooting galleries, and at the lotería tables—there groups still collected either to play or look on.

Mexican lotería—unlike lotto or bingo or keno, whatever they choose to call it where you live—is played with picture cards rather than numbered ones. The lotería tables were the noisiest in the square as everyone scrambled to match and cover the picture squares of their cards, in the hope of planting beans on four squares in a row—in which case they won a bunch of paper flowers or a brandy glass or a comb.

You heard the cry of the man who turned up the cards: "El diablo!" And his assistant repeated: "El diablo!" "El globo!" ——"El globo!" . . . "El alacrán!"——"El alacrán!" . . . "La vaca!"——"La vaca!"—the devil, the globe, the scorpion, the cow they called out, among all the other species and objects portrayed on the cards. The callers liked to greet the names with spicy remarks which they thought witty.

Many of the merchants were now covering their stalls with tarpaulins; others packed their wares away in boxes or simply spread rush matting over them. When that was done they lay down on a mat in the stall or alongside it and went to sleep.

More and more of the lanterns and the lamps of oil-soaked cotton in tin cans were extinguished. The people who still wandered about among the stalls looked like ghostly shadows.

But near the fountain the dancing was kept up merrily.

The mournfully rising and falling flute notes of a marimba could be heard from a distant street. Sometimes it sounded like harps, sometimes like oboes of all sizes, sometimes like the singing of women's contralto voices, sometimes like a soft peal of bells. Some citizen of the town was giving a private party in his house, or a lover serenading his mistress, or a family celebrating the saint's day of one of its members.

"Would you like to dance for a bit?" asked Andrés.

"I'd like to, but I'm afraid," said the girl.

"There's nothing to be afraid of, little girl," he said, encouraging her. "There are no Ladinos dancing, but only Indians like you and me. Come along."

They joined the dancers. No one paid any attention to them. He looked like the other young fellows and she, in her jorongo, like many another Indian girl who had come to the fiesta.

He gave her his colored handkerchief and they danced their Indian zapateado as happily and unconcernedly as the rest. They entirely forgot that they had met for the first time only two hours ago. And it did not worry them that neither knew the other's name. It seemed to them that they had known each other ever since the world began.

10

It was very late. The musicians were weary. They had been playing day and night for three weeks, often right on until daybreak. They did not earn much; those who came to them to dance had little to spend. But they, Indians like the rest, seemed to find much of their reward in giving pleasure to others and enabling all who came along to forget their cares, if only for a few happy hours.

"Now we'll have another drink of coffee, and a cake with

it," Andrés proposed when the girl gave him back his handkerchief.

"As you please, Binash Yutsil," she said smiling. "Command and I obey."

He guided her by the elbow to the kitchen of the old Indian woman, who was now squatting half asleep by her stove. This woman kept open day and night cooking for the hungry Indians who patronized her. She too, like most of the stallkeepers and the gambling-table people, had already attended the fiesta at Sapaluta. It was a question whether she ever lay down to sleep at all. No doubt she had the gift of sleeping while squatting beside her stove.

Her customers were never in a hurry; they never hustled her or made loud and angry complaints if their enchiladas were not ready quickly. And so she could have her forty winks while apparently seeing to her job. If there was no one waiting she pulled her rebozo over her head and was at once so fast asleep that she snored. But one of her daughters had only to say in a whisper: "Madrecita, dos con pollo, dos con res—two with chicken, two with beef, Mother dear," and she was awake in an instant and automatically getting the enchiladas ready without ever once mixing up an order or the various salads and sauces.

Her first act on being waked from sleep was to blow up the fire. The first thing any Indian woman does when she wakes is to blow up the embers which smolder either on the open ground or in a clay hearth; it is the same with the Indian boys who are on the road.

11

The air was now pretty sharp, and the hot coffee and the bizcochos put new life into them.

"It is very late," Andrés said tenderly. "How would you like to turn in and sleep? I'll make you a fine warm bed in a carreta, where you can sleep as long as you like."

"If that is your command I must obey," she replied without thinking.

"Will you always obey me, little girl?" he asked softly.

"Always," she said simply, "always, because you are good to me."

They walked through the long silent streets. The further they left the plaza behind, the darker it became. The street lamps had been put out.

They often stumbled. The municipal authorities were accustomed to spending the money set apart for repairing the streets on other items of more personal interest to themselves, and therefore the streets away from the center of the town were in a deplorable condition. Rough stones, deep holes into which you sank nearly to your knees, ruts full of slimy refuse and noisome mud, puddles and quagmires from overflowing drains, tree trunks, planks, carreta poles, roof wreckage, and tumble-down walls—this was what met you at every step on the outskirts of the town. There were gaping holes in the footbridges; some had broken-down railings, others none at all. By day it was bad enough; by night you risked a broken leg or immersion in stinking pits every ten steps you took.

Andrés took some pine splinters from his pocket and lit them to throw light on the road. He had not yet managed to acquire a flashlight—one of the cherished ambitions of his life— nor could he see the remotest chance of his ever acquiring one.

But he, and the girl too, were used to these splinters of pine. They had had no other light in their homes. Every carreta, certainly, had an oil lantern, but these lanterns were of so little use in practice that the carreteros used pine splinters if they needed a really good light. This relieved their masters of the cost of supplying oil for the lanterns.

The town was very scattered, for every family had a house to itself and every house had a spacious patio. So it took a long time before the two reached the last houses. After this the road was safer, for the wide prairie stretched before them.

12

Andrés sat down on a bank.

"Let's rest a bit," he said, "and smoke a cigarette. What do you say?"

"Yes," she said and sat down beside him.

He rolled cigarettes and gave her one. The deep night sky was dense above their heads, but it did not weigh down and oppress them. It was a wide flood of thick darkness, reposeful and comforting. The crickets, and whatever else lived and took joy in the grass, fiddled and whirred and fluted from the prairie. Now and then from the distance came the deep lowing of cattle or the mournful trumpeting of a mule. The stars twinkled and sparkled with the tropical brilliance of little suns. The bats flitted by them, returning and circling around them, now close, now far.

A few solitary lights glimmered from the town. Now and then belated fireworks sputtered over it, and here and there a rocket soared up to rouse San Caralampio once more. He surely did not wish to sleep on his birthday—that would not be right.

13

"Whenever I see the stars spread so far over the deep blackness of the sky—which all the same is so clear," said the girl, "and sparkling as if they were trying to speak, I can't help thinking of my dear mother. Perhaps she is living on one of those stars now. She loved the stars more than anything else in all nature. She could sit for hours at night watching the stars and rejoicing in them, with me on her lap or between her knees. One of those nights when the finquero had sent my father off for a few days driving cattle, my mother told me a story about the stars. I have never forgotten it. It is always in my heart. That is why I am never afraid at night, however black it is. I have never told the story to anyone, because it is sacred to me as the most beautiful and lovely thing my mother could have left me. But, Binash Yutsil, I will tell you the story. For you are good to me, good as only my mother was good, and no one else in the whole world, not even my father, was so good to me. He was always tired out with his work and always covered with cuts and bruises from his labors in the bush."

After a long pause and while she leaned against him for shelter from the cool wind that had risen, he said softly and tenderly: "This story is the most beautiful present you could give me, and I will listen to it as well and closely as though your mother were telling it to me. I do believe indeed that she lives on one of the stars and looks down on you and protects you from all that could harm you."

She nestled closer to him and he took her in his arms and wrapped her well in his serape.

14

In a voice almost as low as his she began her story:

"It is the story of the god who made the sun.

"The evil spirits who wanted to destroy mankind, because the good gods had made it, conquered the good gods and killed them all. That done they put out the sun with snow and ice and blizzards.

"And then began an endless night on the earth. Everything

was covered with ice. Men froze to death. Scarcely any maize grew, and on this mankind existed in great wretchedness. Many, many people starved and died.

"No trees with sweet fruits grew any more. No flowers bloomed. No birds sang. Crickets and grasshoppers ceased to fiddle and flute. All the animals of the forests and prairies died, so that men could not hunt them any more for food for their wives and children or clothe them in warm skins.

"When man's wretchedness got worse and worse, all the chiefs and kings of the Indian people summoned a great council to decide how a new sun could be made.

"The only light in the sky came from the bright stars. The bad gods had not been able to put them out. On the stars lived the spirits of departed men who had been able to defend themselves. Strength had been given them by the good gods because it was their task to keep the stars alight forever.

"The great council of kings lasted many weeks, but nobody knew of a way to make a new sun. Then the kings sent for a man of great wisdom, who was more than three hundred years old and had learned all the secrets of nature. And he said:

" 'There is certainly a way of making a new sun. A young man of strength and great courage must go to the stars. There he must beg the spirits of the departed to give him a little piece of each of the stars. He must fasten each piece to his shield and carry it with him higher and still higher, adding new pieces of stars, until he has reached the center of the vault of the sky. There, when all the little pieces are at last on his shield, his shield will turn into a large hot shining sun.

" 'I would gladly go and do it myself, but I am old and feeble. I cannot leap as I once did. So I cannot leap from star to star. Also, I am no longer strong and nimble enough to wield spear and shield and fight with the bad gods, who will try to prevent a new sun's being made.'

"When the wise man had spoken, all the kings and chiefs and great warriors who sat in council leaped up and cried: 'We are ready to go!'

"Whereupon the wise man said: 'It is greatly to your honor that you wish to go. But only one can go, and this one must go alone with his shield, because only one sun may be made. Too many suns would burn up the earth.

" 'That one who goes must make the greatest sacrifice a man can make. He must leave his wife, his children, his father and his mother, his friends and his people. He can never again return to the earth. He must forever wander in the vault of the sky with his shield on his left arm; and he must hold himself forever in readiness to fight the bad gods, who will never rest until they have again put out the sun. He will see the earth and his people, but he will never return to them. He will be forever alone in space. Let each man ponder this before he volunteers.'

"When the kings heard this they were deeply dismayed. Not one of them wished to be parted forever from his wife and his children, from his friends and people. Each one of them preferred to die then and there and to rest in his own earth among his own people.

"So there was a long silence in the council. But then at last one of the youngest chieftains spoke:

" 'I wish to say something, O brave men. I am young and strong and handy with weapons. I have a young and beautiful wife whom I love more than myself. And I have a fine boy who is like my heart's blood to me. And I have a good and dear mother whose defense and hope I am. And I have many beloved friends. And I love my people among whom I was born and of whom I am an inseparable part.

" 'But, more than my wife, more than my boy, more than my mother, my friends and my people, I love mankind. I cannot be content as long as I see mankind suffer. Men need a sun. Without a sun mankind must perish. I am ready to go and restore a sun to men whatever my lot and my fate may be.'

"It was Chicovaneg who said this.

"He took leave of his wife, his boy, his mother, his friends and his people. Following the counsel of the wise man, he went to arm himself.

"He made himself a strong shield of tiger skin and snake skin. He made himself a helmet of a mighty eagle. And he made himself strong shoes of the claws of a mighty tiger, which he slew in the jungle.

"Then he went out to seek the Plumed Serpent. He found it after a search of many years in a deep and dark cave. It was the symbol of the world. Therefore it was guarded by a sorcerer in the pay of the bad gods.

"Chicovaneg succeeded, by great cunning, in slaying the sorcerer. First he made him drunk with sweet maguey juice. Then, when the sorcerer lay drunk and all his forty eyes were shut, Chicovaneg crept up to him and killed him with his spear, which he had poisoned with a hundred poisons the wise man had told him of.

"Now he sang sweet songs and played soft melodies on his flute; whereupon the Plumed Serpent came out and followed him, obeying all his commands.

"After this Chicovaneg set out on his long journey, and after many years and many fights with bad gods he came to the end of the world. Here the stars were at their lowest above the earth. He easily leaped up to the lowest of them.

"He told the spirits of the departed who lived on this star, and whose faces were black because they were not of Indian blood, that men had no sun and that he had left his wife and his people to give a new sun to men. The spirits gladly gave him a small bit of their star to be of help to men. Chicovaneg fastened it to the center of his shield, where it began at once to shine with the beauty of a diamond.

"From now on he could see his way better in the darkness of night, owing to the light of this tiny star on his shield. He sprang from star to star, and everywhere he went, and whether the spirits were yellow, white, brown, or black of face, they willingly gave him a little bit of their stars.

"When he came to those who were of his own blood he was greeted with great joy. They were proud that it was one of their own people who was restoring the sun to mankind. They strengthened his weary body and sharpened his weapons.

"At every leap he made from one star to another the shield became brighter. And when at last his shield was so bright that it far outshone the largest of the stars, the bad gods took note of him. They saw that he was on the way to making a new sun for men and they began to fight him with great fury and to try to hinder him from going any farther. They made the earth quake so as to shake the stars and make him miss his jump to the next star. They knew very well that if he missed only one jump he would fall into the blackness of space whence he could never again emerge, because there the bad gods had all power in their hands.

"But Chicovaneg was clever. If a star was too small to be judged properly, he had the Plumed Serpent take a look at it first and it told him the size so that he would not jump short or overjump the mark. If the distance was too great to cover in one leap, he had the Plumed Serpent fly up first and let its tail hang down. Then he could easily make a jump, grab it by the tail, and crawl up the body of the Plumed Serpent.

"As he climbed higher in the vault of the sky and as his shield grew brighter and brighter, men on earth began at last to see him. They knew that he would now restore the sun, and they were merry and held many festivals.

"But they could see too what a hard time he had. When they saw the distance to the next star and knew that he might well jump short, they were filled with terror. And when they saw the bad gods fighting against him they fell into despair.

"The bad gods roused howling storms which deluged their huts and laid their fields waste. The bad gods flooded the earth and made the mountains spit fiery lava, so as to destroy mankind before the sun stood in the sky. And the bad gods flung burning stones down at Chicovaneg as he climbed up. They threw so many that thousands of these stones still fly about the sky at night.

"Nevertheless, Chicovaneg climbed higher and higher. Brighter and brighter grew his shield. Flowers began to grow and bloom on the earth. The birds came back and sang. Mangoes and papayas began to ripen on the trees, and bananas, tunas, and tomatoes were plentiful.

"And then at last when men looked up one day there stood the sun shining down from the vault of the sky right above their heads. And they held a great feast to honor Chicovaneg.

"But the bad gods never cease in their efforts. They veil the earth in black clouds until the people fear the sun will be put out again.

"But Chicovaneg, the brave, is on the watch. He stands behind his sun shield to protect men from the bad gods. And when the bad gods press him too hard he gets into a fury and flings blazing arrows above the earth so as to hunt out and hit the bad gods who are hiding in deep black clouds. Then he rattles on his shield, and the thunder of it shakes the air.

"And when at last he has chased away the bad gods he traces in the sky his many-colored bow to tell mankind that they need not be afraid: he will not give in and the sun will not again be put out and destroyed by the bad gods."

15

The girl, nestling against Andrés all the time, had now brought her story to an end. She said no more.

After a while Andrés asked: "Did your mother also tell you who made the Huh—the moon?"

"Yes," she said, "Chicovaneg's son. When he grew up he wanted to go to see his father. He could not, however, find a plumed serpent, because his father had taken with him the only one there was, and when he had made the sun he told it to coil about the earth where the vault of the sky rested on the earth. There it lies keeping watch against the evil ones who are on the other side of the vault of the sky, trying to break through it so as to strengthen the power of the bad gods under the vault of the sky.

"But Chicovaneg is clever. He does not wholly trust the Plumed Serpent and is afraid it might sleep and fail in its watch. For this reason he climbs down every night to see if by any chance it is asleep.

"Since there is only one plumed serpent, Chicovaneg's son had to seek some other creature by whose help he could climb up to the vault of the sky. He chose a rabbit because rabbits can jump well.

"He too, with the rabbit's help, sprang from star to star. But the departed spirits could not spare him so much of their stars as they had his father. That would have made the stars too small. Therefore his shield is not so large and brilliant as his father's.

"But so as to be near his father he follows him over the whole vault of the sky, and whenever he passes his father he gives him a greeting from his mother, who sleeps on a high mountain under a mantle of snow.

"The rabbit which the son took with him to help him leap from star to star you can see clearly on his shield."

16

Andrés looked away over the prairie and up into the sky. He saw the young chieftain climbing up to the stars.

The poetry he was conscious of as the girl told him this story of her religion was not in the tale itself. He felt it far more from the simplicity of her way of telling it, from her gentle and quiet voice, and most of all from the feeling he had, while she told it, that she felt herself close to him and safe in his arms from every sorrow in the world. The knowledge that he might and could protect her, and that she put herself under his protection utterly and without thought or question, made him feel big and strong.

"She is like a helpless songbird fallen from the nest," he said softly. She made no reply. She seemed to hear without quite realizing what he said, for she wriggled and nestled closer into his arms.

But when he looked up again to the starry roof above, the story immediately became real. At once he saw the young chieftain climbing up, saw him forsake his wife and his child, and saw a molten stone whirl from the hand of one of the bad gods in a flaming arc above his head.

He asked himself whether he would really like to be a god and to live in a glory of light. It might, indeed, be necessary to restore the sun to men when they had none and were in great want; and it was, indeed, a fine and glorious deed that the young chieftain had done. He deserved to be a god and to be honored by men. At the bottom of his heart Andrés was glad, nevertheless, that men now had the sun and that he could never be troubled by the pangs of conscience and valorous intent until compelled to do as that chieftain had done. He felt the warm pressure of the girl on his breast, and it made him wonder whether he would be capable of making the sacrifice that god had made of abandoning his wife and child and people forever. But, thinking and feeling as he did, he understood all the more how great and beautiful a deed that god had done, and what love of his fellow men it showed, to have sacrificed all that makes a man's life worth living in order to be of help to men. And what made the deed all the greater and more worthy of admiration was that the god could never die, never sleep, and never forget; for ever and ever he had to think of the loves he had given up, and the pang of his loss could never cease. For though he knows that all whom he knew on earth have been dead for thousands of years, yet they live in his memory as vividly as on the day when he forsook them for the sake of mankind. It is only a very slight consolation to him that his son is near him and that he can embrace him on those days, few and far between, when for an hour the sun is darkened for men on earth. It was very natural, then, that Andrés should feel no ambition to become a god of his people; for when he considered and pondered the matter he came to the conclusion that the lot of a god is not an enviable one. The greatness and glory of the gods is dearly bought.

17

He wanted to ask something, but he saw that the girl was fast asleep. Taking her gently in his arms, he picked her up and carried her all the way to the camp where the carretas were.

The others were all asleep. Some seemed to have drunk to excess in their recent celebration of the fiesta in honor of San Caralampio. They groaned and grunted in their sleep and lay on the ground like logs.

He put the girl tenderly down. Then he prepared a comfortable bed for her in the carreta, and when he had got it ready to his satisfaction he lifted her carefully into the carreta and settled her down. She only sighed now and then—she was so utterly tired out.

Then he spread his petate on the ground under the carreta and lay down to sleep. His last waking thought was that never in his whole life had he fallen asleep with such joy and content and hope as on this night. With his last glimmer of consciousness before he fell asleep, he knew in his heart that the loveliest and sweetest days of his life had begun—days that would make him forget all the cares and troubles of his hard life.

His drowsy thoughts even got so far that he whispered: "To be a carretero is the finest life on earth."

13

The carreteros were up early, as always. There was plenty to do. The carretas had not yet been made ready to go through the next few weeks without breakdowns.

Andrés was responsible for the good order of the whole train; but he saw that nothing much in the way of repairs could be expected that day. The fellows were still befuddled from the previous day's celebrations. Some of them had fiendish headaches because of the bad and doctored tequila they had drunk—for lack of the money to drink good comiteco. Early in the afternoon they would start drinking again. They knew of no other recreation; or if they did it was not available.

Andrés decided to send the worst cases—those whom the night's boozing had reduced to the condition of wet rags—out over the prairie to see that the oxen had not strayed too far and had no sores. It was light work which the fellows could do all right. He himself would go with one or two others to the pine forest and hew out some poles and yokes to take along as spares.

When breakfast was ready he went to his carreta to see

what the girl was doing. She had been awake a long time and was sitting on a case combing her hair.

"Buenos días—good morning, little girl. How did you sleep?" he asked laughing.

"I slept fine," she replied cheerfully, "better than for months past. I wish you the best of good days, Binash Yutsil."

"You must be hungry," he said. "We haven't got anything very good for breakfast—black beans, tortillas, chile, and coffee."

"That's a meal for a king," she said. "I've got a fine appetite for it."

She climbed down from the carreta. Then she arranged her crumpled skirt, smoothed down her jorongo over her breast, and went shyly to the fire, where the fellows had already begun to shovel up the black beans with their tortillas and cram them into their empty bellies.

They all looked up as the girl approached, but there were no inquisitive glances or shameless stares. Since Andrés had brought her out from his carreta, they knew already whose she was.

"Mi mujer," said Andrés, "my woman. She travels with us now."

That was enough not only to introduce the girl, but also to conclude a contract of marriage, which would be respected by Andrés's own comrades and all other carreteros no less than if it had been solemnized in a church. She was from now on as unapproachable and as far from the thoughts of any carretero as the patrón's wife.

Besides, these carreteros, like all the rest on the road, had too much sense to play the fool. It was as much as their lives were worth. Each man knew that—if not in open fight, then one night in the bush when the oxen were being looked for. Every man of them would have his machete in his hand to cut a way through the bushes—and a machete leaves the guilty man no time to think before it slips between his ribs. Carreteros had their own code of morals and honor. The dead man had had his due. Why had he not left the woman alone? He had known the score. The verdict of any carretero who knew the circumstances was short and sharp. There were no lengthy proceedings or superfluous talk. The culprit was buried. The patrón was told that he lost his life in the jungle while looking for the oxen. And if the deed ever came out, perhaps through a carretero's drunken talk, the worst that could happen was that the man who carried out the sentence had the dead man's debt entered to his own account. No court of law was bothered with it. If the law had once begun bothering itself over the private affairs of carreteros, it would only have been a useless expenditure of public money on matters which once done could not have been undone. And once the law interfered with the carretero's personal liberties, transport contractors would have had no able-bodied carreteros left in their employment. Besides, judges had other things to think of which paid them better. There was not a cent to be made out of carreteros. Why trouble, then, and why add to the accumulation of legal documents which nobody reads, which only collect dust and which it costs time and labor to draft and file away?

2

The carreteros merely said casually: "Cómo estás, Chica—how are you, little one?" without even ceasing to chew as they said it.

It was nothing of importance and nothing new that one of their company should pick up a wife somewhere and take her along with him. That might happen on any day's journey.

Sometimes the woman saw out one trip and then, finding she did not like the life, took a job at some place on the road; or else she came across an agricultural laborer whose settled way of life suited her better or who attracted her more. Then the marriage was dissolved—without tears or sentiment.

The rough and ready life of a carretero left no room for soft hearts and fine feelings. Life was taken as it came. It is the lies and perjuries of romance and poetry that inflate a man with feelings which, in truth, he never has, and never indulges in without embarrassment.

The fellows moved up to make room for the girl at the fire. It was still early. The sun was rising halfheartedly. A thick and clinging mist lay over the prairie and the air was cold.

Andrés squatted beside the girl and handed her an earthenware bowl of hot beans in their own watery sauce, without fat or meat. He put a few chiles on a tortilla and gave it to her. Then he laid some tortillas on the naked fire, turning them this way and that, and passed them to her when he thought they were heated through.

She ladled up her beans with pieces broken from the tortillas and took little bites of the chile to season the plain black beans.

For the girl, Andrés poured some hot coffee into a jarrita—a little earthenware jug. He drank his own coffee from a gourd that is grown in this country especially for its smooth, hard rind.

All carreteros drank their coffee out of gourds, and the same with their bean soup. The little jug and bowl which the girl used were the only utensils at the fire which gave any hint of what you might call civilization.

There was, indeed, a blue enamel pot in which the beans were cooked, but this was so battered that its proper place was a rubbish heap among the refuse that civilization vomits out. It was so blackened with smoke and so battered and bashed that there was scarcely a flake left on it to show that years ago it

had been enameled blue without and white within. The beans
in it were stirred with a splinter split from a spoke.

3

"Make a good meal, girl," Andrés said to encourage her.

She nodded like an obedient child.

"You're thin enough, Chica," Manuel—one of the fellows—
said. "No cushions on your thighs, girl. You're not my style, I
can tell you. I want flesh in my hands to make me happy."

The girl nodded in assent. She did not understand what he
said, for she knew very little Spanish.

"She doesn't know Spanish," said Andrés, "and anyway,
none of that."

"Don't get excited, Andreucho," said Manuel laughing. "All
the better if she doesn't understand Spanish. We needn't put a
gag in our mouths. But, hombre, what can you do with a stick
like that, I ask you? What is there there when you get down
to it? She'll fly right off the hinges, hombre. There's nothing to
her at all."

They all laughed at this. But there was nothing nasty,
nothing disgusting about their laughter. They had no thought
of being obscene. It was as natural to them to speak of such
things as of the state of their carretas. There were no dark
secrets, no repressed sensuality in their lives. No one had taught
them to play the hypocrite about natural things and to regard
plain facts as sinful.

They certainly did not mince their words. They spoke as
they thought and felt. Problems of sex and psychology had no
meaning for them, and so their lives took on no superfluous
complexities. Man is man, and woman is woman; and when the
two come together they know what they want of each other.
That was the sum of their philosophy of sex. They found it a
very satisfactory one, and it never played them false.

Andrés, naturally, knew well enough what they were talking about, even though he had had no personal experience of the sort. He did not even know whether he hoped for such an experience with the girl or not. He was no more certain of his hopes than clear in his wishes. So far, he felt only the strength and warmth of his devotion to her as a comrade, but he also felt very clearly that this affection was not the same as he felt for his mother and sisters. If he had any convinced desire at all, it was that their relation might continue to be as it had been the night before and was that morning. He would be more than content with the situation as it was. If it came to more he would accept it with joy and gratitude, but to press for more had not even crossed his mind.

And when this occurred to him he began to feel superior to his fellows. They would naturally have laid hands on the girl on the way out from the town, so as to know from experience whether it was worthwhile taking her any farther and looking after her.

In this he was wrong, as he was surprised to discover later on; for he found out that Manuel, who now made such a show of going straight for what he wanted, could be held up by his hopes exactly as he himself was now. Manuel found a girl and behaved just as Andrés did. Andrés then saw the two of them together week after week on the road without ever actually becoming man and wife; until at last a night came when they rushed into each other's arms, overwhelmed by a longing which they felt they could not resist for a moment longer.

That was a good lesson for Andrés. It was an experience that taught him he had no right to feel superior to others because of feelings of which he thought himself alone capable, and which were denied to his fellows. He learned that it was only a matter of circumstance for any man to discover feelings in himself which till then he believed to be the privilege of the elect, who alone could have elevated thoughts and noble feelings.

4

The other men, all the more now that they knew the girl could not understand, were determined not to lose the chance of ribbing Andrés and amusing themselves at his expense.

It was all in good fun, though they went at it without any disguise. If the girl had not been sitting there, they would have put on an act that would have been even clearer than their words.

"You didn't let her go thirsty all night, let's hope, Andreucho?" asked José, laughing loudly.

"What do you think?" said Andrés. "What do you take me for? You bet, Pepe, I squeezed the life out of her. I can tell you that."

"And how did it go?" asked Esteban.

Andrés laughed knowingly. Out of his native Indian guile, he saw at once that if he accepted their imputations without more ado, he would quickly put an end to the banter.

"How many times? That's what we want to know," put in Hilario.

"Listen to me, you pollitos," said Andrés, winking. "When I load up cases, I take care to count them; and when I get change for a peso in a cantina, I count it too. But in lots of things I don't count. Do you follow me, hombres?"

"That's the way to talk," Manuel threw in. "When you lose count, then you've something to talk about." He shook the coffee grounds from his gourd into the fire and stood up and stretched himself. "Let's get off now and cut those poles. This afternoon I'm off to the plaza again. Maybe I'll strike it lucky and come back married myself. But I'll want to see more flesh on her, I can tell you that."

They all got up, one after another. Those whom Andrés, on account of their thick heads, had written off for the job went out over the prairie to see after the oxen, and Manuel and two others picked up their machetes and got ready to go to the pine forest.

The girl rinsed out her bowl and jarrita with water from a battered gasoline can and took them to the carreta where she had slept. Andrés followed her.

He took three five-centavo coins out of his pocket and gave them to her as they stood together beside the carreta.

"Tujom ants," he said, "go to the town and buy yourself needles and black thread. Then come back and sew up the holes in your skirt."

"I will do that," said the girl. "I will gladly do as you say."

"And then," Andrés went on, "go down to the river—down there, look—and wash your face clean, and your arms and legs, and when you've done that, come back here and comb your hair till it shines."

She laughed. "I will do it all just as you say."

"If anyone asks you where you belong, say you belong to don Laureano's carretas and that one of the carreteros is your marido—your husband. Then no one will harm you and the police won't shut you up in jail, thinking you've no master and are a runaway. And if anyone asks where your na—your home—is and where you were tocvic—born—then say Chiapa. Do you understand all that, little girl?"

"Yes, I understand all that," she answered, "and I will say and do all you tell me to."

"Vicente, the boy, stays here with the carretas to keep an eye on them. If Vicente goes to fetch water, you keep an eye on them. No one here will harm you—you needn't be afraid. Now I must go," he said, turning to join the others who had already set off. "We have hard work ahead of us."

5

Andrés knew what he was about in giving the girl these strange directions.

The girl was no slave. No one had any right to lay hands on her. She was a Mexican citizen. All the same, if she were found alone in the town and could give no account of herself, a policeman would take her to the town hall, in the hope of earning a peso from a master she had run away from and to whom she was sure to owe money. There was not an Indian, male or female, apart from those in the independent communes, who was not in debt to some master. And if she had no master, all the more reason to arrest her. An excuse could never be lacking. She would be charged with being drunk, or with having stolen a button from a stall, or with being a vagabond with no family or home. Then the mayor or the chief of police or the political resident got a cheap maid-servant. She would get a peso a month—since she was no slave; she would be beaten by an ill-tempered mistress and her ill-tempered daughters; and if the master or sons of the house took a fancy to her they would get her with child whether she liked or not, for she had to obey and do as she was told, whatever it might be.

On the other hand, if she had a marido to look after her, a policeman would think twice before he took her in. Carreteros had the same rights as an Indian girl—but one day or another the policeman or the mayor would be sure to have to ride to another town, and it might easily happen—indeed, was sure to happen—that there were carreteros on the road. And quite inevitably that very carretero, whose girl had been arrested and taken away from him by that officer's authority, would be among them. That officer would never return home. No one would know where he had got to or ever discover the mound beneath which his carcass rotted, and a dozen detectives would never find the culprit—bribe, imprison, and torture as they might. And as all officials, from the jefe político down to the barefooted policemen, knew that well, and not only by hearsay, the wife of a carretero was as inviolable as the chieftain of an independent Indian commune when he had his staff of office in his hand.

The carreteros had no brotherhoods or unions, but they were respected throughout the state. They had only themselves to rely on; yet the measures they took were ruthless ones from which there was no escape.

They were wretchedly paid, wretchedly fed. Their life was one of merciless hardship. All that, they accepted without question as a destiny to which they were born. They were ordered about and exploited to the last drop of blood in their veins. Yet they could only be ordered about and exploited successfully when those who gave them orders and exploited them knew how far they could go and where to draw the line. And the transport contractor who knew this best had the best carreteros and made the highest profit on them.

The carreteros, like so many of the working class in Mexico, Peru, Bolivia, and Venezuela, did not turn a hair if they were hanged or shot. Hence they were beyond the law, and particularly beyond all laws which did not correspond with their own sense of justice.

6

The men returned to the camp early in the afternoon. Next day they would take the oxen along to haul the poles and yokes they had hewn. The fellows who had been sent to look after the animals had not yet come back. "They've been having a lie-down somewhere out there," said Andrés, "and they're still asleep."

The girl showed Andrés with pride her mended skirt. It was as clumsily stitched up as could be, but at least it showed her good will; and in any case it looked a little better than before—a little. To have made a good job of it would have required some patches, and Andrés promised to see about getting some scraps for her.

Her arms and legs were well washed—hands and face too. But the best was her hair. Hours of thorough combing had transformed the tangled mop into long gleaming rich black waves of hair in which the upper half of her body could be entirely enveloped.

Andrés saw her for the first time in the full light of day, and with the dirt and dust and caked mud well removed, which had made it difficult to guess what there might be beneath. He saw with wonder and delight that she was a pretty girl, with white teeth, gleaming black eyes, short straight nose, rounded chin, and smooth deep-bronze skin.

She laughed and asked: "Have I done everything as you told me to?"

"Yes, indeed you have, little girl," he said, taking hold of her by both her arms.

"And are you pleased with me?" she asked, drawing closer to him.

"I am," he replied.

He turned her round and looked at her from all sides. She was nothing but a barefoot girl in a worn shirt and bedraggled woolen skirt. That was all. The embroidered shirt and the mended black skirt and the jorongo were all she had more than a beast of the jungle. But there was nothing to suggest that she wanted more to make her happy; for she showed without a care how glad she was just to be near him.

"Later, after we've had something to eat," he said, "we'll go out on the prairie, you and I, and sit in the open field and tell each other about ourselves."

"Yes, we'll do that," she agreed. "You know such wonderful things. Everything you say, Binash Yutsil, is beautiful. I could listen forever when you talk."

"I will never say anything to you but what is beautiful," he said softly.

"Then I shall always be happy," she answered.

7

The men washed their hands and threw themselves wearily on the ground to pass the time until their food was ready. Vicente had put the beans on the fire in good time and they were now nearly soft.

Then two of the fellows who had been sent out in the morning to see to the oxen came up. They told Andrés they had not been able to find them.

"I guess not," said Andrés. "Your eyes are still closed. You've been asleep down there by the stream."

"Are we under your orders, pollito?" one of them asked in a temper.

"You know well enough you're not," said Andrés. "And I won't give you any orders either. But if we have to scout after the oxen for three days and the carretas are not ready to start when the comerciantes want to go, it's I who'll get it in the neck from the patrón, while you stand and grin."

Manuel, who was lying full length and tired out on the ground, sat up and said to the two: "Andrés is right. It's him the viejo—the old man—will come down on if we're not off in time. And it'll be your fault. You ought to be ashamed of yourselves, you sinvergüenzas, parranderos, léperos, borrachos, cabrones!"

A perfect hail of curses descended on their heads, while

Manuel only grew the more incensed the more he cursed, until at last he leaped to his feet and went for them, head down and fists clenched. "You should have more shame, you droppings of the damned—get out with you and find the oxen or I'll cut you to ribbons."

The two shirkers knew that Manuel was not a pleasant enemy. He did not do things by halves once he saw fit to begin. They turned about and made for the prairie again.

But Andrés called to them: "Better eat and have your sleep. It's late. We'll all go out first thing in the morning and look for the beasts. We want them to haul the poles and yokes and they have to have their feed of maize tomorrow too. Oye, listen, Vicente, are the frijoles soft yet? Bueno. Bring the tortillas along."

8

After they had eaten and taken a nap the men washed up and got ready to go to the town again. The fireworks could be heard popping once more.

Hundreds of thousands of the poorer classes in Mexico have neither a whole shirt nor a whole pair of trousers and have never so much as thought of a pair of shoes. But they always have money for fireworks in any quantity whenever they attend the frequent sacred festivals of the Church, and thus the money they bitterly need for the sheer necessities of life goes up in the air—and this in honor of a Church which never thinks of advising them to make better use of their money, any more than it would ever advise them not to spend their last peso on candles to illuminate the altars of the saints. In their own homes these people have no illumination but splinters of pinewood. Yet it is precisely upon these multitudes of the poor that the saints rely for most of their candles and fireworks. The saints could very well do without these things, for they are long since dead. The worker is still alive and needs a shirt and a pair of trousers far more urgently than a saint needs a candle or a firecracker. But the Church takes and goes on taking, caring nothing whether those on whom it lays the burden of gifts and offerings as the price of getting one day to heaven are without the bare necessities of life. It matters nothing to the Church that through its teachings and its promises of eternal joy in a paradise no one has ever seen or knows anything about, poverty is increased and spread abroad like a wasting disease.

The more poor and hunger-stricken people there are in the world the greater is the profit of all those who know how to exploit their poverty and grow rich on their labors. An empty belly and a torn shirt produce the willing worker, who neither winces nor jibs; for his belly cries aloud and his body craves warmth and clothing. It is the Church that prospers, and with it all those whose rule is: Keep the people religious, for religion is our best safeguard.

It may well happen that, if paradise really exists and if the proletarian finally gets there, he will find the very same persons seated at the table as have already skimmed the cream from life on earth. They don't often come off second best. And if the eye of the needle is too narrow for the camel to pass through, they widen it and there's no further trouble.

Andrés could not have been expected to have any such thoughts when he heard the fireworks popping off in honor of San Caralampio. He knew nothing of a paradise in the life hereafter, but neither did he know of any paradise here on earth. Like other carreteros he was so closely identified as a living person with his lot on earth that it would have seemed paradise enough if he had had twenty-five centavos more a day, if he had found meat in his beans, if his debt to the patrón did not increase at such a rate that nothing he could ever hope to earn by his labor would enable him to reduce, let alone cancel it.

The sum of what he actually possessed on this earth and all that he could hope to enjoy if he ever found the time was his bare existence.

And that was something.

One day when he was still a child on the finca where he was born, a peon answered the finquero back in a dispute about the price of a pig which the peon had reared. A dealer had offered eight pesos for the pig. The finquero offered only five. As a peon he was bound to sell the pig to the finquero for five because the finquero had the right of pre-emption on all animals reared on his property, never mind who reared them, and even though they were fed on maize which the peon had cultivated with his own hands on his plot of ground. When the finquero had had enough of the dispute he lost his temper and gave the peon a blow on the head with his machete. The peon fell to the ground and, while the blood poured from him, he whispered: "Mercy, patroncito, mercy—kill me, patroncito." The patrón gave him a kick in the ribs. "You can be glad, you filthy pig of an Indian, that you have your life. What more do you want?"

Andrés had his life. What more did he want? But the Church, this great savior of souls, had never taught him, or other Indians who lived in independent communes, the first lesson that saviors of souls and liberators ought to teach: Make the best of your own life first, before you bother about anything else.

14

   "Do you want to go to the town—to the plaza?"
Andrés asked the girl.

"No—or not unless you want to," she replied. "I would rather, as we said, go out on the prairie and sit with you, to look at the wide-open world and listen to what you have to tell me."

So they walked through the prairie, and then over to the pine forest. There they sat down on the fringe of it, from where they could look right over the prairie. Behind them trees, sixty and eighty meters high, stood like the pillars of a mighty hall. Ferns a meter high grew in the forest, and in many places there was deep grass. Pine cones as big as melons were scattered about the ground.

"You've only been in the upland country?" he asked her.

"Yes, that's all."

"Then you've never seen palms and jungle and tropical plants?"

She shook her head.

"I'm very glad," he said, looking at her.

"Why?"

200

"Because I can show it all to you and you will see it all for the first time with me. Then your memory of it will be forever bound up with your memory of me."

"Memory?" she asked, opening her eyes wide and looking at him. "Don't you wish me, then, to stay with you always? I want to stay with you always. I want no memory of you. I want to be with you wherever you go, whether for good or bad."

Andrés seized her hand and for a long while sat silently beside her.

"Who knows," he said at last, "whether I shall always please you, little girl. I don't know how I shall be to a wife. I have never had one. Perhaps I am not what you think. You've only known me for a day."

She nodded, and said in a voice deep with feeling: "Yes, I've known you only one day. And you have known me for only one day too. But after many moons we'll have known each other a whole year."

He laughed, and she joined in.

Two great beetles landed at their feet.

"Every beetle has her mate," she remarked without looking up at him. "I don't want to be all by myself. I want to be with you. I want to help with the oxen and all your work. I shall wash for you, and whatever you say I will do—just as I washed myself and combed my hair for you. I don't comb my hair otherwise; it only gets matted again with the wind and from sleeping. But for you I comb it again and again. I also sewed up my skirt for you. I don't care for myself if my skirt is full of holes."

"That is how it ought to be," he said in playful earnest. "I don't want you like the wives that many muchachos have in the carretas, who never wash and are always in rags, who get drunk whenever and wherever they see the chance, and then grovel about on the ground and scream and shout out shameless things."

"Anything like that I shall certainly never do, Binash Yutsil," she replied, setting her lips firmly.

Then she added: "But how am I to know what is good and right and pleasing to you, if you don't tell me? I am not as clever and experienced as you. You must tell me everything I must do so as to be what you wish. You are my husband—and I am glad that it is you and no other. Nobody has troubled about me since my father's death. But you"—she suddenly looked into his face with wide eyes, eyes in which beseeching and sadness and helplessness were all seen at once—"but you, my husband, you trouble about me and care for me. It is you who can, who may, who shall make me whatever you wish."

"I will for sure never forsake you, little girl," he said, weighing his words, "and I want to tell you how endlessly glad I am that I found you and that you want me to be your husband."

He put his hand on her head and drew it to his breast and stroked her hair. She took his hand and drew it across her cheek and kissed it. Then he bent his head down to her hair and touched it with his lips in a caress like an unspoken prayer, and remained thus so long that it seemed to him as though centuries flowed through the universe.

Neither spoke. Neither made a movement, fearing in their tremendous suspense lest they might thereby disturb some unknown beneficent influence in their own beings and in the world at large.

The last faint glow of day died away over the wide plain. The prairie was veiled for the coming of night in a mist which swept up in long waves from all sides at once, with darkness hastening on its heels.

Night came down.

When the two woke at last from their trance of rapture and

opened their eyes and looked about them, they found themselves enclosed in an inky darkness. It seemed to them as though countless eternities had fled past, while they, unaware of all that took place around them, had remained behind alone. They were glad that they had not been torn apart, but rather had grown together in heart and soul and body to form a single part of nature by the kindness of a destiny that meant them well. But the night, now that it had come, inspired no wishes; they continued to feel the deep contentment in which departing day had left them and which they felt in their present mood nothing could ever destroy, whatever might happen and whatever cares and troubles the days to come might have in store for them.

2

She loosened herself a little from his arms and raised her head.

"Shall we go back to the carretas now, or to the plaza, or would you like to sit on here and talk?" he asked her.

"It is lovely here in the black night," she answered. "Unless you have work to do at the carretas I'd rather sit on here with you, until it gets cold."

"Aren't you hungry?"

"No, not a bit. And if I were, it could wait. I have let hunger wait so often that I've learned how to forget it. I have often had nothing to eat for a whole day, and even two—but only since my mother was buried. One day she was dead. We didn't know why. Perhaps it was the fever. The finquero had no medicine, none of that white powder. He told me not to worry, my mother was only lazy and would be all right again next day. But in the morning she was quite still and dead. She had gone without a sound.

"After that I cooked and did everything at home. But one day it was the feast of San Antonio. And the finquero gave every peon some brandy. It was to give them the taste for it. When they had enough taste for it, then they would want more brandy. That is why he gave them the firewater to start with. But then when they wanted more they had to buy it from him. He sold them as much as they liked, but not on credit."

"I know that," said Andrés. "The finqueros daren't sell aguardiente on credit. It's against the law."

She went on with her story: "Then the peons emptied their pockets to buy aguardiente; then they brought their pigs, their goats, their sheep—everything, to get more aguardiente. They could not drink it all. They poured away more than they drank, but still they went on buying. My father drank very little. He was sad because of my mother.

"Next day there was the great feast when the old capitanes of the church were put down and the new capitanes for the new church year were chosen. It was my father's turn that year to be chosen capitán, but there was another man who said it was his turn. And as the new capitanes have to give the people a feast in their houses, this man said that my father could not give a feast, because he had no wife—to which my father said no, but he had a daughter. Then the man said a daughter, and this was me, could not cook and give a good feast, and so the people would not have their holy feast if my father was chosen capitán.

"The men were very drunk, for they had been buying aguardiente all night and until early in the morning. And as soon as it was light they began their drinking again. So it came to a quarrel which of the two, my father or the other man, should be one of the two new capitanes. The quarrel got hotter and all the men, who were too drunk to know what they were doing, began playing around with their machetes. This too grew hotter and hotter and my father, who had no machete on him, got a deep stab in the body from the other man. He died that night. Then the other man got a stab too, but he did not die.

"So then, when my father was in the cemetery, the finquero called my two brothers and showed them my father's account. But they could not pay it. And as the finquero wanted the money for my father's account, he sold my two brothers to a montería, where the Spaniards get mahogany wood from the forest."

"And that happened to your poor brothers?" asked Andrés with deep concern.

"Yes," she said, "that happened to them. They were still so young, one sixteen and the other just seventeen, and being so young they could not have any land on the finca, and of course they had no wives either. And the finquero would not let them work off the debt on the finca. He said he would never get his money back on the few centavos their work would be worth to him. In the montería they could earn more. And because the Spaniards can never get enough men for the monterías they buy peons who are in debt and then they have to work it off."

Andrés was just going to say that a montería was worse than any hell could be, and that any Indian who was sold to one found his grave there; but he did not say what he had been told, because it would have added to her pain.

"The finquero wanted to sell me too, but the agent of the montería did not want me. He said I was too small and weak and no good even to help cook, and I would not be alive at the end of the weeks and weeks of journeying through the jungle.

"Everyone in the village told me I would never see my brothers again, that no one sold to a Spanish montería ever comes back. He perishes there, more wretchedly than a beast.

That is why the agents are always around to buy up more peons and to entice other men who are free into signing on.

"When my brothers had gone, the finquero came to our hut and said: 'I have now given this hut to Daniel. You will come into the house and work in the kitchen. Now, right away.' So then I worked in the house—from early morning, three hours before sunrise, grinding corn and washing laundry and washing up and cleaning the rooms, till long after sunset. He paid me nothing and no clothes or anything at all."

"And so you ran away," Andrés broke in.

"No, not for that," she replied. "All the girls have to work like that. But José, the finquero's son, was always after me and sending me now here and now there at night, and then he'd catch hold of me and tell me to come to his bed. But I was terrified of him. He is so horrible and has such black looks.

"He has eight peon girls, who all have children by him, and then the girls get no husbands of their own people. The young fellows are all afraid he will shoot them, because the girls are his girls. And if one does find a fellow who wants her, he never knows when José may want the girl back; and if he says anything, José beats him or shoots him. He has shot two already. The municipalidad did nothing to him, because the Presidente is his friend, and he said that the two young fellows meant to cut his head off with their machetes when he was looking for strayed cattle with them in the fields, and that he had to shoot them to save his life. He did not shoot them both in one day—one he shot last year and the other this year. He was going to shoot another too, but that one took his wife with him and got away to Tabasco.

"But the girls can do nothing against him, he is so strong, and they have to work in the house. He brings them silk ribbons from the town, and pearl necklaces and earrings, and tells them that he will always keep them with him and they'll live like ladies. The girls know that all that is lies, but they can do nothing. They are only peon girls.

"When I was down by the river washing clothes he came riding by and stopped and said: 'You'll come to my bed to-night, do you hear, you rat?' I said: 'But I will not come. I'm afraid of you. You make the girls cry and beat them.' He said: 'There's nothing to be afraid of, you rat. I'll be very good to you if you're good to me. The girls are dirty liars and that's why I beat them—to stop them carrying tales to the village to their mothers. I'll bring you back red ribbons when I ride to the town.' I said: 'Leave me in peace, patroncito, I won't come and I can't come.' At that he got off his horse and came down on my back with his whip till I fell on my knees from pain and fright. Then he bent over me and caught hold of me by the hair and lifted me from the ground till I screamed because it hurt so much. He pulled me backward and forward by the hair and said: 'You rat, you'll come to my bed tonight. If you don't, I'll drag you out of your corner and tear off your hair, scalp and all, and throw it to the pigs, and I'll shut you up all night in the granary for the rats to eat you up alive, and what's left of you in the morning I'll throw to the pigs. That I swear by the Virgin and Child. So if you don't come to my bed tonight, that's what'll happen to you. I'll leave my window open.' Then he threw me to the ground.

"You see," she went on, turning to Andrés, "there are more than a thousand huge rats in the granary and they eat up whatever they find there at night, and so I was terribly frightened. That's why I meant to go to him at night. But, as I was coming up from the river, I met one of his girls who has three children by him and she said to me: 'Chica, I know that José's after you, but don't listen to him. You won't get a good boy of your own, and you will get a child and you're still too young to know how to look after it and it will die.'

"After dinner when the master and everyone in the house, José too, were asleep, I ran away—first through the great forest, where I was so frightened I nearly turned back again. But then I met an Indian and his wife driving pigs to Jovel, and I went with them for a long way. They were kind to me, both of them, and we spoke the same language. They told me that there was the fiesta of San Caralampio at Balún-Canán and that I ought to go there, because I could easily get into service there and working in a town I would be safe from the finqueros. Then we came to a crossroad which they said was a shorter way to Balún-Canán. If I went with them to Jovel I would be late for the fiesta, because it was a long way around and they could not go as fast with the pigs to drive as I could going alone and with nothing to carry.

"They told me what to do and that I was sure to fall in with traders on the road—Indian dealers in crockery, hat-makers, petate weavers, dealers in skins—who would all be going to Balún-Canán to sell their wares. I was to join up with the ones that seemed most friendly, and if anyone asked me why I was traveling alone and whether I had run away from a finca or from service, I was to say I had made a vow at my mother's deathbed to go to San Caralampio and offer up a candle to him and kiss the soles of his feet so that my mother would go to heaven. If I said that, everyone would believe me. And I was not to say I had come from a finca, but from Bachajón, because that is a free Indian village.

"They gave me some tortillas and frijoles and a few chiles for the journey, and off I set. But the first day I met no one, not for the whole day. Late in the afternoon I came to a corn field where there were two huts in which lived some Indian families to whom the corn field belonged. I told them I was on my way to Balún-Canán to kiss the soles of the great and holy god Caralampio, because I had made a vow to my dead mother, and I told them everything else the man and woman with the pigs had told me to say. The people gave me some food, and I spent the night in one of the huts, near the fire where it was warm.

"In the morning when the sun was up I wanted to go on, but they said I could not go alone, because there were tigers along that way and perhaps even mountain lions too—though they had never seen lions in the neighborhood yet, but plenty of tigers. So I had better wait, they said, until the afternoon or next morning, for there would be many Indian traders passing with their wives and children, all going to Balún-Canán with their wares, and there were a man and his wife waiting to go from that very place, who were taking parrots to sell at the fiesta.

"And so it turned out. By midday the traders came along with their families. They were from Cancúc, Oshchúc, Chiilum, Hucutsín, Sivacjá, Tultepec, Chanjál, and all over the place. They had collected at Achlumál, and there the presidente of the town refused to let them pass. They had first to pay a tax for the right of passage, for the right to use the roads. They had not known that the presidente would take all their money, otherwise they would have gone another way around and avoided any place where there was a presidente. That's how presidentes all get rich and then they can soon buy a large finca.

"So then I came on here with these traders. But I found no work. No one here asked me whether I wanted to go into service. Whenever I stood at the door of a house meaning to ask for a place someone came out and gave me angry looks. So I was afraid and did not ask for a place. But all the same I stood waiting at the doors of houses, from hunger, hoping that someone might ask me if I wanted to go into service in the house. Then a woman came out and gave me a push and shouted at me: 'Get off with you. We want no thieves here. Get off and don't let me see you here again.' So I got more and more frightened, and didn't know what to do and what to eat.

"At last I crept into a dark corner to die, because I was so miserable. And while I was sitting there in my misery and thinking I'd soon be dead, there you were and you were good to me, and you made me your wife without knowing who I was or where I came from. You are good, Binash Yutsil, and I will always be good to you and never be a sorrow or a pain to you."

3

Andrés drew her to him and stroked her face. He resolved to make up for all the hardships she had suffered the last months, so that she would forget that she was ever alone on the earth. She came to meet him so willingly in her helplessness and loneliness, doing whatever he asked, that he began to feel poor beside her.

He did not know what to do—whether to stay as they were or to take her in earnest as his wife. There was no one whom he could ask what he ought to do to make the girl happy. Perhaps if he had had his mother there she could have told him what was best. Yet, when he thought it over, he came to the conclusion that not even his mother could have given him any advice. It became clear to him that it was a matter for himself alone, and that only he could decide what his feeling for the girl required and how to behave accordingly. But the more he weighed it and debated it with himself, the more uncertain he became. He could not make out what this meant. It was not his way to be irresolute. As a carretero, particularly, hesitation was not in his line. Carreteros have to make up their minds quickly and act at once. The time it takes to think things carefully over may be as much as a carreta and its load and a pair of oxen, and perhaps even the life of a human being, are worth.

Even though Andrés had had no personal experience of women up to now, he felt instinctively that with any other woman he would have known without thinking what to do and what was the right thing to do. But with this girl he was irresolute, just because of his affection for her and because he did not want to lose her affection for him. He was afraid that if he did the wrong thing he might lose her trust, but what the wrong thing was he could not tell.

The girl had not understood when Andrés represented her as his wife to the other carreteros, because he had spoken in Spanish. But her instinct and feelings had revealed to her what he meant. She herself had told him that she was now his wife.

Even so, Andrés did not know what it meant to her to be a man's wife. He got the impression that all she meant by it was that a wife obeyed some particular man and treated him as her master; that he cared for her and that she helped him in his work in any way she could.

If he could only have guessed what the girl expected—but since he knew that she had no clear idea of what it was her feelings half suggested, he could not hope by any stratagem to gain a hint of what was in her mind. There might have arisen in her during the last hours a half-dreamed, half-urgent desire; but it might be just as fatal to their present happy state if he fulfilled it as if he left it unfulfilled.

The one impulse or urge which she quite definitely inspired was the desire not to lose her and not to disturb what he thought of as the stillness of her soul.

So at last, when Andrés had thought it over this way and that until his thoughts seemed to go in circles, he decided that he would not do anything to alter or influence the terms they were on at the moment. With that his confidence returned; and he became convinced that whatever it might be that he or the girl really wished would happen of itself one day or one night with an inevitability of its own. It would then have a beauty which could come in no other way and at no other time. To experience this beauty at its right and imperative moment seemed to him so complete a delight that it was not worthwhile to endanger it now in uncertainty of mind and uneasiness of feeling.

This may have been what the girl thought too. True, she was innocent and inexperienced, but she was not so ignorant as all that. She was an Indian girl, as natural in her instincts and feelings and impulses as an animal of the forest. And she had been with older girls, already married, who had spoken of such things as frankly as they did of eating, sleeping, working, or dancing. They were necessary and unavoidable parts of life to be enjoyed without a thought when the desire for them was aroused.

In the stillness of her heart she may have been questioning her own feelings during the long silence while Andrés was debating his thoughts within himself, and she may have come to the same decision Andrés reached. For her happiness was complete when Andrés desired and demanded nothing, but only sat close beside her and held her in his arms.

It was because he expressed no urgence or desire that something was born and allowed to mature in her heart. It was a feeling she could give no name to, a feeling which warmed her through and through and made her soul light and gave her a strange creative power, a sense of deep certainty and security. She felt that her heart grew larger and larger until it filled her whole body. She felt it beating not only in her breast but in every part of her. She was overcome by the mysterious knowledge that in heart and spirit and soul and body she had become tremendously and inseparably one.

At last it came to her that there was only one wish which put into words could make her wish clear. "I want him to kill me—that would be the sweetest thing that could happen."

She kissed his hands and nestled further into his arms, so as to be nearer to him. It was a pain to her not to be able to creep inside him so as to be wholly one with him.

He stroked her hair and said: "Tujom ants, my dear little wife, you are like a little, a quite little star. Whenever I look at you or feel you or think of you, I can't help remembering the story you told me, the one your mother told you. You are a little star in my heaven, the most beautiful, the dearest little star I can possibly imagine to myself. If I were a king who set out to restore the sun to men, I would fasten you to my shield as my first shining little star. Then you would always be with me when I climbed up into the great blue vault of the sky. Then I should never be alone, but always glad, and I would shout for joy from the dome of heaven, so that the whole world heard how happy I was. I would send down nothing but gladness and laughter on mankind, and there would be no more sorrow anywhere on earth and no peons would suffer and labor on the fincas, but all take their joy in the land. With you, my little star, on my shield, I would defy all bad gods, and I would never be sad up there in the midst of the sky, far from the earth and everything else. With you on my shield I could conquer all worlds that ever were, to bring joy to men wherever they might live. You have no name, little girl, and I will give you a name—Estrellita. Do you know what that means, little girl? It means 'little star.' Estrellita mía, dulce Estrellita, my sweet little star which has fallen from heaven into my lap."

She, unable to put into words what she felt and what was in

her heart, said simply: "And you, Binash Yutsil huinic, you are my Chicovaneg; you have given me the sun. But I cannot give you that name, because it is another's. For me you will always and forever be Chicovaneg, but I will give you a name to call you by—Viltesvanel. For you are really Viltesvanel, because you can give beautiful names to all things on earth and can tell wonderful stories. And now, my Binash Yutsil huinic, how does your name please you?"

"It is the most beautiful name, and I will take it because you have given it to me, my little star."

15

Andrés's train of carts was ready for the start. Shortly after midnight they were to break camp on the prairie and pick up the rest of the goods in town where the traders waited with their crates and bales. Andrés wanted to be on the road long before sunrise.

The carretas were now all in good order for the journey, and the oxen had been brought in and were kept close at hand, ready to be yoked the moment word was given. So there was really little more to be done in camp that night.

And as the camp had no attractions to offer—indeed, they were all sick to death of it—the carreteros got ready for a final trip to the town to make the most of what was left of the holy fiesta and to seize upon what pleasures its last dying hours could offer them.

Manuel, Andrés's friend and fellow worker, was one of those who went to the town. When he got there he found that the market place was almost deserted and that the town was relapsing into its peaceful smugness after the weeks of uproar. It almost seemed, to judge at least from the dreary aspect of the square, that the town and its inhabitants were at bottom glad to have the mad fair well over and to be able to give themselves up once more to a pleasant stagnation, in which nothing could occur to amuse and distract them except the nosing out of scandals to spread abroad and the provocation of hatreds and jealousies among themselves and their families and the fanning of them to a good, steady, lasting glow. For the rest, the worthy citizens set about propagating future citizens, many of whom were condemned to bear for the whole of their lives the name Caralampio, distasteful to many a Mexican ear if for no other reason than that the parents believed that any child who had this chosen name would benefit to an outstanding degree by the special protection of San Caralampio in all that could conduce to his well-being on earth and in heaven.

Most of the traders had already shut down, and their stands and stalls were by this time either cleared away or being taken down by those who had hired them out; only the gambling tables and refreshment booths were still doing good business, and of course the cantinas, where the girls were being frantically urged on by the old bawds to make the most of the last night.

As the hours ran out and the moment drew near when these girls too, after providing the hungry men of the town with such a feast of pleasure, would have to be ready to join their carretas, the scenes in the cantinas got wilder and wilder.

2

Everyone in authority, or in its immediate employment, was drowned in bliss and beer and comiteco. The authorities rejoiced with all who rejoiced. Their eyes and ears were closed. San Caralampio gave his indulgence and blessed this year's windup.

The worthy and honest citizens' modest wives were safely

stowed away in the marital beds. And as in Mexico it is an unheard-of thing for a wife to hurry along the streets at night looking for her husband in the cantinas—although she knows well enough how he spends the happy hours of night time— the husbands were left undisturbed and could do their utmost to pay a last heartfelt and pious tribute to San Caralampio. The husband, who does the work, deserves his pleasure; and the husband who does no work deserves it even more.

The majority of Balún-Canán's respectable citizens do no work. As soon as they grow up and face life in earnest they set about raising five hundred pesos in any way they can. Once they have these five hundred pesos, or four hundred—no matter if they're short a peso or two—they marry. When they have been married for a couple of weeks and have skimmed the cream off married life, they buy a little tienda where the ordinary necessities of life are offered for sale.

Somebody has to be in the store, so they put their wives there. The wife gives her husband two pesos a day—sometimes three, sometimes one—out of the proceeds. After this she has to meet all the expenses of a house and a family out of the store. She adds to her profits by molding candles, making clothes, haggling with Indians who come to sell their wares, making rompope—eggnog—retailing contraband comiteco in the room at the back, and bargaining by the hour with smugglers from Guatemala who smuggle silk over the frontier.

The husband gives her sturdy children. That is his only job, the sole function of her lord and master. He is always cheerful, amiable, and pleased with the world in general and with all his fellow citizens in particular. He goes in for politics, and always carries a revolver in his belt. When the elections come around he tries to get the job of mayor, or chief of police, or assessor or collector of taxes, or postmaster. If he becomes mayor, all his close friends get good jobs. Not one is forgotten. In a life like this and in a climate whose incomparable perfection never varies all the year through, where tuberculosis and cancer are unknown, he reaches an age of eighty, a hundred, or a hundred and thirty years; and he never looks his age. He dies before his time only when the elections are inconclusive and because the revolver is the surest way of voting—not, of course, the revolver which is worn for display in the richly adorned belt, to show that the wearer is really a man, a macho, but the revolver which is set off on those who are unable to reconcile their political views with those of their fellow citizens who aspire to office. But, as all voters have revolvers, the freedom to vote is not the exclusive privilege of any one gang; the best marksman, who has the best marksmen in his party, is chosen to wield civic authority, after the manner of the celebrated and admirable republic of Rome. Murder Caesar and you will be first consul; murder Francisco Madero and you will be president of the most beautiful and the richest country on earth, president of the most lovable and patient people on earth, President of the United States of Mexico.

So, when there are no elections, there is nothing left for the men of the charming and hospitable town of Balún-Canán but the feast of San Caralampio, if they want a change from the quiet and contemplative and not very exciting round of daily life.

In a good republic the civic authorities hail from the people. They are no different from the other citizens of the place. Those in authority are citizens again tomorrow and the citizens of today are in authority tomorrow. Why then be a spoilsport when everyone recognizes pleasure as the bright spot in an earthly existence which otherwise is so gloomy? That men live to work is the philosophy of the sanctimonious, of the moral eunuchs. If life has any meaning at all—which may be doubtful—its one and only meaning is: Enjoy yourself to your heart's content and let others do the same in their own manner, and as long as they don't make themselves a nuisance to you or your fellow men, leave them in peace; you are no better than they and they are no holier or worthier than you, for the nonrighteous and the evildoers are only those who are caught.

Tomorrow the feast of San Caralampio will be over for a year. So let us be happy today while we are still under his saintly protection. It is in his honor that we enjoy ourselves, and to his glory all our sins will be forgiven in return for a confession or a well-paid Mass or a trundle on our knees from the church doors to the altar. People would not put up with a religion for long which did not allow them carnivals and all the license of revelry.

3

What a pity, beloved San Caralampio, you couldn't see all that went on in the cantinas in your honor on the last night. Perhaps it was just as well and just as wise to have put your wooden image in a quiet, dark corner of the cathedral and to have bolted and barred the doors, in case, like Harun, you went on your rounds by night to see what your believers were up to.

In the cantinas no one any longer wore any disguise. The girls danced to please all customers, in any fashion and without clothing. When one had done with them they were ready for the next comer. And since the very last pesos had to be raked in now or never, with the carretas already waiting, no time was lost in drawing curtains, closing doors, or shutting windows. Many, for fear of losing business, did not even take the time to run along to one of the houses which let rooms para un ratito—for a short time—or the time even to go to the room which the cantinero kept for such occasions and let out at a high price. This room was generally occupied by two or three or four couples at the same moment for lack of time and other accommodation. But now there was not even time for that—with the old dames crying aloud for their percentage. Any corner would do. And if every nook and corner inside and outside was occupied, then across to the church to a dark corner beside one of the doors—in the more immediate protection of San Caralampio.

It was the orgy round the golden calf, a public exhibition, and anyone who had the time and the inclination could take his pleasure in looking on. For as the hours ran out, the indulgence was stripped of all restraint and all disguise. One bellowed, another shouted, another sang, but all were of one mind. And everybody seemed to pay up, for there was no disputing over money to be heard. But the climax came at last. The inhabitants of the town had tired themselves out or spent all they had. Fewer and fewer of them were to be seen. Finally the field was occupied only by finqueros, agents and contractors of monterías, and the traders, who were now free at last to enjoy their share of San Caralampio's blessings.

4

Compared with the wild uproar in the cantinas the public dance by the fountain was a modest and decent scene; for here those who enjoyed themselves in San Caralampio's honor had every centavo to earn by the sweat of their brows. It was not that they were any better or more pious than the rest; it was simply that they had not the money to carouse in the cantinas. Even if they had had the money, they still would have lacked the proficiency in pleasure of those others who were used to having more money than they knew how to spend. To be able to enjoy yourself properly and thoroughly needs long and patient practice—like any other activity.

Here too a couple now and then withdrew into the shadows of the church, to study its architecture. But most of the dancers seemed to take more pleasure in dancing for dancing's sake than in anything else. Perhaps they knew that these other pleasures could be had any night they liked; but they could not have dancing every night—the marimberos would not play for a dance as cheaply as these strolling Indian musicians.

Manuel turned up there at last. There was now nothing else left on the plaza worth looking at. The gambling tables, where, as in the cantinas, there was a wild scramble to take the last bent centavo out of the pockets of the good people of Balún-Canán before it was too late, were boring to Manuel. He understood nothing of the play and he did not feel enough confidence in his luck to try and win a fortune with the few centavos in his possession. He found the dancing, where there were only people of his own class, a great deal more entertaining.

As he looked about him for a partner he noticed a girl with a small bundle in her hand standing apart from the other girls. She looked like a girl who might be employed by one of the female traders who were leaving for home with the carretas in the early morning.

He went toward her but then stopped irresolutely. He thought that one of the fellows dancing might be her husband and that she was waiting for him. But when several dances came to an end and still none of the fellows came up to her, he went a little nearer to her.

Again he came to a stop. Then she seemed to notice him, and when she looked at him he laughed. She laughed too. At that he said: "Shall we dance, muchacha?"

"Cómo no?" she replied. "Why not? But where shall I leave my bundle? I can't very well dance with a bundle."

"Oh, that—" he answered. "I'll take it for you."

He held it while they danced. It looked foolish, although none of the other dancers cared whether a man danced with a bundle in his hand or a box under his arm, and if anyone had given the matter a thought he would have said to himself that someone who danced with a bundle in his hand must have a good reason for it, since he wouldn't do it from choice.

At the end of the first dance he invited her to have coffee with him. She seemed very glad to, and she swallowed it down so thankfully that he said: "You must be hungry."

When she said she was, he bought some enchiladas. Then he asked the old Indian woman whether they might leave the bundle in her stall for an hour, and they went back to join the dancers.

"What's your name?" he asked between dances.

"What do you want to know for?" she came back at him.

"Well, I can't always call you muchacha if I take you along with me," he said, laughing.

"So quick?"

"Why not?" he said. "I have to be quick. We leave soon after midnight. I'm a carretero, and you can come with me if you like."

She only took a moment to think it over, and then asked: "Where are you going?"

"First I'm taking my carreta to Jovel," he replied, as though it was his own property, "then to Niba, and then Chiapa. There I get fresh orders. Probably it'll be Tuxtla after that and down to Arriaga and perhaps as far as Tonalá."

"That would suit me very well," she said. "Tuxtla's a big place and I might get a good job there, at ten or even fourteen pesos."

"Certainly you could," he put in, "and if you don't get it there and want to go farther, Arriaga and Tonalá are fine places too and there they're always wanting criadas. Servant girls are in demand down there. But if you won't tell me your name, I won't take you and you'll stay here."

"Rosario López, su servidora—your obedient servant," she replied in jest.

"Rosario then," he said. "Chayo, querida mía——"

But she stopped him short, laughing at the same time: "Mira, mira, caballero—not so fast! Querida suya—your dear girl. We'll see about that. Not so fast. You don't even know whether I like you. Pero, pensando, but thinking about it— yo creo que sí."

"*Creo* que sí?" he asked. "What do you mean you '*think* so'? Either you like me or you don't. So out with it."

She flushed and smiled in confusion. "Perhaps I do."

"That's better. Then it's a bargain," he said abruptly. "Then I'll take you along. We can see about the rest on the road. There's no sleep for me tonight. We still have goods to load and we have to yoke up. But maybe you can get two or three hours' sleep. We have another girl with us, Andrés's wife. You can sleep with her and keep warm. We've no time tonight, either of us, to bother with our wives. We shall be hard at it. They're dancing again. Come on, Chayo, stir your legs and get to it."

While they danced he had the chance to consider his rapid courtship and engagement calmly. He took a look at her now and again without her noticing, for she looked down at her feet, as a modest girl should when dancing an Indian zapateado.

He liked her better the more he saw of her. She was an Indian, but she spoke good Mexican Spanish. She was obviously experienced and no longer entirely ignorant of life; for she had acquiesced without false modesty in the proposals he made, although he had no more than hinted at them. She had cut him off merely because of the suddenness of his suggestion, as it is the part of any girl to do who wishes to keep a hold on a last shred of her modesty. No woman likes to have it thrown in her face by the man she honors that she fell into his arms at the very first moment. She does not like it, on her own account, if she has waited and looked forward to nothing more worth her desiring than taking the first chance that came along as soon as it presented itself.

And when he thought all this over, he only took a stronger fancy to her. Never mind a girl's past when time presses and nothing better offers. After a while it is always found that it makes no real difference. Any woman may be the right one and any can be intolerable, whatever her past may have been. A woman is far less influenced by her past than a man by his. A man is too much inclined to be pedantic, moral, and respectable through and through, to be plagued by his conscience, and to sacrifice everything, including his wife, to his narrow-minded and strait-laced respectability. If you leave out the desiccated holy women and withering spinsters, a man is far more of an intolerable and stinking pharisee than a woman.

5

After Manuel had danced a few more times with his newly won girl, he looked up at the sky to see by the stars what time it was.

"We can have two more dances, querida, and then we'll go," he said. "They'll be looking for me at the camp."

When the two dances were over, Manuel took the girl by the arm and they went to pick up her bundle. On leaving the little restaurant, they passed by one of the cantinas.

"There, muchacha, have a look at that," he said, stopping. "The finqueros and the big shots from the monterías are chucking their money about in grand style. They're giving San Caralampio the time of his life. Damned if every one of them hasn't a couple of girls riding on his knees. Now, look at that—they've got three of them sitting on the table in front of them, stripped to their stockings—their clothes are all hanging on the hat pegs. There's life for you. The cantinero's getting it in by the sackful. That's the style."

"Why do you look at them?" she asked, pulling him on by the arm. "You'd like to be there too. You'd enjoy it, I'm sure."

"Celosa? Jealous?" he asked with a laugh. "You're shaping up well, querida mía. Wait a bit, Chayo, we'll get along all right together. You'll have no complaints to make. But," he went on, "when I see all that carrying-on, I can't help thinking of the slave-driven peons on the fincas and the wretched muchachos in the monterías, who have nothing and go to wrack and ruin like mules and dogs. And here the money's chucked about on women and drink, and the women take it any way they're asked as long as it's gold pieces. Not that the women ever see much of it. Most of it goes to their dueñas, those madams who steal it from them when they fall down drunk on their beds. And what's left their boy friends take, the fellows who live off them in Tapachula, Veracruz, Frontera, El Carmen, or wherever else these girls come from. And those fellows spend the money these girls earn for them on other girls around the corner. There was a gang of these girls who came along with the carretas. I listened to them talking and quarreling among themselves and heard all about it. It's a hell of a life they lead."

Suddenly he gripped her by the arm and pulled her toward him and held her tightly. "To the devil with it, querida, let's go. When I think of the carretas and look at all this and then think how we founder in the mud and never have a whole shirt on our backs—yes, to hell with it all. I'd just like to know who made this damned world!"

They went on their way. But his bitterness rose again now he had started. With the feel of the girl's warm body close to his own, stumbling along the dark street, dodging stones and holes and puddles and quagmires, he began, probably for the first time in his life, to take a clear view of the world, of his place in the economic order, and, indeed, of his whole wretched existence.

The girl was strong and healthy, quite unlike the child Andrés had taken for his wife; and while he danced with her, stood about with her, and drank coffee with her he had seen something in a woman he had never seen before. The open-heartedness of the strong healthy girl whose hands were hardened by toil, her free and easy way with him, and the warm and womanly feeling that streamed out from her inspired him with a wild and, at the same time, almost diffident desire.

He stopped and took her tightly in his arms. "Chayo," he said, "I've only known you for an hour or two, but it's nothing to me what you are and why you're running away. I want you to be my wife."

"But—" she stammered, "well—but wait till we're on the road, or—not just here—there's plenty of time—and of course I'll—you're taking me to Tuxtla and I know well enough why you take me. I will—I promise you. You know that—but——"

"No," he interrupted, "that's not what I mean. Yes, of course I mean that too. But I mean something else. I want you to be my wife altogether—I mean, for always. What I mean is—I want to live in a hut with you on a piece of land. Or we'll go to a town where I can get work and where you'll be with me always, and have children and be properly man and wife. I'll see to it that I get hold of a little money. As soon as we get to Arriaga, I'll clear out with you and make for the next station. There we'll buy tickets and go along the line to a town where no one will know that I'm a runaway and owe money to the patrón. I'll say I'm from Tapachula. And after a time we'll go on to a bigger town. There no one will know anything and I'll work in a factory. Then we'll have a life of our own, you and I, just you and I and the children. Would you do that, Chayo?"

"I think I would," she said simply.

As soon as he had said all this, and still more when he heard her honest and unromantic reply, Manuel was overcome by a deep and serene contentment, which released the pressure of his immediate desires. It was something like what had occurred in Andrés, though the cause and grounds of it were quite different—as different as Andrés was from Manuel and Estrellita from Rosario.

It was no novelty for Manuel to be with a woman, and he could tell that Rosario too was not a novice. Neither for one nor the other was there any mystery left in these matters. Yet, in place of the importunate desire which had tormented him for the last hour or two, he now felt the aspiration to something beautiful. He might not be clear about the beauty of it, but he felt it was the best life had to offer, that which gave it its real worth. As a carretero he had thought a hundred times over that he might as well not live at all as carry on in that life of hopeless toil which could never change or come to an end.

At the sight of this strong, healthy, and openhearted girl there flamed up in him the wild longing, which is in every Indian's blood, for a family—a family to bind him to home and country—and for work which he could see living and growing under his eyes and which gave him an aim and a return. It was that unquenchable yearning of man for a point of rest, for a core to his life, without which life is nothing but a ceaseless flux.

The calling which had him in its grip stifles such yearnings in the men who are trapped in its toils. And until this day, until this very hour Manuel had scarcely known such a yearning at all. The carretas had almost succeeded in killing it for good.

As soon as he recognized all this he no longer felt that unabashed, aggressive desire for the girl which he had given signs of all evening. No longer did he see in her just a stray girl he had picked up, to be taken and kept, or discarded as he chose. He wanted now to have this woman for good, and the first step was to win her.

It was not sentiment that moved him, and he knew nothing of ruses and stratagems. He was as innocent of soft and tender feelings as she was. If he meant to win her, it was not with long discourses and fine words or with gallantries and chivalrous service. Nothing of all this entered his head, any more than it would enter the head of any Indian who had not given up his natural and healthy attitude to life.

His instinct told him that the way to win her was not to take what was now his for the taking, but even to give up all thought of it. It was not that he was plagued by any notion of its being hateful or unclean or that it would be taking an unfair advantage.

What he felt suddenly was the longing to be free, and it came to him that only through and with this woman could he attain freedom. So long as this woman was the core of this longing, he could never surrender the aim of freeing himself from the carretas. It might be that, if he let himself go, the woman might cease that very night to be all that he wished her to be. Whether or not, he had no wish to gamble on it. His desire for a home and a family was bound up in the desire to store up something beautiful for an opportunity less casual and meaningless than the present moment.

If Manuel had been of a highly civilized race he might be suspected of thinking of his pleasure and how to enhance it. But Manuel was an Indian—and a carretero. He knew nothing about the enhancement of pleasure by cunning preparations and delays. Even if any such ideas had occurred to him he would never have taken the trouble to carry them out. It would have taken too long. His notion was to reach his goal by the shortest and surest path without any fooling about.

He could not have said why he behaved as he did. It was instinctive. If he could have attached the woman to him by not delaying for an hour, he would not have delayed. But he felt that if he delayed he would be on better terms with her and they would be better friends. She would wonder why he did not do as she expected he would; and that would show her that his feeling for her was more serious than she had thought it.

He behaved in this way because he did not know how otherwise to express himself and to tell her what he felt for her and that what he felt came from the depth of his heart, for he had no words for this feeling. He was as incapable of expressing deep emotion in words as of forcing tears from his eyes when he felt sadness or pain of mind.

6

Meanwhile they had been walking on. Manuel no longer had hold of her. They had separated without thinking, while he debated within himself and came to his decision.

The real reason may have been the stones and holes and puddles and quagmires and pits and pieces of timber, which made hard going of the dark streets. They had fallen apart as they stumbled along; it was easier like that to fight their way on.

When they left the outskirts of the town and had the open

prairie before them, the going was better. Rosario now walked beside him.

A thought struck him. "Chayo," he said, "don't say a word, not even to one of the muchachos, about me clearing out. If the patrón hears of it, I'll never get down to Arriaga and the railroad; or he might sell me to a montería, to be sure of what I owe him, and that would be a thousand times worse. There's no escape from a montería. The muchachos there are better guarded than convicts."

"I won't say a word, you muchacho," she promised him. Then she added: "But what is your name? I don't know what to call you. . . . Oh—Manuel. I give you my promise, Manuel. I won't betray you."

It bound him closer to her to have her promise of secrecy. They were now conspirators. He could tell from the tone of her voice that he might rely on her promise. They were not only conspirators but loyal comrades. It needed only these few and apparently trivial words to bind them closely and firmly together. It was not the words themselves so much as the tone and the way she spoke that told him he was on the way to win a woman to depend upon.

So far she had said very little. She did not seem to be a great talker. She was like that, he supposed.

She was no longer a girl. She might be twenty-five or so.

7

He saw her now only as a shadow as he went along beside her in the darkness dimly lit by the bright stars. She was barefoot and walked with a long firm stride. She was only a little shorter than he.

He was still carrying her bundle. For the sake of saying something instead of walking along in silence he asked her: "What's in your bundle, querida?"

"Only my Sunday dress, two shirts, a towel, a pair of shoes, and a pair of long cotton stockings," she said. "Not much to bring you, but I didn't steal them and I don't need much."

Then, without beating about the bush and without fear that she might lose him or that he might despise her for it, she told him all that had happened to her. She saw nothing tragic in her experiences any more than he saw anything tragic in a carretero's lot—not even bad luck. To them, as to all their kind, whatever came their way, every calamity and every pleasure, belonged to the natural order of things; if unpleasant it might be avoided, granted you were smart enough, but otherwise it had to be put up with once it came and could not be eluded in time. And if they sought an explanation they fell back on the submissiveness which they had had well hammered into them, and said: "It is God's will." It never occurred to them to say that God's will is merely what man wrests for himself by the exercise of his reason, his perseverance, and his will. If they had reasoned thus they would not have belonged to the lowest and most wretched class.

8

Rosario, as they walked across the prairie, told him that at the age of twelve she had had to leave the Indian village where she was born, because there were too many children at home. It was a village of free Indians, and the land which the commune allotted to her father was stony and barren and too small for sustaining a large family. The more fertile land had been taken away bit by bit from the commune by don Porfirio's political chiefs and sold by them for their own benefit to Spanish and German landowners.

Rosario went into service at Yajalón with a Mexican shop-keeper. She got a peso a month. Her employer got her with child before she was fourteen years old. She stayed on there and was given fifty centavos more a month. Her baby died and her employer wanted to give her a second one.

The first had arrived without her knowing anything about it. She was very much surprised when one day it suddenly made its appearance as she was cooking over the fire; it just fell to the ground at her feet. She knew whose the child was, so she stayed quietly on in the house, since the child really belonged to the household. In this country such events are not taken tragically. The wife pitches into her husband for an hour or two, and then they are reconciled. She never for a moment thinks of separating from him. They are good Catholics, and though the Catholic Church tolerates every sort of beastliness in marriage—wife-beating, scandals, and whatever you please—it does not allow divorce, no matter to what lengths of hatred the married couple may go. For God has joined them in heaven even when the marriage was merely a question of money, or a maintenance policy, or an impulse which did not last.

But when her master approached her again, thinking that she would now easily admit his right to her, Rosario showed more sense. She had learned by experience where children came from and the reason. So she made a commotion in the dead of night and her mistress came along and the husband got his discharge.

Rosario stayed a few months longer in the house, but it became more and more intolerable, for the man gave her no peace. At last she left and went from place to place, taking jobs at two, three, and four pesos a month. Finally she arrived at Balún-Canán. She worked in various houses as cook and maid-of-all-work.

After several changes she settled down with a widow whose temper was getting worse from month to month from the exasperation of having no man in her bed. There were times when she became confidential with Rosario, and sometimes so confidential that this Indian girl, whose instincts were entirely normal, could not make out whether the woman was more man than woman. She made proposals which confused the girl and even nauseated her, so that by degrees Rosario became far more afraid of the widow than she had been of her first master—though it was only because she was so afraid of him and because he beat her that she had submitted to him.

She gave notice. The woman, who had reached the most difficult crisis of her life, lost all control. She thought she had found in Rosario a suitable victim, whom she could win over in the course of time by presents and other favors, and so indulge her abnormal cravings. When Rosario stood by the notice she had given, the woman took her revenge, still in the hope that the girl would prove amenable. She went to the police and accused the girl of a theft of money. The money was found in the dark hole where the girl slept.

If it came before the court the girl would of necessity be sentenced to a term of imprisonment. The woman, however, still in the hope of bringing the girl to her knees, came to an understanding with the chief of police not to press the charge if he would put her in the lockup and fine her fifty pesos. The chief of police very much preferred the fine. It was no profit to him to put anyone in prison, but he could always wangle a fine so that the greater part of it found its way into his pocket. These fines are one of the reasons why in the course of the municipal elections in the smaller towns from five to fifty voters, according to the fervor displayed, are left on the field of battle—dead, or, if they are lucky, crippled.

The woman expected that Rosario would wilt in jail and implore her mistress to pay the fine for her release. She intended to do so only on condition that Rosario went on her knees before the Holy Virgin and swore unconditional obedience, an obedience which was to cover every order the woman might give. But Rosario was not by any means in such dread of jail as her mistress supposed. She preferred to remain in jail rather than fall in with her mistress's wishes.

Another reason was that Rosario was not badly treated in jail. It is true that most of the jails in the small towns of Mexico are infested with rats, fleas, lice, and every sort of pestilential filth, but that is more than made up for by the absence of all discipline. The occupants are mostly outside in the yard all day. They can play games or cards and smoke and generally do as they please. They may have visitors if they like and for as long as they like. They may have presents from their friends of food, drink, cigarettes, clothing, books, newspapers—all of which are allowed in after a merely perfunctory examination. Women usually have their children with them; infants at the breast are never taken away from them, not even as a rule in the large and well-organized state and federal prisons. It is regarded as an unnecessary cruelty to take her children away from a female prisoner. Even convicts of the worst type are allowed visits from their wives and to be alone with them all day long and sometimes even during the night. The State realizes that this is of benefit to the health and mental condition of the prisoners and conduces to orderly and normal behavior on their part.

Rosario was more favored than she had ever thought possible. As she was a strong girl and a good and willing worker she was employed the very first day in the house of the chief of police. On the second day she was already going out alone to the market to buy provisions, and the mistress of the house felt no hesitation about trusting her with the money required. On the third day she was sleeping in the house, and the chief of police was as pleased as his wife to have a maid for nothing.

Indeed, as the cost of her keep was entered on the books, he could pocket those centavos, which just paid for his cigarettes.

Her former mistress was entirely balked of her revenge and still more of her hope of getting hold of a willing tool. There was now nothing more she could do as she had come to an agreement with the chief of police over the prosecution and sentence.

He, however, was more concerned about the fine of fifty pesos than about the cheap servant he had got. There were always plenty of women and girls in prison whom he could employ in his house for nothing. It was for his wife to pitch into them if they knew nothing of housework. That was not his affair.

In the third week of her imprisonment the chief of police met a doctor one day at a bar. This doctor had recently come to live in the town. He told the chief that his wife complained of being unable to find a decent cook. They talked it over and the chief of police offered the doctor Rosario, if he cared to pay her fine of fifty pesos, plus eight pesos as costs; the doctor could charge this fine to the girl and deduct it from her wages, as the law allowed in the case of all debts incurred by wage earners. The chief of police told the doctor frankly that he did not believe the girl was a thief. It was a false accusation, but he could do nothing because her former mistress was a reputable citizen, whose word counted for more than that of an Indian girl.

The doctor said he would speak to his wife. His wife said she would give the girl a trial. She took Rosario into her home and was so pleased with her work and her cleanliness that she told her husband he might pay her fine for her.

In this way the chief of police sold Rosario to the doctor for the price of her fine and the costs. The doctor's wife was no skinflint. She gave the girl seven pesos a month—an unheard-of wage which gave rise to much talk in the town, although the girl, as the doctor's wife openly declared, was worth twenty, since she relieved her mistress of the entire work of the house.

Rosario, however, had now to work for eight months for nothing, in order to pay off her debt. She was still a prisoner and could be shut up again if she ever made the attempt to run away before this debt was cleared. The chief of police had had to give his word to this before the doctor would go bail for the girl.

Rosario naturally needed a few things, such as shirts and dresses, and therefore she had to borrow from her mistress and so add to her debt. But at the end of eighteen months she was clear of debt and free to go where she pleased. She thought of going to Tuxtla, where higher wages were paid than in up-country towns. But when she gave notice the doctor's wife offered her ten pesos and she stayed on. The doctor's wife was cut by all the women of her acquaintance for this outrage against the current rate of wages. She was beginning to make it impossible for the worthy ladies of the town to get servants on proper terms—for they were used to treating them as slaves.

Rosario spent two years in the doctor's house, and might have spent two more if she could have had it her own way. But the doctor began to tire of his wife and, finding her inadequate, he longed for a change. So he cast his eyes on Rosario in the hope that she would have more to give him.

One day when his wife was out and the doctor was alone, he summoned the girl to his consulting room.

"Rosario," he said, "I notice your lungs are not sound. You might easily get tuberculosis."

He explained what this meant and frightened her by telling her that she might die. She would get thin and ugly and no one would marry her. If she did marry, her children would perish in infancy and her life would be a misery.

The last threat was decisive. Rosario wanted to marry as soon as ever she found a man to please her—she was too much of a woman to remain unmarried—and the first thing she asked of marriage was children.

She let him examine her after he had talked to her long enough to make her thoroughly frightened. He then told her that her lungs were, as he had suspected, in a very bad way and there was no time to be lost. But the treatment would cost a lot; for though he would charge her nothing as a member of the household, he had to buy the drugs and injections.

He gave her an injection on the spot to arrest the disease and told her that the injection cost three pesos. "For you I will make it two. But I shall have to give you at least three every week, if I am to save your life and restore you to health."

"But, señor Doctor," she said, "how can I pay you six pesos a week when I earn only two and a half?"

He busied himself with his instruments—or pretended to. Then he turned around. "Yes, I see you can't pay that. But I can't do it for nothing. It is my profession, and it is against professional custom for doctors to work for nothing. The training costs a lot of money and instruments and medicines are very dear. But why should you die when it is so easy to be cured? Do you want to die or not?"

"No, I don't," she said in alarm. "Dear señor Doctor, help me and don't let me die."

"That's right," he said more kindly. "That's the way to talk. Why die when you can be saved to have a happy life with husband and children?"

Rosario laughed, but her eyes were moist all the same.

"I'll tell you how it is, Rosario," he went on. "Now listen to me—I want to tell you something. But don't say a word to my wife or she'll kill you. My wife is not in good health, although she looks well enough. What I want to tell you is this—she can't sleep with me. You understand what I mean?"

"Yes, I understand," she replied, and it dawned on her what was coming. It was the same as with her first master, though he had put it more brutally; he had used force and beaten her and threatened to strangle and shoot her unless she took the place of his wife.

"And look here, Rosario," said the doctor, "you'll soon know what I mean. I must have a wife. I can't be going every week to Tapachula or Tonalá. I'll give you the three injections a week you need for your cure and you can pay—I mean, you can make me some return for each injection. I should think your life and your health and the children you will have some day are worth that much. Or do you think not?"

The mention of children, however, made a difficulty. "But I don't want to have children with you, señor Doctor. It won't be so easy then to get a good and honest husband. You know that yourself, señor Doctor."

He patted her on the shoulder. "I am a doctor, after all," he said reassuringly. "I am a doctor and you need have no fear. I know how to prevent that. I don't want any fuss with my wife, so you can leave that to me. If you have children the señora will know all about it. Don't worry about that."

She made no reply.

"Well, there it is," he said, becoming impatient. "If you want to die, it doesn't matter to me."

"I don't want to die," she said, sobbing. And then she added reluctantly in a low voice: "Yes—well then, I must do as you say, señor Doctor."

Three weeks went by.

Then one evening the señora came home earlier than the señor Doctor expected and found him and Rosario in a situation which left no doubt whatever, though he swore by God and the Holy Virgin and all the saints besides. The doctor's wife did not cry out or make a fuss. She kept all that, apparently, for the doctor.

"Rosario," she said without ado, "pack your things and come to me at once for your wages. I'm sorry I have to let you go. You're a good servant. But you must leave my house. You are perfectly healthy. There is no need whatever for the doctor to treat you."

This was news to Rosario. So she was not the first whom the doctor had set out to cure of a fatal disease. And in spite of the shame of being surprised by the señora, whom she honored and reverenced, and thrown out like rubbish, she was all the same delighted to know that she did not have a mortal disease and could forgo any further treatment.

In five minutes she had packed her things, and then she presented herself rather timidly before her mistress. But the señora was not angry with her—she knew her lord and master too well. She could not divorce him since she was a Catholic. She had to put up with it and overlook the señor Doctor's exploits in intimacy. For a moment she thought of keeping Rosario, for she knew that the next girl would certainly arrive at the same degree of intimacy with him.

But she said: "Here are your wages, Rosario, and thank you for the way you have worked for me. I am giving you ten pesos over and above your wages. But you must leave the town first thing in the morning, or else I will have you put in prison. And if you say a word about what has happened, I will see to it that you spend a year in prison for defamation of this house. So now you know. Adiós, Rosario."

Rosario took the money. She stood barefoot before her mistress, wearing her woolen workday dress. "Mil gracias, señora, a thousand thanks for the kind way you have treated me while I have been with you. I will always remember you.

And mil gracias for the money. I will go away early in the morning, as you bid me, and I will never say a word to anyone—that I promise you in the name of the Holy Virgin."

She did not attempt to defend herself by saying that she had been the doctor's victim against her own wishes. She thought it would only hurt the señora.

Kneeling down she kissed the señora's hand. Then she picked up her bundle, which she had left in the passageway by the door, and left the house.

She walked over to the square and stood near the dancers with her bundle in her hand, hoping to find someone in whose company she could leave the town early in the morning. Her idea had been to join a party of traveling peddlers so that she would not have to travel alone.

"So there you are, Manuel," she concluded. "That's the whole story. You can take me with you now and make me your wife, or if you don't want to, say so and I will go with some other people. I have told you all about it, because I wanted to be honest with you. Be the same with me and tell no one what I promised the señora I would tell nobody. I had to tell you, so that you should know me as I am. No one else on earth shall ever hear a word of it. The señora was always good to me. She is a santa, a saint, and I honor her far above all Holy Virgins, for none of them ever did anything for me."

Manuel let go of her bundle and put his arms around her. "Querida linda," he said, "I have already forgotten every word of what you told me. Now I think of it, I wasn't really listening and most of it I didn't even hear, because I kept thinking all the time how much more you were my wife for telling me it all. I was thinking of you and what I could do to make your heart glad. A new life is beginning for you and for me. I know now what I want, and I know it through you. I want to get away from the carretas, where there is no hope for me. I want to go with you as far as ever our feet will carry us. For freedom, we must go far away."

Without being aware of the truth of it, speaking only from her heart, she repeated: "Yes, freedom is far away."

9

They stood clasped in each other's arms on the vast prairie. They said not a word more and thought no more; they merely felt and understood and trusted in one another.

The stars were above them and around them the velvet darkness of midnight. Not far away the carretas and the resting oxen were blocked out against the deep blue horizon. Then campfires leaped up in tongues of flame and brightened to a red glow, and carretas, oxen, and the carreteros going about their work stood out in the flickering light.

He let her go, picked up her bundle again, and together they walked on toward the carretas. When they got there the fellows were all stirring. The rusty coffee can and the large battered enamel pot of black beans were already on the fire. The carreteros were bringing up the oxen and yoking and harnessing them.

Manuel stood looking on for a moment at the lively scene. He felt already that he scarcely belonged to it. In his thoughts he was far away with his wife.

"Hola," Andrés shouted cheerily, as soon as he saw Manuel, "good you've turned up, Manuelito. You're the man we want. You know what a lot of use the rest of them are and we've got a job on with the oxen—they'll have it and then they won't have it. They don't know what work means by this time."

"Don't you worry, Andreucho," said Manuel, falling at once into the old rut again. "We'll soon put some go into them."

"I'd made up my mind," Andrés said laughing as he pushed his hair from his face, "you'd taken on a cargo as a farewell to

Caralampio and we'd have to load you up with the rest of the gear."

"Not far off it," said Manuel, "but I had other fish to fry."

"Ay, hombre!" Andrés now shouted in professional style. "Hombre, look where that damned Amarillo's got to—the one with the broken horn. He gave us the slip just when we'd got hold of him, and now there he is along with Luciano's."

Then Andrés saw Rosario.

"Buenos días, muchacha," he said, greeting her.

"I am Manuel's wife," she said, introducing herself, "and I am going along with you down to Arriaga."

"Felicitaciones," Andrés cried out with a laugh, "congratulations to both of you. Bienvenida, welcome." He took her hand and said: "So my little star will not be alone. Go over to her, muchacha. She is lying in that carreta there. Lie down beside her and have a sleep. We've half an hour's hard work before we take off. Have some coffee, if you want some, and take the can to Estrellita."

She went over to the carreta and crept up close to Estrellita, who woke up; and Rosario out of the fullness of her heart talked to her in whispers in their own native tongue.

They were like old friends at once. They understood each other immediately, for both were full of the same joy and hope, in which for both a new day dawned after many days of cloud and sorrow.

But before they could fall asleep the first carretas, swaying, creaking, and rumbling, began to move off, leaving the prairie behind them.

16

The carreteros had a hard time of it in the early hours of the morning. There was a stretch of more than three kilometers through primeval forest where the road clung to the edge of a stream and was nothing but a marsh. On the other side was a sheer cliff from which at every twenty feet springs welled out over the road, which was covered with decaying leaves, rotting branches and twigs, and the soil always silting down from the face of the cliff. At low-lying places on the road the stream flooded it every few days and the volume of water was so great that instead of running off at the sides it ran all along it and turned it into a bog; and the shade of the huge forest trees prevented the sun's ever penetrating to dry the road thoroughly once in a while.

This stretch of road gave the carreteros so much to do that they could not for a minute think of anything except how they were to come through without broken wheels or the foundering of the oxen. But by nine o'clock they had reached the good part of the road and now it ran high and dry as far as Jovel.

So, by the time the sun began to blaze down, they had left

the soft, difficult road far behind them. The oxen, owing to the heat and the attacks of huge horseflies, could work no longer and Andrés gave the word to halt.

The drivers took out their animals, lit their fires, and cooked their food. They wasted no time; they were tired and wanted to sleep.

Their camping place was not large, but it was covered with good grass. It was triangular in shape.

The road to Jovel met it at one corner, traversed its left side, and then left it at the next corner to go around a hill. The next side of this triangular parcel of grass bordered high ground covered with gnarled trees and bushes. The third side fell away steeply. This steep descent was grassy and clothed with bushes and stunted pines.

Far below, a stream, with clear drinking water, wound its way through thick undergrowth. On the other side of the stream began the great bush.

2

This little camping place was to enshrine for Estrellita one of the most beautiful memories of her life.

It was the first place since she had left her home where she felt secure from all pursuit. She breathed freely for the first time, like a young animal of the forest who has escaped from its cage and smells again the familiar trees and bushes in the bliss of being with good and trusted friends once more.

After he had rested, Andrés took her down the steep descent to the stream below. There they found a clearing in the thick undergrowth which gave them just enough room to sit side by side. As they sat together he took a scrap of paper from his shirt pocket. On it was a poem of a few lines. It pleased him because of its simplicity and its tender melody and because its whole meaning was clear to him and found an answer in his feelings. He had carefully torn it from a printed sheet he had picked up on the road somewhere—he had long forgotten where. It was now yellowed and worn from being so long in his pocket.

He unfolded it carefully and read to Estrellita: "Blue flowers by the way / Red tunas at Nopal / They are part of you, Prieta / Since I looked into your eyes."

He had read it in Spanish. When she looked up at him inquiringly because she did not understand, he translated it into Tseltal for her.

"It is like a bird singing among the bushes when he wants a wife and wants to build a nest for her," she said.

"That is just what the man who wrote it meant," said he, moved by the simple explanation she gave to the lines.

"Wrote?" she asked. "Why did he write it when it is a song to be sung aloud?"

Then he began to explain to her what writing was, what its use was, and how by means of it you could speak to people who were not present.

"Then I have no need for writing," she said impulsively, "for you will always be with me and I with you, and there is no one else in the world I want to speak to. I can say everything I want to you with my mouth and don't need to write."

"That's true, Estrellita," said he, and he was quite sure she was right.

But he felt so rich in the knowledge he had so painfully acquired that it hurt him not to be able to share it with Estrellita. He wanted to share with her all he possessed, to possess everything in common with her.

In his impulse to share all he knew with her and to make her a partner in all he possessed, Andrés looked for another way of making her understand how important reading and writing, and arithmetic too would be for her.

"You see, Estrellita," he said, "if you can write and read you can't so easily be deceived with contracts, accounts, and government regulations. If the peons on the fincas could read and understand figures, the finquero could not keep them in slavery and debt and sell them when he liked."

She did not understand why this could free a peon, because she did not see the connection. To understand this connection she would have first had to understand reading, writing, and arithmetic and thus recognize their advantage. But since he said so she believed it without understanding.

"Can you write?" she asked.

"Yes, I can write. Would you like to see how it goes?"

He found a scrap of paper in his pocket and wrote on it in pencil: "I found Estrellita when she was poor and forsaken and had not a single friend in the wide world."

She watched attentively while he slowly traced the letters, and was full of admiration. It filled her with great joy that he, who was the whole content of her life, was so clever and could do everything and knew everything that was to be known and done on the earth.

When he had read what he had written, she said: "That is true. It is as true as the stars in heaven." She seized his hand and pressed it against her face.

"Take this paper and keep it," he said.

As she folded it and tucked it into the top of her shirt, she said: "I will wear it next to my heart where I keep all you say."

Then she said: "I'd rather than anything in the world write you something as beautiful and dear as you have written for me."

"Well," he said, smiling, "if you'd like to write me something beautiful, then I'll teach you writing and Spanish at the same time. We can't write in Tseltal because it has no letters.

The letters are of the language of the Ladinos. They made them so as to be able to write up contracts and debts."

This was how their lessons began; and they began down by the stream, a hundred feet away from the carretas and their drivers, while the last rays of the sun grew pale. The first word Andrés taught her to write was the name he had given her—Estrellita—though she got no further that day than writing an E with much difficulty.

Since that day Estrellita had been back to this camping ground four times, when Andrés was in charge of carretas and halted there. And each time they had gone down to the little clearing beside the stream, and she had knelt and kissed the grass in greeting and in remembrance.

Whenever in later times she heard the word "home," she thought of this little piece of ground.

3

It happened on this fourth journey when Andrés and Estrellita had made their ascent from the little stream that they heard their native Tseltal being spoken in low tones. The voices came from a campfire nearby, around which sat a group of Indians.

These Indians were on their way from their native district in the north of the state to the villages and settlements of the fertile south and southeast, and had just stopped to rest on the grassy meadow.

It was music to their ears when Andrés and Estrellita caught these Tseltal words.

"Buenas noches," Andrés called out, and then added in Tseltal, "are you from the Bachajón district?"

"Yes, that's where our pueblo is," one of them replied, "but we don't live near Bachajón. We come from farther on, nearer the great jungle."

"I'm from the finca of Lumbojvil," said Andrés, walking up and introducing himself, "and Estrellita, my wife, is from the same neighborhood, but nearer to the road to Simojovel."

Estrellita was a few feet behind him. It is not the custom for Indian women to thrust themselves into the company of men and join in their talk. She stood where she was.

"And where are you bound for?" Andrés asked, squatting down by the fire and lighting a cigarette from one of its smoldering branches.

"We are after young mules," one of the men said.

"Mules are very expensive in these parts," Andrés told them.

The eldest of the Indians, who seemed to be in charge of the party, laughed. "You must be a fool yourself if you think us such fools as to buy any mules here. I have been on this job four times now since I earned my first money on an American's coffee plantation in Soconusco and was able to buy my first two mules. No, muchachito, we are going down to the railroad and then further still to the lagoons on the coast. Then we shall keep going along the railroad. That is the best hunting ground for us, for there the people have plenty of young mules and sometimes they're only too glad to sell them as soon as they're born; for, don't you see, the people down there by the railroad are always hard up for money. They're always seeing something they'd like to buy whether they need it or not; and that is good for us, because otherwise it would be very difficult to buy up enough young animals to bring back from these long trips."

These mules were not so easily bought as it might seem, for the farmers and owners of haciendas were not very eager to sell; they preferred to rear the animals themselves, since a good mule brought ten times, often twenty times, as much as a fat pig. So the Indian buyers sometimes went from one ranch to another for a week or more without being able to purchase a single animal, and they were often months on the road before they had bought up all the young mules they had come prepared to buy.

Then again, they often had a stroke of luck. They would come upon a young mule which its owner did not want to sell, but while they lingered on the ranch a trader would arrive and set out his wares. Then the ranchero, but a hundred times more his wife, felt wretched not to be millionaires and able to buy up everything in one sweep. The ranchero would catch his wife smiling at him as she never had since their marriage and at the same time would become aware of the Indians still standing about with ready money in their pockets. Half an hour later the Indians were the possessors of a fine young mule and three hours later the money they had paid for it was in the hands of the trader.

The Indians bought mules even when they were not yet weaned and had scarcely begun to graze, for at that age the animals were cheapest; and these men could only buy at the cheapest prices if they hoped to bring home a few animals each, for money was a rarity with them.

They had an unwearied patience and kindness in rearing these young mules. When, after three years, the mules were offered for sale they often brought ten times what had been spent on them. Indians living in independent communities on barren soil were able to earn a tolerable living by rearing mules, and it gave them a life they enjoyed.

4

"Did you come through Lumbojvil?" Andrés asked the men.

"We spent a night there," said one of the men as he stirred up the fire.

"Didn't you say you were from Lumbojvil?" said the Indian who appeared to be the leader, scrutinizing Andrés.

"Yes," Andrés replied. "I come from Lumbojvil and my people live there, although it's a long while since I've seen them."

The man's question already hinted that he had news to tell which might interest Andrés. Now he took a flaming branch from the fire and threw the light on Andrés's face.

"Yes, now I know who you are," he said. "You're Criserio's son who lives on the finca there. You're the son of Criserio Ugalde."

"That's my father, yes. How is he? And my mother and all of them?" asked Andrés.

Lázaro—for that was his name—made no answer. Instead he reflectively pulled out some tobacco leaves, which he rolled in his hand. Then, selecting a larger leaf to wrap them in, he slowly and carefully made himself a cigar which, when it was at last completed, was almost twelve inches long and two inches thick.

It gave Andrés a queer feeling to see this cigar. It was eight years since he had left home. During this time he had become Mexicanized. He spoke fluent Spanish, though with the peculiar accent of this remote southern state of the Republic. In these years, moreover, he had also grown accustomed to the habits of the Ladinos, even though he could not himself copy these habits—he had to lead the hard and meager life of a carretero, who is always with his carreta on the roads of the state, which are forgotten by God and engineers alike. But he was used to the cigars that he saw for sale in the tiendas in the towns, cigars of the same shape and size as are familiar throughout the civilized world. He could not himself buy cigars; they were too expensive. He had to stick to cigarettes, which he rolled himself. Now, when he looked at this immense cigar, his home rose so clearly before him that he saw his father sitting on the ground with one of those huge cigars between his fingers. Andrés's father had smoked nothing but cigars of this size, which he made for himself, as did all the other men of his race in that region.

While Lázaro with infinite pains rolled his cigar, and did it with an air of not having heard Andrés's question, another Indian, Emilio, said: "I know your father Criserio very well, and your mother and all your people. I bought five little pigs from him two years ago, but I had to pay the money for them to the finquero because your father was in debt to him. All the same I managed to slip your father a peso on the quiet when the finquero wasn't looking, otherwise he'd have had that peso as well. That finquero of yours is a bad one, es un hijo de la chingada, bad luck to him. What's his name? Don Arnulfo? Yes, that's it, don Arnulfo. Wolf would suit him better."

"We say in the pueblo that don Arnulfo must have had a tiger for his father," said another man.

"And a stinking coyote for his mother," Emilio threw in.

Lázaro had at last put the final touches on his cigar. He licked it all around with the tenderness of a connoisseur and smacked his lips as though ready to eat it slowly instead of smoking it. When after an ample pause he had lighted it and made sure with equal care that it was well lit, he exhaled a few thick clouds of smoke, his head thrown back and his eyes half shut in order to savor his delight to the full. After he had taken several puffs, he looked steadily at Andrés, letting his glance pass over and about him, as if he wanted to appraise his worth.

Andrés looked into the fire. He felt now in every fiber of his being that things at home were not as he would like. But he did not break in, because he knew that men of his race say what has to be said when the right moment has come. They are not babblers who speak without thinking.

"How much do you earn with the carretas?" Lázaro asked.

"Since I am now encargado I earn seventy centavos a day and rations," answered Andrés.

"Does your wife earn anything as well?"

"No," Andrés replied. "I buy her what she wants, but she does not want much more than a little bird."

"Seventy centavos a day," Lázaro repeated slowly, as though comparing this sum with another in his mind. "Seventy centavos. That is damned little. Then you can't help your father out of the mess he's in. Hell take it. That would need more than a hundred and I don't know how many pesos."

Andrés gave a violent start. He gulped and swallowed and could not open his mouth. His lips were clamped together.

Lázaro pushed some branches further into the fire and shut his eyes tightly when a cloud of green smoke was blown into his face.

Estrellita was now squatting on the ground about five feet behind Andrés, because she felt that the conversation by the fire would go on longer than at first seemed likely. None of the men paid any attention to her or called to her to come nearer the fire. This was not out of any disrespect to the girl, but simply because she was free to sit by her husband at the fire if she felt any desire to do so.

5

Andrés had looked around several times toward Estrellita while this talk went on and had nodded and smiled to her to show that he had not forgotten her. Now, under the shock of this terrible blow, when his lips seemed to have lost the power to form words, he turned around toward her again. He did it unconsciously, as though he looked to her for refutation of what he had just heard, as though she alone could release him from the anguish he was suffering at that moment.

The men around the fire had spoken in undertones and

Estrellita had been able to catch only a word here and there, so that she knew nothing of what they were saying. That was why, when Andrés turned to her, she only nodded carelessly and smiled as she had before.

At this Andrés had a strange experience. He saw her not just five feet from him but so far away that she might have been sitting on the opposite shore of a sea. And with this peculiar optical illusion there rose in his heart the conviction that he had lost her.

He moved his neck as though he were choking, and then took a deep breath and asked: "How do you mean help my father, hombre?"

Lázaro did not lift his eyes from the fire—not for a long time. Then he stretched his shoulders. He looked at his companions. When he saw that they all stared into the fire—some poking at the burnt-out ends, others putting on fresh wood, and all occupying themselves in case Andrés might call on one of them by name for an explanation—he became restless. He moved this way and that, held an ember to his cigar although there was no necessity, and said nothing.

Then Emilio spoke up. "What is the good of beating about the bush?" he asked roughly. "It's not our fault that we've met you here. We were not looking for you. It's you that ran your head into us. No one told us to tell you the news."

"Of course not," said Andrés. "It is no business of yours. But it's my father, and I've heard nothing of him for so many years."

Emilio replied as though with indifference. "This is how it is: Don Arnulfo has sold your father to the monterías—to an agent. I believe his name is don Gabriel."

For minutes Andrés sat there stunned. When his brain began to work again his first thought was to take the quickest way to Lumbojvil and murder don Arnulfo. This thought, however, quickly passed. He saw at once that by murdering don Arnulfo he would be unable to help his father, whose situation would then be even more hopeless.

Slowly, the full weight of his father's plight pressed down upon his consciousness. "My father . . . sold to the monterías," he kept repeating in a scarcely audible voice, "sold to the monterías because I was not at home to help him work off his debt."

In the turmoil of his thoughts and feelings he recalled the day when he saw his father for the last time. It was the day when his father had bought him a petate, and a serape to keep him warm. He had bought these things for him because he could not bear to see his son suffering. His father had to buy the petate and the serape on credit from the finquero and had thus greatly increased his debt.

Andrés recalled also the day he had said good-by to his father on first leaving the finca. His father did not utter a word and no tears stood in his eyes. All the same he looked at his boy in a way he had never looked at him before. The deep love which the father felt for his boy and which it would have shamed him as an Indian to express; the shy veneration an Indian feels for his child and for the mysterious link in the chain of generation stretching from eternity to eternity to carry on the family characteristics, making him, an aging man, feel young in the thought of this life after his own death—all this was in the father's eyes as he took leave of his son. Only an Indian, slow and measured in his words and loath to give expression to his feelings, can put a whole religion and life's philosophy into his expression; and again it is only an Indian who is capable of reading this expression rightly and of understanding and seeing in it all the years that have been before and all the years that will follow.

It was this look on his father's face, never forgotten and always carried within him like a song of home, which Andrés now had before his eyes.

He saw it in the embers of the fire, written there in fiery characters. He saw it on the faces of the men, where it paled and grew brighter as the fire flared up and died down. He saw it even in the dense night which rested over the wide field, shining out like a star seen in a dream.

After a time that seemed to him infinite, he sighed deeply and turned to Estrellita. But he did not see her, though she crouched there waiting for him. In place of her he saw his father's face, which extinguished everything else in the world and fell on his soul like a darkened sun.

6

He got up heavily. "I must get back to my carretas. We have to be on the road just after midnight. I haven't a day to lose. Good luck to you all, amigos." He held out his hand to each one. Not one did more than just touch the tips of his fingers; but in this light touch of the fingers they put, like all their race, more sincerity and true feeling than others do who nearly pull each other's arms out of the shoulder sockets, so afraid are they their cordiality and candor will not pass muster without.

Estrellita got up when she saw that Andrés was taking leave of the men. Andrés went up to her, stroked her hair, and said simply: "Come along, Estrellita, we have an early start."

7

A few hours later, a little past midnight, Andrés's train of carretas was on the road to Jovel. Estrellita sat beside him. She had not asked about the talk around the campfire. That was among the men. If anything was said that Andrés wanted her to know, he would tell her in his own time. They sat silently. The oxen pulled on.

Andrés rolled himself a cigarette. He did it very slowly. Then, after lighting it, he said without prelude: "The finquero has sold my father to the monterías. I must go and take his place."

Every drop of blood left the girl's face. Her mouth fell wide open and remained open for some minutes. Then it grew hard and dry. She drew her breath in sharply. She shook her head violently as though she wanted to shake it from her neck. Her eyes protruded and went red, till it seemed that they might burn in their sockets. She clenched her little hands and beat her thighs. A cry broke from her and was strangled in her throat. She swayed her body to and fro as though being swept by a storm.

And then the tears began to rush from her eyes.

But Andrés neither heard her cry nor saw her tears.

8

If one Indian says to another, "My father is in trouble," there is no need for either to say another word; for the part of a son in the matter is as unalterable and as entirely outside his will as death. Those who have to express their feelings in hard cash before they can know that they have any, command or have their God command: "If you want to prosper and live long in the land and be successful in business and make plenty of dollars, then honor your father and mother."

And it is never said in our Hebraic religion in sermons about the Son of God that His reward was the reward of deep content after completing His life's task, and the satisfaction a man feels in having never purposely and deliberately done any living creature harm; on the contrary, it is always emphasized by preachers and in religious instruction that the Son of God was after a good seat at an excellent symphony concert, which gave the right to wear wings and now and then to play on the saxophone, the percussion instruments, and the lyre. It must always be made clear what rewards in ready money or privileges after death good conduct will fetch, and it is worth mentioning that a childlike faith is repaid by the not inconsiderable pleasure afforded by the thought of those who smolder and roast to all eternity.

The Indian knows no divine command and he has known none in the long history of his race. Nevertheless, he is acquainted with the facts of this life, and one of these facts is: "He is your father and she is your mother." Whether he honors these two persons or not is no concern of his gods. His blood tells him what he has to do for these two. He does not need to be promised dollars or to be menaced with red-hot tongs.

9

"When will you go?" asked Estrellita.

"As soon as we reach Jovel we'll unload the carretas. I have a load of coffee and tobacco and a few thousand empty bottles for the breweries. Tomorrow we'll be on our way to Chiapa. When I have the carretas safely back at don Laureano's, then I'll go off that same night in case I reach my father too late."

"I am going with you, my dear," said Estrellita. "I am going with you to the monterías. I am going with you wherever you go, to the end of the world and beyond. No place is too far, no road is too rough, no work is too hard, if I can be with you."

"If you could do that, Estrellita mía," Andrés replied in a choking voice, "then I would not have spoken to you about it. We would go and it would not matter where and with what object and what end. I have been thinking it out all night. You cannot come with me. You cannot—for your sake and for mine. I certainly never thought I should ever bring such sorrow on you. It is not my fault, still less my father's, that I have to leave you alone, my little star."

"You promised me at the very first when we sat at night on the prairie and were so happy, that you would never leave me. Didn't you promise me that?" asked Estrellita.

"I did," Andrés admitted. "You come first after my father. And but for my father no one on earth could separate me from you. My mother could never be in such trouble as my father is now. For my father is old and tired out. He has spent a life of labor. He could scarcely stand the march to the monterías, and would be likely to die on the road and be devoured by vultures and wild dogs. And that is why you come next for me, and I cannot take you with me, because you might then be in even greater trouble than my father is, and I don't want it to be worse even than my father's."

The girl did not understand what he meant. "But how," she asked, "can my trouble be greater if I am always with you than if you leave me?"

"My father is oppressed by trouble and I must free him from it. It is the bitterest fate that could ever overtake him. But I could never free you from the troubles which would certainly overtake you if you came with me. I could only murder—but then I would be shot and you would be left alone and it would be worse for you than before."

"But I should also die," she said quietly.

"Yes, if they let you die, Estrellita," Andrés corrected, "and if there was enough left of you to make it worthwhile to die and if you had enough will left to die of your own accord. For you would be broken, body and soul."

She did not know what to say. The vision of an unknown

terror rose before her eyes, like a monstrous beast with innumerable claws and long hairy arms which writhed in all directions to seize his victim.

She could not imagine what troubles Andrés could mean. But she gave way to him because he knew so much and everything he said was always right. When she thought of this the parting from him seemed only more painful. The quiet resolution with which he had said that he had to go alone without her took away all hope of there being any other way out.

He had thought it over hour after hour and weighed every alternative. She remembered now that he had not spoken a word all evening, whereas usually, even when the road was worst and the labor hardest and curses buzzed in the air like flies, he always found time for a few friendly or joking words whenever she was near. At the sight of her, anger died on his lips and instead of a curse let out over an unexpected break-down at the most awkward part of the road, a cheerful laugh took its place on his sweating and dusty face.

Since his experience of life was so much greater than hers and since she knew in the depth of her heart that he was one with her to the roots of his being, she knew that he must have thought everything over and over before giving up the possibility of keeping her with him.

10

Fate is incontestable—and far more so for an Indian than for a European, who lives under the influence of many conflicting philosophies, from among which he selects the one which promises him the best return or the most harmonious existence. The Indian is not so happily situated. For him fate is the decision from which he cannot escape and against which he does not even fight.

Yet Estrellita grasped at the last ray of hope which seemed to flicker across the turmoil of her thoughts.

"I have heard," said she, "that men sometimes take their wives with them to the monterías."

"Yes," Andrés admitted, "many men do, but in most cases, in fact always, particularly when their wives are young and pleasing to look at, the man does not come back—because of his wife."

Andrés knew that Estrellita had not understood him. And he could not have made her understand if he had wanted to, for she lacked an important premise without which understanding was impossible.

She took him to mean something else. She said: "Then of course I will not go with you. I will certainly not make it my fault that you never come back. I want you so much to come back as soon as you have worked off your father's debt. I shall wait for you, wait and wait."

"Yes," he said heavily. "That's what I want, that you should wait for me. I have been thinking about that too. But where in the world can you wait for me? In the whole wide world, as far as I know, there is no single spot, however small, where you could quietly and safely wait for me."

"I will wait in your mother's house," she said gleefully.

"You might do that, Estrellita," he explained, "if my mother lived somewhere else, far away from the finca. In less than a week the finquero from whom you ran away would find out that you were on don Arnulfo's finca and he would have you brought back by the police. Apart from everything else which you would certainly undergo, you would have to work two years for nothing in order to pay back the costs of getting you back. And what do you think his son José, whom you told me about, would do to you? I need not tell you that."

She shut her eyes and shuddered with nausea and fright.

"That," Andrés went on, "is another reason why I cannot take you with me. The road to the monterías leads through the districts where the finqueros are almighty gods, and where the officials will sentence a peon to be shot then and there in return for ten pesos and a few glasses of comiteco, if the finquero asks them to. What do these finqueros care whether an Indian, even a dear little Indian girl like my Estrellita, perishes or not? There are so many Indians, and they cost a finquero less than small calves."

"You're right," Estrellita nodded, "you know everything in the world and it is as you say."

"And now, my little star," he said gently, "you will obey me for the last time and do what I tell you."

"Not for the last time," the girl interrupted, "not for the last time. I will obey you for ever and ever—as long as I live."

For a time he was lost in reflection, as though considering step by step all he had thought out for her. "Tomorrow we shall be on the way back to Chïapa. There I shall settle up with don Laureano. I still owe him a good deal—about ninety pesos, I daresay. He will enter it against me with don Arnulfo; and don Arnulfo will enter it against me with the montería. I shall see if don Laureano will lend me another ten pesos. He will certainly do it. I have served him well and never caused him any loss. I will give you the ten pesos. You must hide them well in your dress. Then you will go with the carretas that Aurelio is taking down to the railroad. I know Aurelio well. He is my friend. I will talk to him. He is a good fellow, who will certainly look after you on the way down there. Then you will take the railroad to Tonalá. That will cost you only half a peso. There you must find yourself a good place. You can speak Spanish well enough now and can even read and write a little. You will easily be able to earn six or eight pesos a month. If you don't like it after a time or you're badly treated, then go on farther, perhaps to Tapachula. That is a big town where you will get good wages. But never go to any town that's not on the railroad. Then I shall be able to look for you and find you when I come back one of these days. If you go anywhere else I shall never be able to find you again."

"No olvidaré ni una palabra," she said in Spanish. "I will not forget a single word. I will always do as you say." She spoke it like an oath.

11

The next day the train of carretas, on its return from Jovel, pitched its camp on the same little meadow. It arrived when night had already fallen.

The oxen had been seen to and the carretas were in good order. The evening meal was over and the carreteros sat around the fire smoking and yarning. Bonifacio played a little concertina he had bought in Jovel. Pascual accompanied him on the guitar. Two of the others danced together.

Then the moon rose. It rose above the high country near Jovel. It swam slowly into the clear sky, looking so deep red and large and round that it might have been going to swallow the earth.

Andrés got up from the fire. He went over to his carreta. Estrellita was sitting there on the plank where the driver sat. Dreaming or lost in thought, her eyes were gazing widely at the moon.

Andrés got up and sat beside her for a moment. He stroked her hair, which she had carefully combed before the meal and which now hung around her, smooth and silken.

"Come, Estrellita," he said, and lifted her down from the seat.

When they reached the edge of the meadow, Andrés took

Estrellita in his arms and carried her down to the stream to the little open place, which had been the first home they had ever had together.

The moonlight flooded the stream in long quivering strands. In front of their eyes was the black and impenetrable bush. Here and there in it were gold discs with jagged edges wherever the closely interwoven foliage caught the light of the moon. Behind them and close to them on every side were bushes, shrubs, and gnarled and stunted trees. Some of them were wholly bathed in moonlight, others only lightly draped in its silver, and others again were armed with little golden shields. Their shadows lay strewn about in the gold-flooded open patches of the steep descent, as though they were their breath left behind after the day.

As the two sat there in silence holding each other's hands, the idea came to them that this scrub was alive in a world of its own, with its own being, its own forms, like those enchanted little people who were and were no more, who were born awry and could never quite establish themselves in the real world.

The bush sang, each bush fiddled, the grass fluted, and the stream played deep oboe notes.

From above, where the men sat around the fire, scraps of music floated down, seeming to come from so far that they might have been the echo of songs sung by other carreteros who had been there nights before.

Andrés and Estrellita were so full of their thoughts they would have felt it as a wound in their very souls to have had to speak. Each felt that the other was thinking the same thought.

The sweet and painful necessity came over them to lose themselves in each other, so that they might win and hold each other for as long as the universe existed, and remain forever bound up with one another in the experience of one feeling and one event. And without their willing it or wishing it they both came a long step nearer to the knowledge of the essence of many things in the life of men.

The carreteros were singing "Amapola del Camino." They sang it draggingly and full of melancholy. And the song encircled the two of them and mingled with their warm breath, so that it became their wedding song.

"Don't be afraid, little star," said Andrés, "be brave. Although hundreds of men never come back but perish and leave their bones in the monterías, yet I shall come back. I shall come back to you, Estrellita mía, even though the world goes to bits for it."

"I will wait for you for ever and ever," she said.

FOR THIRTY-FIVE YEARS, *from 1876 to 1911, power in Mexico was in the hands of one man, Porfirio Díaz. Mexico's constitution had been altered to give sanction to his re-elections, which were assured by his appointment of state governors and other officials. Opposition was controlled by a ruthless federal police, called the* rurales. *It was a reign of peace and prosperity for the few and dire poverty for the many—half the entire rural population of Mexico was bound to debt slavery. Big landowners and foreign capital were favored as more and more Indians lost their communal lands.*

In the final decade of Díaz's rule, however, opposition strengthened, and before his last engineered re-election he promised a return to democratic forms—which after the election he gave no sign of honoring. In 1910 revolution broke out; independent rebel armies under the leadership of Pancho Villa, Emiliano Zapata, Francisco Madero, and others upset the power of the landlords and eventually overthrew the Díaz regime.

In what have become known as the "Jungle Novels," B. Traven *wrote, during the 1930's, an epic of the birth of the Mexican revolution. The six novels—*Government, The Carreta, The March to Caobaland, The Troza, The Rebellion of the Hanged, *and* The General from the Jungle—*describe the conditions of peonage and debt slavery under which the Indians suffered in Díaz's time. The novels follow the spirit of rebellion that slowly spread through the labor camps and haciendas, culminating in the bloody revolt that ended Porfirio Díaz's rule.*

In the 1920's, when B. Traven arrived in the country, peonage, although officially abolished by the new constitution of 1917, was still a general practice in many parts of Mexico. The author observed the system at first hand in Chiapas, the southernmost province, a mountainous and heavily forested region, where the jungle novels, as well as many other of his stories, are set.